Downers Grove Public Library

1050 Curtiss St.

Downers Grove, IL 60515

(630) 960-1200

www.downersgrovelibrary.org

GAYLORD

DRAGOONS

DRAGOONS

An Ensign Early Novel
of the Anglo-Zulu War

Garry Douglas Kilworth

This first world edition published 2011
in Great Britain and the USA by
SEVERN HOUSE PUBLISHERS LTD of
9–15 High Street, Sutton, Surrey, England, SM1 1DF.

British Library Cataloguing in Publication Data

Kilworth, Garry.
  Dragoons.
    1. Great Britain. Army. Regiment of Foot, 24th (2nd
    Warwickshire)–Fiction. 2. Zulu War, 1879–Fiction.
    3. Duelling–Fiction. 4. Historical fiction.
    I. Title
    823.9'14–dc22

ISBN-13: 978-0-7278-8004-8 (cased)

All Severn House titles are printed on acid-free paper.

Severn House Publishers support The Forest Stewardship Council [FSC],
the leading international forest certification organisation. All our titles that
are printed on Greenpeace-approved FSC-certified paper carry the FSC logo.

Typeset by Palimpsest Book Production Ltd.,
Falkirk, Stirlingshire, Scotland.
Printed and bound in Great Britain by
MPG Books Ltd., Bodmin, Cornwall.

This novel is dedicated to
mis amigos
Ruth and Ben Connor

One

Young boys in any neighbourhood instinctively know when a fight is about to take place. The boys of Landman's Drift in Natal were no different. They gathered at dawn in two large mahogany trees like monkeys about to witness a battle between big cats. They hung silently in the branches, unseen by the duellists below: black boys, white boys, boys of mixed race and one single albino who was not sure to which group he belonged, all equal under the sky at least for the duration of the encounter below them.

One of those boys was Thomas Tranter, an orphan adopted by Ensign Sebastian Early, the Provost-Marshal for Lord Chelmsford's army in the invasion of Zululand.

Tom stared wide-eyed at the men below. Two were stripped to their white silk shirts and trousers, while two others were in full uniform. A fifth man was also in uniform but he carried a black leather bag and did not look like a real soldier. Tom was spread along a thick branch like a lazy leopard. Other boys were in similar positions, or nestled in crutches between branch and trunk. Tom could hear them breathing heavily. His own heart was hammering so loudly in his chest he was sure the men underneath could hear it. Then a parrot started squawking in one of the higher branches and Tom almost fell out of the tree in shock. Fortunately the duellists below were too intent on their purpose to take any notice of nature's sounds. Not one of them looked up into the mahogany.

'Gentlemen, take your places.'

The voice floated up from one of the men below. The two men in white shirts each holding a pistol pointing upwards stood back to back. At a signal from the man who had spoken they strode away from each other. When they were twenty paces apart they turned. The slimmer one, the man with the ginger hair, immediately fired into the air. The dark-haired thickset man, who looked the older of the two, took careful aim at his victim. There was a shout from one of the other men but he squeezed the trigger and fired anyway. The slim man folded to the ground, the front of his shirt stained bright red. All the others, except the one who had fired, rushed forward and bent over him.

After a few moments one of them looked up.

'He's dead,' came the cry.

Tom's eyes went blurry and there was a thick lump in his throat. He started trembling violently and had to grip the branch, fearful of falling. He was shocked to the core. One of the other boys made a gagging sound, but the parrot started up again and smothered this noise. Down below the men were arguing loudly. Finally, the man who had shot his victim put on his coat and went away. The other three men took off the dead man's trousers and coat and pushed staves through the leg and armholes. They placed the body on this makeshift stretcher and carried him away.

Some of the boys who had been holding their breath now expelled it noisily.

'Did you see that?' cried a tight-voiced drummer boy from the 24th. 'Shot him through, clean as a whistle.'

One of the black boys asked excitedly, 'Why dee killim?'

'It's a matter of honour,' explained one of the colonial boys. 'His honour was impunated.'

'But,' Tom pointed out, 'the other man din't fire – he just shot in the air.'

'Deloped,' said the knowledgeable drummer boy, who was a bit older than the rest of them. 'That's what it's called.'

'Moonies,' said another colonial boy. 'All of 'em.'

A moonie was a white man straight from Europe, his skin still pale and untanned by the African sun. Those below had had a touch of redness to them, a certain amount of sunburn, but clearly they had just arrived with the new regiments from England. It was May 1879 and Lord Chelmsford was building up his army again after it had been cut to pieces by the Zulus. Reinforcements had been arriving since mid-March, trying to acclimatize before the second invasion of Zululand took place. As always many had fallen ill, especially those who had not been abroad before, and quite a few were feeling homesick. Moonies looked sickly at the best of times, but these soldiers had suffered a long voyage aboard tubs of ships and were a miserable bunch.

'Him on the rack,' said a small Bantu boy. 'Him no go home

forever now. Him dead sojer, for sure. Stay in Africa, for bury, eh? Gottim dead-squire in th'heart.'

Lord Chelmsford's army was busy preparing for the second invasion of Zululand from Natal. The general had under his command fifteen Imperial infantry battalions, two regiments of British cavalry and a naval brigade: in plain figures sixteen thousand Europeans and seven thousand Natal Kaffirs, plus a few thousand civilians with the wagons. Chelmsford intended giving Cetshwayo a good hiding. As with the first expedition, hundreds of ox-drawn wagons and carts were being assembled. They were packed full of supplies, including water and ammunition. Everything that was needed had to be taken with the troops. There would be cattle out there, in Zululand, and game, but for the most part the army would rely on the stores they were carrying. Once again even officers knew they would be called upon at times to assist when wagons were bogged down in mud and many soldiers – ex-farm hands – would be placing aside the rifle for the pitchfork to revisit their old work of feeding the cattle.

There was a certain amount of revenge in the hearts of most of the soldiers. A massive defeat had been inflicted on them by the Zulus just a few weeks previously. Two thousand men had been massacred at the Battle of Isandlwana by an impi of twenty-five thousand warriors. There had also been one or two smaller failures after the big battle. The salt had been rubbed into the wound and it stung mightily. Indeed, Isandlwana was the worst defeat ever suffered by the British army fighting against an enemy using primitive weapons.

There had been another massacre, back in 1842 in Afghanistan on a retreat from Kabul. Gleeful anti-British historians often write of the slaughter of around sixteen thousand British troops. However, this is an incorrect account of the campaign. There were in fact only three and a half thousand soldiers in that column, of whom only six hundred and ninety were British: a single battalion of the 44th Foot, the Essex Regiment. The others were Bengalis of the Honourable East India Company, fierce fighters and admired for their warfare skills and courage, but not the British army.

And the remaining twelve and a half thousand dead?

They were camp followers: women, children and male civilians. Since the massacre in Afghanistan was not a massive defeat of the British army per se, it did not compare with Isandlwana.

Isandlwana's two thousand was more significant.

And more importantly, after Isandlwana the British were facing more than primitive weapons. The Zulus now had two thousand of the latest Martini-Henry rifles, along with many boxes of ammunition. This sobering thought was in the minds of many soldiers about to re-invade the inhospitable land beyond the Buffalo River. Rifles were not difficult to operate and the Zulu warrior was not stupid. A soldier in the next battle would face more than spears and the odd musket.

This time the iron wind would be blowing in both directions.

Sam Weary, Seb's self-appointed Xhosa batman, was sewing a tear in the ensign's uniform outside the tent Sam shared with Corporal Evans, Seb's Assistant Provost-Marshal, when young Tom came up looking hot and bothered, and short of breath. Sam remained intent on mending the tear but he was aware of the boy's agitation. He said nothing. Tom sat down on a log nearby and with bowed head, stared at the ground.

'Them ants is interestin', eh, Thomas?'

'What?' Tom looked up quickly. 'What ants?'

'Them ants you starin' at,' replied Sam, calmly, biting off the thread and sticking the needle into the cotton reel. 'Interestin' fellahs, to be sure.'

'Oh.' Tom looked down. 'I s'pose so.'

'You want to splash some water on you? On you face? You look hot, Thomas. Hot and dusty. You been runnin' out this mornin'?'

'I – I just went with some other boys. We went lookin' for snakes with his mongoose.'

'Whose mongoose?'

'Jimmy Spates'. He's got one, you know.'

'And the mongoose? He ran away?'

Tom frowned. 'No.'

'Then why you runnin'?'

'Just to get back here, see. Look, when can we have breakfast? I an't had me breakfast yet.'

'Whose job is it to fetch water for the breakfast?'

'What? Oh – mine.'

Sam raised his eyebrows.

Tom seemed pleased to have a job to do and went trotting away with a canvas bucket to fill.

'That boy's been up to somethin',' muttered Sam to himself, 'an' we'll find out soon enough what it be.'

'WHERE'S THE BREAKFAST THEN, EH?'

This bellowed question came from the lanky corporal who hove into view from behind the nearby bell tents.

In finger-language Sam signed to Evans that he should keep his voice down because the officer was still asleep.

'Time he was up, then, isn't it?' said Evans, but this was delivered in a much more subdued tone.

'He is up,' came a voice from inside the neighbouring tent, 'and I'll thank you to keep a respectful tone to your voice, if you please, Corporal.'

Sam passed on this message in sign language.

'Sorry, sir,' yelled Evans, then much more softly, '*I ddweud y gwir, 'd oes dim drwg genni o gwbl.*'

The officer in the tent came back with, 'Evans, I have to tell you my hearing is a lot better than yours and also I'm learning Welsh, you insubordinate man.'

Sam kept this last to himself, for the prospects of future clashes between the officer and his NCO might prove quite entertaining. There was not a lot of fun in a Xhosa man's life in the British army, so Sam intended to make the best of a poor situation. He enjoyed these encounters between the invaders who had defeated his people in battle, finding some comfort in the idea that underneath they were as vulnerable as any local man. Not that he disliked either the corporal or the ensign: they were both men he admired for certain aspects of their character. The ensign, in his early twenties, was eager, honourable and had a kind heart. The older corporal was sage, bold and the longer he was in Africa the less he came to care whether a man had a lime-green skin, let alone black or white. Sam treated the officer like one of his sons. Evans, though, was a man full grown and Sam enjoyed minor battles with the Welsh ex-shepherd. Evans was a good adversary and kept Sam interested in the world.

★　★　★

Seb rose from his makeshift cot with aching limbs. Sleeping near the ground was not good for his joints, even at his young age. He rubbed his hairy face briskly to wake himself up, catching his fingers in those long silky moustaches that all soldiers of Chelmsford's army sported. Seb was quite proud of his whiskers. They hung a good three inches either side of his chin and proclaimed him to be quite a fellow. A few months ago they gathered him compliments, but since he had been made a policeman for the army they had dried up. No one likes a provost-marshal, the equivalent of the chief of police in a civilian capacity. Even some of his old friends tried to avoid him and those who had been merely army comrades actually cut him dead. He cared about this, deeply, but he was certainly not going to hand in his post because others thought he should. No one was going to tell Ensign Sebastian Early what to do with his army life. Seb had not been fond of provos himself, when he was not one, but now he was and any comrades with criminal tendencies had better watch their damn boots.

Seb emerged from the tent feeling a little better. Sunlight soon banished the aches and pains of the cold ground. And Sam was a treasure. Always on the button. Bacon was frying in the pan and the smell was intoxicating. Eggs, too, sizzled on an iron griddle. Not for the first time Seb agreed with himself that the Xhosaman Sam Weary was an invaluable servant and deserved every farthing of his pay.

'Morning, Sam. And to you, Corporal.'

Seb made sure Evans could read his lips. There was a relaxed discipline between the NCO and the officer. When everyone else despised you, it brought down barriers between ranks. Such familiarity was frowned upon by the army and any staff officer present would have blown out his cheeks and reprimanded both men. But then most staff officers were pompous prigs and to be held in contempt.

'Mornin', sir,' shouted Evans. 'A fine day.'

It had rained heavily during the night and there were puddles everywhere, but the sun was rapidly drying the planet.

'I need to wash,' said Seb. 'Where's the water?'

'Boy's fetching water,' explained Sam, scooping a fried egg onto a tin plate. 'He will not be long, boss.'

'Fine. Thank you, Sam.'

Seb sat down on an upturned crate and began to tuck into the breakfast. When he was halfway through, a thickset, dark-haired man approached him, coming out of the row of tents behind. It was Jack Spense, a war photographer and one of those friends who had not deserted Seb, possibly because Jack was a civilian even though subject to military law while he followed the army. He sat down beside Seb and stared for a moment with longing eyes at the fried breakfast.

'You want some?' asked Seb. 'Sam, have we enough?'

'Yes, boss, I do some more for the picture-man.'

Jack thanked everyone in sight and then set about swatting the insects that seemed to plague mainly him. Indeed, he did seem always to be followed by a cloud of gnats and midges. Jack was convinced it was because he stank of the chemicals he used to produce his photographs and had sent for protective clothing in order to rid himself of the smell. He was sure that once he could peel off the odour he would be free of flies and other bothersome creatures of the *arthropoda* world. There was a lieutenant, Henry Charles Harford, who collected bugs but when Jack had asked him if he had an answer to their bothersomeness Harford had come up short. What was the point of studying insects, Jack had complained to Seb, if there was no practical or useful result in the exercise?

Once the food was in his hands he spoke quietly to Seb, using his nickname.

'Had a job this morning, South-East. Called to photograph a body.'

'Oh yes?' Seb was only mildly interested. Death was not uncommon in a war zone rife with disease. 'Someone I know?'

'Someone *no one* knows, apparently.'

'What?' Seb looked up and frowned. 'Meaning?'

'Meaning the officer, a lieutenant, rode in last night and almost immediately got into an argument with some cavalry officers. This morning he's dead. When they went through his personal effects, which amounted to a few items in his saddlebags, they were still no nearer to his identity.'

'Surely he reported to someone?'

'Yes, to Major Gambolini, adjutant of the 90th – the new man was of that regiment.'

'And?'

'Gambolini says he was very busy and distracted at the time, he perfunctorily acknowledged the new officer and told him to report this morning.'

'And?'

'The major has forgotten the name, if he ever registered it at all, since he was, to put it in his words, "too bloody inundated with work to bother noting a new man".'

'Gambolini? Sounds Italian.'

'Father was, but the major was born in Glasgow, which makes him a Scot, I suppose. Anyway,' continued Jack, 'I was asked to take a photograph of the dead man which could be sent to his family, if they ever find out who the man is. Gruesome sort of request you might think, but some relatives like to be sure their loved ones are actually dead and not just missing in the bush. They find these death-mask pictures help them. An actual death is not so upsetting as a mystery never solved, if you know what I mean.'

'I think I do, Jack. The misery of uncertainty is worse than the certainty of misery.'

'Exactly. Who said that?'

'Don't know. Not a scholar, old chap. Just unearthed it from somewhere in the recesses of my skull.'

'Well, anyway, I took a couple of photographs of the man lying pale as you would expect on a blanket in his full-dress uniform, eyes closed of course. Took them from bird's-eye view, so it looks as if he's standing up straight. When I asked how he'd died, they said a hunting accident this morning, out in the bush. I was told this unknown officer was shot through the heart when he got between the quarry and the shooter. When I asked about the weapon a young cornet, clearly very disconcerted and upset, blurted something about a pistol.'

'A pistol?' said Seb, his eyebrows going up.

'Precisely. Who goes hunting with side arms? Only someone like Mad Henry, who is . . .'

'An absolute lunatic. Precisely.'

Jack continued, 'Anyway, one of the other officers interrupted the boy quickly with a short laugh and said, "No, Cartwright, you've got it wrong, you booby. It was Ryan's hunting rifle that did for the poor devil – he was hit by a .760 from a Blanch sporting gun. Poor chap didn't stand a chance, getting one of those in the chest." ' Jack paused before adding with his mouth full, 'There's something mighty strange going on. I just thought you ought to know. Ryan and his friends didn't seem to know the man's name either. They told me he never gave it, but just asked to join the early morning hunt.'

'Sounds unusual. A gentleman not giving his name.'

'Or a bunch of other gentlemen not asking for it. Then there's the pistol thing.'

'Well, Jack, it could be the cornet was simply just confused.'

'True, but I got the feeling everyone was uncomfortable. And you know what snobs the cavalry are. Why would they let an unknown infantry officer join them on a hunt? Yes, if he was a friend of one of them they might bend a little, but no one knew him. It all sounds like a mess of beans, if you ask me.'

'A conspiracy?'

Jack said, wiping up the egg yolk with his unleavened bread, 'If there is, you're the man for it, eh? Anyway, can't send the blasted picture to the family if we don't know who he is. We *may* have a conspiracy but we've certainly got a mystery.'

'Can I have the photograph? I'll need to find out if any of the other officers in his regiment, or indeed any regiment, knows who he is. Perhaps a chest or two will arrive later? It should do. No officer travels with just his horse and his saddlebag. I'm sure we'll find out who he is when his luggage arrives.'

After Jack had gone, Seb sat and brooded on what his friend had told him. It was thin stuff. Was there enough there for him to make further enquiries? He was disliked enough as it was, without fabricating reasons for other officers to hold him in contempt. It seemed a ludicrous thought that a bunch of British serving officers should get together to murder one of their own. That was beyond belief. In which case the whole scenario fell apart, for clearly there was more than one witness to the so-called accident.

Tom had returned with the water and gone off again to see his young friends.

Sam walked over to Seb in that languid way of his and settled his dusty body on the box beside him.

'Sir?'

Seb looked up. 'Yes, Sam?'

'It's about the boy.'

'What is?'

'Well, boss, he came this morning all *dwaal*. He was hot too, from runnin' Sam thinks, and upsetted about something.'

'Do you know what it was all about?'

'No, boss, but I hear you talkin' with the other officer . . .'

'Civilian, but go on, Sam.'

'He speak about a man who was killed. Somethin' upset the boy this mornin'. I think he maybe . . .'

Seb straightened. 'You think Tom saw something?'

'Maybe, boss.'

'Right, thank you, Sam.'

When Tom returned at lunchtime Seb observed the boy closely. There was nothing about him now that raised any suspicion of having been upset. He chattered in the normal way, going on about playing cricket with his 'pals'. Later in the day, Seb had Tom to himself. He then carefully opened the subject, anxious not to send Tom scuttling into his shell, for the boy was quite difficult to extract once he disappeared inside that carapace which so many of the boys from remote farms used to protect themselves from intense questioning. Also Tom had suffered the terrible shock of witnessing the death of the last member of his family, his older brother, at Isandlwana.

'So, Tommy,' said Seb, pretending to be interested in the firewood the boy had collected, 'what have you been up to today?'

'Playin' cricket.'

'Ah, cricket. Wonderful game. Did you know our village back in Britain beat the local town two years ago? It's true, Much Wenlock brought the great double-sided metropolis of Bridgenorth to its knees. I ought to know, I was the wicket-keeper.'

'You were?' cried Tom. 'How many runs did you score?'

'Ah, you know better than that, Tom. A wicket-keeper isn't expected to be a great batsman. You young boys, your only heroes are batsmen – and at a pinch, the bowler. Let me tell you I stumped three of the opposition. Caught them from behind out of their crease. They went home crying to their mothers.'

'They did?'

'Well, not exactly. You mustn't take every word I say as gospel truth, Tom. I exaggerate in order to make the story more interesting. Listen, didn't you go hunting today with the lads? I thought one of you had a shotgun?'

'Yes, Ricky Piers.'

'So you did go hunting.'

'No – I meant he's the one with the shotgun.'

Seb said, 'Ah, that's the boy, eh? Some of the men went out this morning, though. Maybe you saw them? Hunting impala?'

'No.'

Seb studied the boy's face from under his arm. Tom did not look flustered at all. There was no sign that he was not telling the truth, not in his expression or demeanour anyway.

'Well, Tom, that's strange. Did you know a man was killed today, out on a hunt?'

Now the boy's head came up. Tom's face went bright red. He looked as if his tongue had curled up and jammed his throat. He *did* know something about the death.

'There's nothing to worry about, Tommy. I'm not going to tell you off for watching a hunt, you know. All boys are interested in hunting. Can you tell me what happened?'

'I din't see no hunt.'

The words came out emphatically. Seb did not think the lad was lying. His words were too strong for that.

'What then? You saw the men come back from the hunt? Is that it? You saw the body brought in?'

'It weren't no hunt,' blurted Tom, 'it was a fight – a dool. This one shot the other one, after the other shot in the air. He din't stand no chance, the other one. He was just stood up straight an' tall when he was shot dead. I know I shun't have watched, sir, but all the boys was. He was shot an' then they started shoutin' at each other.'

Seb was stunned for a moment. 'A duel,' he repeated.

'That's it, sir. One o' them. Both had on these white shirts and the other one, he just fell down with blood all over here.' Tom rubbed the spot above his heart. 'It made his white shirt all red. He din't stand no chance, sir, 'cos he put his arm down with the gun in it and din't try to shoot no more, not after the one he sent up in the air.'

'Tom,' asked Seb, after a moment, 'would you recognize any of the men at this duel if you were to see them again?'

'Dunno, sir. Maybe. An' the other boys. Maybe they would, or not. I dunno.'

Seb stared away into the distance. Duelling was illegal. Therefore this was manslaughter, or at worst, murder. A man may go willingly to a place to risk death from the hand of another, but if that man died as a result of a deliberate attempt to kill him then a crime had been committed. This was no hunting accident. This was a major crime and Ensign Sebastian Early was the Provost-Marshal, whose job it was to uncover the truth of such crimes and arrest the perpetrator of the deed.

It was a hot afternoon. A fat, bored-looking sergeant was sitting outside the shack used as a temporary mortuary. He looked up as an officer approached. This surprised him. Most officers would not come near a place where men lay who had died of disease. Most officers were more frightened of yellow and blackwater fever than they were of a Zulu carrying a captured Martini-Henry. The sergeant stood and saluted, his left lazy eye on the red sash that denoted Seb's office. Did the Provost-Marshal want the sergeant or the mortuary? He began to run through all his misdemeanours of the last twenty-four hours and could find none that would interest the army policeman. He had even paid that whore a bit more, since she had been quite athletic.

'Sir?'

'How many bodies have you inside, Sergeant?'

Relief was released in the form of gas from the sergeant's rear, which made the officer wince.

'Sorry, sir, too much beer last night. Three, sir. Three cadavers.' The sergeant was never sure what the official term should be for the bodies under his charge. 'Corpses, as it were.'

'You have an officer that was brought in this morning?'

The sergeant flicked a fly from his nose, before it managed to climb up into the cave of his right nostril.

'No, sir.'

The officer looked a little stunned by this answer.

'No? But wasn't an officer killed in a hunting accident this morning?'

'So I understand, sir. But they took 'im straight off, and buried him in the graveyard.'

'Sergeant,' said the ensign, looking very angry, 'I wanted to examine that body. Did you happen to notice the wound in his chest? Was it made by a large-bore weapon, would you say? Or a pistol?'

The sergeant began to feel agitated. Why was he at fault? He just did as he was told, like most soldiers.

'Din't see nothin', sir. Them troopers just came and took 'im as he was.'

'Did you actually see him buried?'

'No, sir, but you can look for yourself – up there in the graveyard.'

'Sergeant, you are an ass.'

'Yes, sir.'

The sergeant did not feel like an ass. He felt put upon by this provo, who was blaming him for not doing something no mortuary sergeant would do. Inspect a putrid dead body, he thought, awash with pus and maggots? Not on your life, Ensign. I wouldn't touch the bloody things with a twelve-foot washing pole, not when most of them are rotten through to the bone with some foul disease. Not me.

'Sorry, sir.'

Seb was now convinced of a conspiracy of some kind. Why would cavalry troopers rush to bury the body of an infantry officer who was not known to them? Why? Only because they had been ordered to do so by one or more of their officers.

When he got to the makeshift cemetery he found the area full of fresh mounds. Most of them had a rank and name, but one or two were marked 'UNKNOWN'. These were men who had been found mutilated beyond recognition after a battle with the Zulus and had escaped identification. One might know from a roll call who was missing after a fight, but if several bodies were chopped into bits, their uniforms stripped from them to the underwear, who was whom?

And if Seb was dealing with a conspiracy here, the murdered man's body would be hidden. If he ordered all the 'unknowns' to be exhumed, he had no doubt the duellist's body would not be among them. A simple but clever way to hide such a corpse would be to bury it under a false name, or even change his marker for one already buried. There were hundreds of graves. It was an impossible task, even if Seb could get permission, which was seriously in doubt.

No, the dead would keep their secrets.

Two

A man crazed with hunger and thirst had been picked up by a patrol in Zululand. He gave his name as Henri Grandier, French of course with a name like that, but a lost member of Weatherley's Border Horse. Grandier had a long tale to tell, of becoming separated from his comrades without his mount. The Zulus had captured him and taken him to their king. Cetshwayo had at first allowed him to live, but then changed his mind and ordered his execution. Grandier escaped by killing a guard and threatening another, so he claimed, before being found by the patrol in the veldt just east of Kambula.

Sam Weary scoffed at this story.

'If he be captured by Zulus, they kill him dead where he stand, or they send him away.'

'You can't be sure of that,' said Seb. 'Why wouldn't Cetshwayo keep him while deciding what to do with him?'

'Because this king make quick decision and he keep them, not like Shaka who dance this way and that, before saying yes or no.'

'Sam, you weren't even born when King Shaka died.'

'I hear things. My father tell me things.'

Seb was not a man greatly interested in modern history. As far as he was concerned, anything that had happened in the last fifty years was current affairs. He had studied ancient history: the Roman Empire, the Greeks and the Persians, all of which excited him because it had occurred in a time long past which shone through the dull centuries that followed like a bronze shield in the sunlight. Peter, his predecessor, however, had gathered information about Shaka with an unquenchable thirst and naturally Peter felt obliged to tutor his friend on the knowledge he had gained from speaking with locals. Seb listened because it was Peter, but in truth he only took in half of what his friend told him and the rest spilled over.

'I take it, Sam, from what you say that you regard Cetshwayo as a greater king than Shaka?'

'Oh, sir . . .' said Sam, shaking his head in that way which indicated that Seb had hit a bullseye with his first shot.

King Shaka was the founder of the Zulu as a nation, the man who had welded together the northern Nguni tribes into a large powerful kingdom. He was widely thought to have invented the iklwa, the stabbing spear with the long sword-like blade that had been given the name of assagai, a word of unknown origin: definitely not Zulu, but possibly French or Arabic. Before Shaka, warring tribes had stood a hundred yards apart and thrown a few spears before hurling insults and then going home to dinner. After Shaka's reorganization of his warriors into highly trained regiments, who attacked as a great massed body of men, hooked their large shields round the shield-edges of the enemy and opened up their chests and abdomens, the battlefields were places of carnage and it was no wonder that other indigenous peoples feared the Zulu. An impi consisted of thousands of fierce warriors, it was home to the fearless, it was trained militarily to a high standard and getting home to dinner was the last thing on a warrior's mind.

'I would have thought, Sam, that Shaka was regarded by all Africans as a brilliant general and king.'

Sam made a face which registered his disgust with that idea.

Seb should not have been surprised, because Sam Weary was an amaXhosa, one of the southern Nguni, who looked back to an earlier king, uXhosa, from whom they took their people's name. Sam's people were as annoyed with Shaka's reforms as the Royalists were with Cromwell and his Model Army, or the Athenians with the Spartans, or the Carthaginians with the Romans. Some men took warfare far too seriously. Kept as an occasional game, with a few cattle at stake, it was acceptable. But to turn it into a wholesale killing machine for the aggrandizement of a power-mad few? No, that was not on.

And Shaka had, according to many, been utterly mad. He had marched regiments over cliffs to their deaths. He had ordered mass executions and the killing of all pregnant women and their husbands. He had starved his people by forbidding them to plant crops or draw milk from the cows. In short, Shaka was like many men who have absolute power and control. He became a mad tyrant who turned on those who had raised him up and treated them worse than dogs.

Tom suddenly appeared from behind the tent.

'Ah, young master,' said Seb, 'I've been looking for you.'

''Ave yer?' came the surprised reply. 'I bin here, but you was talking deep stuff wiv Sam.'

'Naught but idle chatter, child. Come with me. We're going visiting.'

Seb set off with Tom trotting at his heels like an obedient spaniel.

'Where we goin'?' asked Tom.

'Medical Unit.'

Tom skidded to a halt and looked alarmed.

'Waffor? I an't sick.'

Like many wise young men, Tom was not just wary of doctors, he thought them agents of the Devil. All you heard from a medical unit were screams and groans, yells of utter fear and bellows of pain. All you saw of such places were men with wide frightened eyes dying of some dread disease, or having their limbs sawn off. Doctors walked around with aprons covered in blood and pus, and large knives in their hands. Only a madman would want to visit a doctor voluntarily.

'It's not for you,' said Seb, turning round. 'It's about that duel this morning. And you don't have to say anything if you see one of the men you saw. I don't want you to. Just stand by me and look bored. You're very good at that, normally.'

'Oh, thassall right, then. It ain't a trick to get me there?'

'I don't play those kind of tricks, Tom, and you know it.'

The boy seemed satisfied with this answer, nodding his head.

They began their walk again. All around them the camp was in a state of activity. Men were digging and constructing. The army had begun to build a fort and lumber was being brought in, while earthworks were being dug. Rope and wire was piled high. Cairns of rocks and stones stood ready. After Isandlwana, Lord Chelmsford was taking no chances and wherever the army had a post it was being fortified. After the first invasion there were only a handful of military forts: Clery, Tenedos, Pearson, Thinta, Eshowe. Now they were springing up overnight, like mushrooms, but made of sterner stuff than fungus. There were ditches, dry-stone walls, redoubts, gabions, stockades, palisades, even drawbridges. All those impediments were needed to halt a Zulu charge in its tracks and protect the defenders within. The Zulus had always had thousands of firearms, but they were generally muskets or worn rifles. Now Isandlwana had made the impi a present of enough Martini-Henrys to arm a tenth of their men, along with ammunition aplenty.

A fort with strong walls and deep trenches was necessary after so many defeats, even though the last two battles had resulted in victories for the British.

The Medical Unit was a wooden hut which had once housed cattle. An officer stood leaning against a wall smoking a yellow-and-brown-stained clay pipe. Seb recognized him as a surgeon he had seen when investigating the murder of a captain.

'Can I have a word?' he asked, with Tom at his heels.

The surgeon, a subaltern in his thirties or thereabouts, looked up with lazy eyes and stared into Seb's face. He had stiff wiry hair, which apart from covering his head to within an inch above his eyebrows ran down the sides of his face and fell in a tangled cascade below his chin and halfway down his breast. If you counted the eyebrows there was more hair than skin above his shoulders.

The officer continued to puff for a minute more, then sighed. He removed the pipe from his lips, tapped it firmly on the heel of his boot, and in so doing broke the stem. The smoking bowl fell into the mud at his feet.

'Now look what you've made me do,' he said, shaking his head. He looked up again. 'Anyway, what is it? Blackwater fever? Foot rot? Syphilis?'

'No it bloody is not,' replied Seb. 'None of those. We've met before. I'm the Provost-Marshal,' Seb flicked the red sash which he wore around his shoulder, 'as you can see.'

'Oh yes, I remember you. Interrupted me while I was pollarding some poor blighter. What is it? Another murder?'

'Could be.' Seb resisted the impulse to look down at Tom, to see if there was any spark of recognition in the boy's eyes. 'I've yet to find out. It's come to my attention that there was a duel this morning, out beyond. One of the parties was killed. They tried to disguise it as a hunting accident, but I've got a whole parcel of boys who watched it from the safety of a high tree.'

'And?'

'And as you and I know, there's always a doctor in attendance at a duel, unless the combatants are totally irresponsible.'

The officer jerked upright, the lazy attitude instantly shed.

'Are you accusing me . . .?'

'I'm not accusing anyone at the moment. I don't know any of the facts. What I'd like you to tell me is how many surgeons are here in Landsman's Drift, and who they are.'

The subaltern shrugged. 'People are coming and going all the time. If you'd asked me that before the invasion I could have told you precisely. There were only a handful of us. Now there are quite a few. You'd be better off asking the surgeon-general.'

'General Woolfreys?'

'That's the man.'

Seb said carefully, 'So you can't help me? I mean, the general isn't here, is he – whereas our duel-doctor must be. Unless he rode out this morning? Did any AMD staff leave today?'

'Not that I know of. But your problem might be more difficult to solve than you think. There are many more civilian doctors attached to the army now. From the towns and cities. The general brought them in to help with local diseases – they know more than we do about African illnesses.'

Seb was aware that in any campaign, more men usually died of disease than were killed on the battlefield.

'Damn, I forgot about those,' he said. 'But, you know, it's more likely to be a regimental surgeon.'

'More likely – but not certain.'

Seb thanked the surgeon, but then told Tom to go and take a quick look inside the hospital hut. Tom did so, then came out, shaking his head. Almost immediately the boy realized he should not have indicated anything. Seb however told him not to worry. The pair then walked back towards the tents where Sam was working. On the way they passed a Boer who was grooming a handsome-looking gelding.

'Pieter Zeldenthuis,' said Seb with an edge to his voice. 'Killed any more innocent Zulus lately?'

The leather-skinned Boer, wearing a wideawake hat with a lion-skin band, and with two bandoliers of bullets forming a St Andrew's cross on his chest, curled his lower lip in a sneer.

'Ah, the Provost-Marshal,' he replied, in the clipped tongue of his countrymen, 'to what do I owe the pleasure?'

'Just passing by.'

'And as to your question,' said Zeldenthuis, 'there are no *innocent* Zulus. They're all bloody guilty, as far as I'm concerned.'

The Boer's father had been killed by warriors when Pieter was a young boy. Zeldenthuis said he could recognize the shield markings of the warrior that struck his father the fatal blow. He had joined the British army in order to find his father's killer, and destroy him, but Seb knew that already two Zulus with similar shield markings had been slain by Zeldenthuis. He was assassinating any he believed was carrying such a shield. Had the two killings been committed during battle, it would not have mattered too much from a legal point of view, but that was not the case. Zeldenthuis had shot – Seb was almost certain of this – a Zulu in captivity just before he was about to reveal some information that would have helped the British.

'Not guilty of the crime you're killing them for – not all of them.'

'Ag, they've all committed some sort of crime or another, it's in their nature, my loskop friend. While this war's going on I can shoot as many of them as I like. And I will, just watch me . . .'

At that moment a wagon was going by, hauled by oxen. On the back was a large fearsome-looking gun with many barrels and a crank handle near the breech. It was a dark monstrous-looking weapon.

'What the fuck is that?' said the Boer.

A captain was riding by the wagon, obviously escorting it. With some pride in his voice he said, 'This, sir, is a Gatling gun.'

Seb and Tom were equally fascinated by the machine. Seb had heard of such a weapon, but had not seen one before now.

Tom asked, 'Why's it got all them barrels? Is it so that when one barrel gets too hot, you got another one?'

'Ah, well you should ask, young man. And no, you have it completely wrong. All the barrels are used for firing, one immediately after the other. This, sir, is a *machine* gun. It will fire two hundred rounds per minute. We will mow down Zulus like corn.'

'Jesus,' exclaimed Zeldenthuis. 'Now *that's* murder.'

The captain stiffened in his saddle, but Zeldenthuis had taken his horse by the bridle and led it away. Instead, the officer addressed his remark to Seb.

'I assure you, Ensign, this is not murder at all. This weapon was invented by a doctor. Dr Richard Gatling, an American. He believes it is the invention to end all wars. And for two reasons. One, there will be no necessity to send battalions of men into the field when one of these will do. Two, the carnage on the losing side will be so great, future war will be unthinkable.'

Seb, whose opinion of doctors had fallen quite dramatically over the last few hours, thought to challenge this idea.

'Is he of addled mind, this doctor?' asked Seb, politely enough. 'Has he completely taken leave of his senses? I mean, there will be progress with regard to weapons of war, that much is certain. Machines for killing men will improve all the time and new ones will be invented. But to attribute the invention of such a weapon of mass destruction to a desire for humanitarianism is a little beyond the pale.'

The captain lifted his nose. 'I can't stay here listening to this prattle. You, Ensign, have no idea what you're talking about.' He spurred his mount forward, to catch up with the ox-wagon.

Seb stared after him and muttered, 'And I thought the Martini was the ultimate weapon. How wrong I was.'

'The Martini's a good rifle,' said Tom, loyally. 'But that thing in the wagon. Why, a man couldn't lift it, could 'e?'

'They don't need to lift it, Tom – they just set it down and create a wind of iron with it.'

Seb was very unsatisfied with his morning's work. He had got absolutely nowhere with his investigations. It was true what the surgeon had said: civilian doctors had been recruited by the army for their expertise with local diseases. On reflection Seb thought it was more likely to be a civilian than a military surgeon. The duellists' seconds might risk their careers for a friend, but a regimental surgeon was unlikely to. There was not a lot the army could do to a civilian doctor, especially if he said – as was most likely – that he was just passing by when he heard a shot and was called to assist a dying man.

So Seb's next move was to find this Cornet Cartwright, of the cavalry. Seb had not asked Jack which regiment Cartwright was from, but there were only two full British cavalry regiments in Africa, the 17th Lancers and the 1st Dragoons. Both were prestige regiments.

The Lancers had been in the charge of the Light Brigade at Balaclava and had therefore gone into the annals of the Great and Glorious. They had been raised in 1759 as the 18th Light Dragoons and had been renumbered and went through a series of re-namings to become the 17th Lancers, the Duke of Cambridge's Own. Their motto was 'Death or Glory', with a skull as the symbol for Death.

The 1st King's Dragoon Guards were third in seniority in the list of cavalry regiments, topped only by the Life Guards, and the Blues and Royals. They had been raised in 1685 by Sir John Lanier and became the King's Own Regiment. Their headdress badge was the double-headed Austrian eagle of Emperor Franz Joseph. They had fought at Waterloo and in the Crimea. Like all 'Guards' regiments, they were higher in status than non-Guards regiments such as hussars and lancers or plain dragoons. In yet another of those idiosyncrasies prevalent in the British army, Guards officers were privileged to be promoted not just to lieutenant but to 'lieutenant and captain' and thence to 'captain and lieutenant-colonel'.

So, two regiments, but there was also a detachment from the 5th Dragoons, which had joined the army very recently.

Both regiments were considered to be amongst the cream of the army's elite forces and therefore difficult for outsiders to deal with, especially a jumped-up infantry ensign in a mediocre regiment of foot. Even a private trooper in a Guards cavalry regiment considered himself superior to a junior officer in a foot regiment. That was why Seb had gone for the doctor first. But he was going to have to bite the bullet and interview this stammering cornet that had let slip something to Jack. At least it was not a colonel or even a captain. The young man was equivalent in rank to Seb, but Cartwright was cavalry and Seb was going to have a sticky time with him.

Three

First, Seb went to see Lord Chelmsford, who would need to know that a murder investigation was in progress. The lieutenant-general would not be pleased to see his Provost-Marshal. The commander of the army in South Africa had a myriad of problems to attend to, connected directly with war, but he had indicated that he wanted to be kept in the picture regarding serious crime.

Seb was lucky that he was visiting Landsman's Drift that day and was inspecting the preparations for the building of the fort. Unlike Lord Wellington, Chelmsford did not mind junior officers approaching him without going through hierarchical layers of staff. Wellington's mistakes, though few, were almost always attributable to poor communication with his spies and juniors. Chelmsford, though lacking in Wellington's brilliance, was not going to make that mistake. Seb did of course approach one of the general's aides-de-camp first and was shown into the general's presence.

The lean and intense Lord Chelmsford looked up from a table of maps and papers.

'Ah, my Provost-Marshal. You have something to tell me?'

Seb was stiffly at attention. 'Yes, sir, sorry to catch you while you're so busy.'

'As to that, young man, I'm *always* busy. I doubt I get four hours' sleep a night. My problem at the moment is not to do with who I take with me into battle, but who to leave behind. I have four major-generals and sixteen thousand troops, plus irregulars and thousands of transport conductors. I don't need 'em all. Those I leave behind will hate me for it, those I take with me will at first be happy but will later hate me for it. Still, a commander should not seek approval of those below him, only hope for it from those above.'

'Yes, sir.'

'And on top that I've got the bloody Prince Imperial of France wandering around my army. Another headache, trying to keep that hothead out of trouble. I'm trying to lead an army to victory here and I have precious youths of precious mothers put in my care. What am I? A kindergarten head? A schoolmaster? God help me . . .'

'Sir?' Seb had gone red, remembering an earlier incident involving the prince. An incident he wanted to forget.

Thankfully the general had not noticed his discomfort.

'I'm sorry, Ensign, I'm prattling. It helps to relieve my stress. You have something to report, or you wouldn't have asked to see me alone.'

Seb cleared his throat and gathered his courage.

'Sir, I believe a murder, or at least an unlawful killing, has taken place in the form of a duel.'

The general gave no indication that he had heard this remark, for he picked up a sheet of paper from his desk and silently began to read it. Seb waited for quite a while, until the general looked up again. His face was more composed than it had been when Seb first arrived.

'I had heard about an accident, but a duel, you say?'

'Yes, sir. I have reason to believe cavalry officers were involved, though I'm not yet certain of that. A man was killed. I'm – I'm afraid we don't know who he is, as yet. He reported to Major Gambolini, the adjutant of the 90th, who it seems cannot recall the officer's name.'

The general blinked. 'A dead man and no one knows who he is? Has he a rank, or is that a secret gone to the grave with him?'

'Lieutenant. But there was nothing amongst his personal effects which pointed to an identity. The dead man only arrived last night and the duel took place today – this morning. I was earlier told that he died in a hunting accident, though the wound was from a pistol, but I have reason to believe that was a lie.'

'It would seem unusual for an officer to arrive late in the evening and then go hunting in the very early morning.'

'Exactly so, sir.'

'Do then investigate this matter thoroughly, Ensign, and report your findings to me. If there was a duel and this officer was killed, then the man who shot him will need to go to trial.'

'Yes, sir, *all* the men.'

For the first time the general frowned deeply.

'All? What all?'

'Why, sir, all those present at the duel. I imagine there were seconds and a presiding officer, as well as a doctor. Every man there was complicit in the unlawful killing. Everyone present at the scene was involved. They would, therefore, all be guilty of the same crime, no matter who squeezed the trigger.'

'You believe this to be true? A common *blaze*?' The general was using the army euphemism for a duel. He had grown up in an era when duelling was acceptable even to British Prime Ministers. Wellington himself, while still PM, had fought a duel with Lord Winchilsea back in 1829, when Lord Chelmsford was a toddler. 'I suppose these days . . .'

'I know it to be so, sir. The men at the scene of this crime have to be regarded as accomplices of the man who shot the victim, and an accomplice is just as culpable as the killer himself. Since taking up my post I've been studying various aspects of the law. No one at that duel made any move to prevent this killing, in fact they encouraged the act to take place. Moreover, I have a witness who saw the exchange of fire and that person tells me the dead man deloped before being shot.'

'*What?*' the general thundered, his attention at last grabbed. 'And his opponent still aimed at him?'

'Carefully and deliberately, according to my source.'

The general growled in the back of his throat.

'Find me these men,' he said. 'We'll discuss how many of them are guilty later. Who is your witness? Is he a serving officer?'

'He's not a soldier, sir. He's a young civilian.'

'You don't wish to give me a name?'

'I – I would prefer to withhold it for the moment.'

The general stared at Seb for a long while, before saying, 'Thank you, Ensign. That is all.'

'Yes, sir.'

On his way to the civilian lines, Seb ran into Lord Henry Wycliffe, a mere subaltern like Seb himself, otherwise known as Mad Henry. He was one of those members of the peerage who gamble their estates away, are regarded as rogues and thieves by their creditors and live their lives as if tomorrow is not an option. Mad Henry might have been a stereotype of his kind, except that he was an archetype. No other peer was actually as crazy as Henry, though many foolish young blades aspired to be. As a baron he was in the fifth degree of the peerage, but as an officer in the army he was destined to remain a junior rank, unless he did something extraordinary on the battlefield. Though a lunatic he was intelligent enough, and certainly brave enough, all he lacked was the opportunity. In fact a mad exploit would be just up his street.

On this day, Henry was dressed in a top hat with an elegant peacock's feather waving from its band, a burgundy smoking jacket, jodhpurs and brilliantly polished brown boots.

Seb winced at the sight.

'Afternoon, Henry.'

'South-East, old chap, how's the head?'

Seb was prone to migraines.

'Fine, touch wood.'

'Good lad. I'm just off to see the chief.'

'Lord Chelmsford?'

'That's the fellah – Baron Wycliffe's off to see Lord Chelmsford. One of the newer nobles, he. I beat the old boy to it by at least five years and yet he's a general.' Henry's face dropped a little. 'Think he wants to tick me off for riding my nag through the mess tent last night.'

'Henry, I heard you *galloped* through. Very dangerous thing to do, Henry. You could have trampled someone.'

'I know, didn't think. Never do. Just go for it. Somebody wagered me I wouldn't dare, so I did. Colonel's already had a go at me. Now it's Thesiger's turn. Wouldn't bother with me if I wasn't a peer of the realm, now would he? Thinks I bring the nobility into disrepute.'

Seb said gently. 'Henry, you must go back and change into your dress, or even undress uniform – anything but what you're wearing.'

Henry looked down at himself in surprise.

'What? Oh, see what you mean, South-East. Can't do it, though. Late already.' He then spat on his hands and smoothed down his hair and his beard. 'There you are, transformed into a handsome prince. Now our lord and master will not be able to point the scinger of forn and say, "Get thee hence, Mad Henry, leave this pleasurable garden and go out into the wilderness, and never touch my precious apples again." '

Seb laughed. 'You're outrageous, Henry. Good luck.'

'Thank you, old chap.' Henry placed an affectionate arm around Seb's shoulders. 'Always liked you, South-East. Something very genuine about you. Of course, now you're a policeman you're a bit of a pariah, an untouchable, but I'm something of a social outcast too, at least amongst the greybeards. We're brothers in arms, you and me. We'll show 'em all, yet, eh? We'll shake the world like the orgasm of a god. I can sense it in the wind. When we're both generals I'll remind you of this prophecy and you'll say, "Henry, old bean, how right you were." '

With that Mad Henry ambled off towards headquarters, whistling an old English folk tune, while a tribesman who now wore the top hat with its peacock feather walked in the opposite direction with poker-straight back and affecting a tall and dignified figure. Those of his friends who had witnessed the passing-over of the hat showed their appreciation of it with their mirth.

The civilian lines were a heaving massive fleet of carts and wagons, some being loaded, some being maintained, some in a state of disrepair. Oxen and horses were crammed into the corrals beyond the cart area. One wagon would need at least sixteen beasts to draw it, once the army was on the move. Men, mostly transport conductors and their assistants, were either asleep under the wagons or working furiously. There seemed to be no in between. No one strolled. It was either the quick or the dead.

The conductors and their assistants were both black and white, and many carried long flexible whips with which to manage their stock. They wore a variety of garments, mostly wide-brimmed straw hats, nankeen shirts and breeches. Some of the blacks were barefoot, though others wore boots or sandals. The whites, with their tender feet and fear of jiggers, always went well shod. Their wagons were huge and cumbersome. At eighteen feet long, with rear-axle span of nearly six feet, a fully laden wagon weighed something in the region of three tons. This sort of load very easily stuck in the mud and with the beasts attached it spanned about thirty-two yards of the track. A battalion of say one thousand men needed nearly twenty of these wagons to carry its supplies. Chelmsford's columns were around five thousand, which meant a hundred wagons. The length of a hundred wagons was therefore in the region of two miles. Dragging this unwieldy supply train, with the necessary cannon and soldiers, Lord Chelmsford's column was lucky to make between five and ten miles a day.

As he passed through the lines, Seb asked where he might find any civilian doctors. He was given various locations, some of them at the far ends of Natal, and eventually gave up that particular avenue of enquiry. He decided it would probably be best if he asked in the officers' mess. Civilians were not welcome there, but many were thick-skinned enough to ignore cold shoulders. They were part of the war too and many decided they were at least equivalent to captain, if not superior, since they had at least undergone some sort of training, whereas a lieutenant might have been a schoolboy one day and purchased a lieutenancy the next. Many officers learned on the job and relied on their NCOs for expertise.

The sun was going down now and Seb admired the blaze of red and orange that filled the African sky. There was a trim of clouds on the horizon which made a line of fire all around the edge of the world. In the distance were the Drakensbergs, their scaly heights piercing the belly of this burning sky. Seb never ceased to wonder at the majesty of the African scene, which was large enough to swallow England in a single small bite. He felt humbled by a landscape that was vibrant with wildlife and a heavenly ceiling that was forever brushed by the wings of birds and polished by soft swarms of various insects.

The musky scent of the African earth was overpowered by the aroma of Sam Weary's outdoor kitchen as Seb approached his tent. Tom was there, helping Sam with the cooking. And where there was food on the hob, Corporal Evans was not far away.

'Evans,' Seb called to his corporal, 'can we speak?'

Sam nudged the tall, willowy artilleryman and repeated with exaggerated movements of his mouth the officer's request. The deaf corporal had been to a church service and was dressed in his finest raiment: that is to say, his only clothes. His red tunic was patched in three places: at the right elbow, on the left shoulder and on the right breast. Evans had used what was to hand to make these repairs and all three patches were of different cloths, including one of goatskin. His white helmet was now mostly a dung-coloured brown, having been used variously as a pillow, a rugby ball and a water carrier. Wadding was visible in several places through splits in the helmet cover. Some of the holes had been made by local birds obtaining nesting material when the owner was absent. Below the waist his trousers were ragged affairs with patches of skin showing through and his boots were laceless and had gaps between sole and upper. He was by no means unusual. One 24th boasted that he had not taken off his boots in three months, let alone any other part of his uniform.

'Sir,' said Evans, saluting smartly, 'you can speak and I shall listen, eh? That's the way of it in the army.'

'I hope that's not insubordination.'

'No, sir, it's the truth of things, which don't bother me in the least, since people have been talking at me all my life.'

Evans then ran his fingers down through his enormous beard to clear it of the evening insects that had been caught in its tangles.

'You've been to a service?'

'Memorial service, sir,' said Evans, trying to control the volume of his voice, but failing. 'Our losses at Isandlwana.'

'I didn't know that was on,' remarked a worried Seb, thinking his presence would have been marked by his colonel. 'Why wasn't I told?'

'Wasn't a parade, as such. Just some of us got together, like. We got to askin' ourselves why the savages kept jabbing an' poking at dead bodies, which we know they did, sir, for they was seen by the fugitives even while they was running away. Couldn't understand it, see, all this hacking of the soldiers when there was no fight left in them. Mutilation, that's what it was. Chopping at the dead body. Desecratin' the departed.' Evans' voice rose even higher as he said the last sentence, his anger rising up inside him like boiling water.

Sam Weary looked up from his cooking.

'Sirs, I can tell you what is the Zulu way. This is not desecrating. This is setting free the souls.' Sam stood up and criss-crossed his abdomen. 'Zulu man will cut here and here, to open up the belly, so that spirit of the warrior he has killed will escape and fly away.'

Evans was not satisfied with the Xhosa's explanation.

'Then why,' he shouted, 'did they keep stabbing the corpses with their spears, eh? Answer me that! Lettin' pixies out, was they?'

Sam was ever patient with these newcomers to his land.

'No, sir,' he said, quietly, 'that was not to let pixies escape, though Sam does not know what are pixies. Zulu man shows respect for his dead enemy by stabbing him many times. It is called *hlomula* and it is one warrior's way of saying, "You died in a brave way, my enemy, and I think you have the courage of a lion." '

'Oh, is it?' cried Evans, the wind taken out of his sails. 'That's what it is, is it?'

'Yes, sir, it is.'

Evans gave a deep sigh and began to follow Seb into his tent, while Sam asked Tom what 'pixies' were.

'They's these little fellahs,' explained Tom, 'like hoomans only small.'

'How small?'

'Maybe six inches, or nine. Some of 'em have got wings, like hornets, and they'm packed full of magic.'

Sam's eyes went round. 'Magic?' he repeated in a hushed tone, and crossed himself in the Christian manner. 'What sort of magic?'

'Oh,' replied Tom, airily, 'nothin' like leopard-men or witches and such. More like spoilin' the milk, makin' it go sour. Stuff like that. They don't come around in the night and cut your throat, nor tear you open with claws, like African magic. All they do is be there, hidin' under leaves and bits of bark, and doin' mischief. I seen one once, when I was very small in England. It went down a rabbit hole.'

'What was it wearing, Tom?'

'Oh, stuff that pixies wear. Green tunic, green leggin's, red hat and oh, yes, a white owl's feather in the band.'

'There won't be any in Africa,' Sam said, almost to himself. 'These are creatures from England.'

'Oh, you never know,' said Tom with some conviction. 'They could've stowed away in men's kit and got here that way. I been expectin' someone to open a hofficer's trunk and a pixie to hop out and say, "How dee-do," and then turn hisself into a frog.'

Sam crossed himself again and turned back to his cooking, clearly deciding he would never open an officer's trunk ever again.

Inside the tent Seb was using sign language for the deaf to speak to his corporal.

Seb: *Evans, we have a murder on our hands.*

Evans: *Good, it's about time we had another one.*

Seb: *That's a bit callous, man, but I know what you mean. A policeman needs crimes to solve, or there's not much use in having him. This one concerns an officer who arrived late last night and was killed − I believe − in a duel this morning.*

Evans: *That was quick work. Who was he?*

Seb (slightly irritated by the lack of formalities he had to undergo while talking to his NCO in sign language): *No one knows.*

Evans: *Who shot him, then?*

Seb: *No one knows that either, or he would have been arrested.*

Evans: *Don't know much, do we?*

Seb: *Not yet, no. But Tom saw the duel. I want you to walk him around camp tomorrow, take two or three days if you want. Take him especially where there are cavalry. If he recognizes anyone, I don't want him to give himself away. Just quietly come back to me and then we'll go from there. Understood?*

'Yes, sir,' shouted Evans.

'Why are you speaking out loud now?' asked Seb, blinking under the blast.

'Important stuff is over, sir, and I could see you getting a little irked with me not calling you sir – sir. It seemed a bit silly when we was conversing in silence, so I thought I'd better go loud again.'

'You know what I said. I don't worry about that sort of thing,' Seb said, stiffly, 'since we have to work so closely together.'

'You said it, but you don't mean it.'

Seb admitted, 'Well, it's difficult to get used to. An officer needs the visible and verbal respect of his soldiers in order to maintain discipline.'

'That's why you make the coalman call you "sir" at home, is it, so that he'll take orders without thinkin', like?'

Seb bristled. 'I don't *make* anyone call me anything . . .'

'But they do.'

'Yes, yes they do.'

'And your bootmaker. And your tailor. They do it because they know you expect it. You think they'd do it otherwise? If you appear to expect it, sir, that's blackmailin' 'em into doing it. They know they don't call you sir you'll take your trade somewhere else.'

'Evans, this conversation is getting very close to insolence – we will leave it there.'

'Yes, sir – I just thought you liked a discussion.'

'We'll leave it there.'

Afterwards Seb was wondering, as he always did after such an encounter with his corporal, why he felt he had come off worst. Evans had that superior way with him that made Seb feel he had to defend himself all the time. Surely there was nothing wrong with maintaining a level of respect from the ranks? Or from tradesmen back in England, if it came to that? Seb was a gentleman. Evans was a shepherd. God and biology were responsible for that, not Seb. There had to be a class order or everything would go to blazes. Indeed there were still aristocratic officers who believed that men like Seb were guttersnipes, simply because his father had no title. Lord Wellington, for example, gave privileges to those of his officers who came from nobility and the gentry and scorned those who were from lesser families.

No, Evans had got it wrong.

'One of these days I'll prove to that man that there's a chain of being here in the army, as well as amongst creatures of the wild,' he muttered to himself. 'He needs to acknowledge that fact or he'll never progress through the ranks.'

Seb knew there had been generals who had begun life as a lower form even than a shepherd. Men like General Colin Campbell, whose father was a Glaswegian carpenter. Seb then tried to imagine Evans as a general and found, to his great discomfort, that his image of Corporal Evans in the uniform of a general was quite imposing, since the corporal was tall and stately in appearance, quite unlike the shorter Seb.

Seb had written three names in his notebook:

Major Gambolini, 90th Foot
Cornet Cartwright, 5th Dragoons
(?) Pearson (17th Lancers?)

Seb made to his way to where the 90th were camped and sought out the adjutant. He was not a hard man to find: a corpulent fellow with a large nose and jet-black hair almost reaching his eyebrows. He wore a jovial expression, almost clownish, but his eyes showed a sharpness of intellect. If Seb had seen him in a street of civilians he might have put him down as a shrewd innkeeper or shop owner. As it was, the adjutant seemed to be wading through a sea of paper, his shining apple-cheeked face glistening with sweat, though he was not actually doing anything but staring into space.

Seb saluted. 'Major Gambolini?'

The major stared at Seb and leaned back in his rattan chair, making it creak ominously.

'Who wants to know?'

'Ensign Early, sir, of the 24th.'

'Can see that. I'm not daft. Provost, is it?'

Seb glanced down at his red sash. 'Yes, sir. I need to ask you a few questions, if you have the time.'

'And if I haven't?'

'I'm afraid it's rather important.'

'Tea?'

Seb was confused. 'I'm sorry . . .'

'Do you want some tea, man. I'm about to have my elevenses.'

'Sir,' said Seb, 'it's 4 p.m.'

'So what? I have 'em when I feel like I need 'em. Tell the black fellah standing outside I'll have cake with my tea today, as well as biscuits, and ask for one yourself. You eat cake?'

Seb, who had not seen confectionery for a very long while, replied that he did on occasion, eat a little cake.

The servant, quietly sitting on the ground making cats' cradles with a dirty piece of string, was given his instructions and very, very soon the two officers were enjoying a pleasant repast.

'That black fellah outside, never remember their names, is the fastest runner this side of the border.' The major tapped the side of his head. 'All cultures love to run, no matter where you go. When I get to a new posting, I always ask who wins all the races. When I find him, I grab him for myself. That fellah outside can fetch me anything within two minutes. Runs like the wind. Got wings on his feet, like that Greek messenger fellah, Hermes, only he wasn't black of course – sort of olive colour, I suppose. Two minutes, tops. Never keeps me waiting any longer, unless he's got to have time to make a fresh brew, of course. You have to use your head in the army, or you get left with duffers who bring you cold tea. Can't stand cold tea.'

'You haven't asked him his name, then?'

The major sipped his drink from his mug.

'Oh, asked him once, but forgot it straight away. Can't keep names in me head, especially some of the names of these fellahs. Tongue-twisters. I think they do it deliberately, make up names we can't pronounce, just to annoy us.'

Seb said, 'You can't really mean that, sir?'

The major looked surprised. 'No, of course I don't – it's a joke.'

'Sir,' said Seb, getting down to business, 'an officer of your regiment reported to you last night. Apparently he rode in fairly late in the evening?'

'The fellah who's been shot? Yes.'

'Can you not recall his name?'

The major leaned back again and sighed. 'Tried. Won't come. Didn't really listen, see. Didn't think it all that important. Told the lieutenant to come back in the morning. Would then *write* down his name and then we'd have it in black and white. Didn't come back, of course, being dead as a nail by that time. Men reporting all the time, coming and going like Venetian ships. Dozens of 'em. Can't be expected to remember all the names they throw at me. Too many of 'em. Wish I had a better memory for names, but I don't. Pick up your crumbs or we'll have the ants in here in no time. Can't stand ants.'

This whole speech was delivered without any change of tone throughout, so the last two sentences caught Seb unawares. Then he realized he was scattering cake crumbs on the major's table and he scooped them up with his hands and looked around for somewhere to put them. There was no rubbish receptacle evident, so eventually under the careful scrutiny of the major he put them in his pocket.

'So, young man – Provost, eh? – can I do anything else for you? Tea nice and hot?'

'Yes, thank you, sir. No, if you can't remember the name, you can't, and that's that. You would have thought he might have a letter or something in his pockets, or in his saddlebags, with a name on it, wouldn't you?'

'If it were up to me,' said the major in a confidential tone, 'we would all have our names embroidered on our chests. Fellah comes up to you in the mess and says something and you search your mind for his moniker and all you come up with is a blank, so you um and ah for ten minutes, hoping someone else will come up and say, "Peterson, you card, where have you been these last few days." Dreadful business, trying to remember names in an army of thousands. If I had "Hamish Alphonso Gambolini" written all over my bosom, no one would forget it, would they?'

From this speech Seb deduced the major's first names were Hamish Alphonso and left him to finish his tea and cake. As he left the tent the 'fast runner' looked up at him and showed him a perfect string figure of an Apache Door, before changing it in a flash into Jacob's Ladder, then swiftly again into A Moon Gone Dark. So, apart from having flashing feet, this local wizard had flashing fingers too.

'You should do that for money,' Seb advised, 'round the camp-fire at night.'

The man grinned at him and nodded.

Seb's next call was on Cornet Cartwright, of the 5th Dragoons. He went to their lines and enquired after the cornet. He met a lieutenant leading his horse and asked the man a question.

'Young Cartwright? He's been sent home.'

'Home?' repeated Seb, a little stupidly. 'What home?'

'To England, of course. Silly fellow broke his arm in two places. Can't ride a horse with one arm. Well, you can, but you need to hold a weapon with the other, what? No one goes into battle without a weapon in their hand, now do they, Ensign? Not that I know of.'

Seb had been told by his uncle Jack, who had witnessed the charge of the Light Brigade at Balaclava, that several men caught smoking pipes before that famous charge were deprived of their swords. At least two unarmed troopers were killed in the attack on the Russian guns. Perhaps more? He was on the point of passing this information on to the flippant lieutenant when he realized he was getting side-tracked.

'Sent back to England? His arm would have healed just as well here, wouldn't it?'

'Resigned his commission,' said the lieutenant, in a bored tone. 'Anything else you'd like to know, Ensign?'

So, they had got rid of Cornet Cartwright, undoubtedly after breaking his arm for him to teach him to keep his mouth shut.

'No, thank you, Lieutenant. You've told me all I want to know.'

'Glad to be of service. Now, if you don't mind?'

Seb left the man to mount his horse and trot it around the perimeter of the camp, presumably to give it some exercise.

Four

The following dawn the sky was ablaze again, with streaks of fiery red flaring up from the edge of the world. The red-dust plains burned again, with a harder light than they had done in the evening, making black figures of soldiers and locals look like toys. A distant lion, seen through a spy glass, walked with a coat that shone like polished amber. Foliage on the tall trees burst into blood-coloured blooms that seemed to startle the birds. Rocky outcrops had a bright fringe of light dancing around their edges, giving them a trim of false gold.

Seb wondered about the old British saying, 'Red sky in the morning, shepherd's warning. Red sky at night, shepherd's delight.' Here there was clearly a mix-up. Red skies at both ends of the dark hours. Was it going to rain, or was it not? He asked Evans, the ex-shepherd, what he thought of the old saying.

'Load of old twaddle if you ask me, sir,' bellowed Evans. 'I've known it to rain hard enough to bring on Noah's flood, and both ends of the day 'ave been as grey as granddad's head.'

'Oh, there must be something in it, surely?'

'Suit yourself, sir.'

'Well, it's such a common saying, after all.'

'If you like, sir.'

Infuriating. The man could be utterly *infuriating*. Here was Seb, an officer and a gentleman, trying to be friendly with his NCO, and getting rebuffed for it. Why should he bother with the man? It just went to show that the army regulation of non-fraternization with the rank and file was a good one. The ordinary soldier was just too crass and unmannered to recognize that you did not just wave another man's opinions away in contempt. You discussed it with him in a sensible, even forthright way, putting across your view but respecting the view of the other person.

'So you think all sayings are rubbish, do you, Corporal?'

'Not all of 'em, sir. Just that one for the moment.'

'What about, "Ne'er cast a clout, till May be out"? Is that an empty phrase too?'

Evans shrugged. 'There's more reasonin' behind that one. If the weather's cool for the time of year, the hawthorn won't blossom, will it? Therefore, it's best to wait until the may blossom of the haw is out, for that'll mean the warmer weather has come . . .'

Seb, who had thought 'May' meant the month and not the blossom on the hawthorn, collected himself very quickly.

'So, you admit that this particular saying is useful?'

'Well, my gramma liked to use it, when we was little, to amuse us like, but when you come to think of it, sir, any sensible grown-up can tell whether it's cold enough to put on a coat or not, eh?'

At that point Seb was saved by the appearance of his uncle, Major Crossman, who came striding towards them. Jack Crossman was a veteran of several wars, an army intelligence agent from the 88th Connaught Rangers, though he rarely served with his regiment. Instead he reported directly to General Lovelace, the shadowy figure who headed a dark nebulous cloud of individual spies, agents and saboteurs who supplied commanders in the British army with information on the enemy without and within, and destroyed things when they needed destroying. Jack was a strangely quiet man bearing enough scars of old wounds for several men. His left hand was missing, having been crushed by a siege ladder in the attack on the redan at the battle for Sebastopol in the Crimea. His skull had been split by the stone axe of a Maori. He had bullet wounds, knife wounds and various other holes in his flesh. He limped. But his heart was whole and his spirit was as clean and strong as a twenty-seven-year-old's.

Jack was this morning accompanied by a huge black man carrying an ancient-looking musket.

'Sebastian,' said Seb's uncle, 'how are you?'

They shook hands, the tall major with his smile twisted by a face wound, looking down on the shorter ensign.

'Fine, thanks, Jack. And you?'

'Equally fine. Have you met Xolani? He's my Zulu bodyguard. Shake hands with him.'

Seb to his credit immediately reached out, but awkwardly. To shake hands with a Zulu? Even Sam Weary, sitting in his accustomed spot by the campfire, widened his eyes at this. He was watching Seb's face closely and Seb was also aware of Evans' gaze on him.

Seb's uncle had always been unorthodox. Not in the crazy way of Mad Henry, but just very unconventional. Seb guessed it was because Jack had worked with natives and savages all over the world, out in the field, and saw them as equals. Quite an unusual viewpoint for an aristocrat whose baronet father would have died rather than shake the hand of a middle-class white man, let alone someone as lowly as his gardener or cook, for that was the status of Xolani.

Seb's fingers were immediately swallowed by the thick callused hands of the Zulu. There was great strength behind the black man's shake. Enormous strength. A broad smile accompanied the gesture, delivered in full before their palms parted.

'Xolani,' said Jack, 'like so many of my assistants, would instantly kill any man who so much as thought about harming me. I'm lucky like that. I had a Bashi-Bazouk in the Crimea, a fierce Maori in New Zealand and a bloodthirsty Rajput in India, all prepared to destroy anyone who threatened me with the slightest harm. It's probably the reason I'm alive today. I certainly could not have relied on my own skills, not in all the scrapes I've been in. Everyone should have a Xolani.'

A Welsh voice broke in very loudly, 'I know what you mean, sir. I have to look out for the ensign.'

'Evans, please be quiet,' ordered Seb, mouthing the words elaborately in the direction of his corporal.

'I was just informin' the major,' said Evans, 'that he don't need to worry about you, sir. I'm your Xolani, see? Anyone who has a go at you, has me to answer to . . .'

Seb was embarrassed.

'Thank you, Corporal, but the major has more important things on his mind than my general welfare.'

Jack was grinning, but said, 'This is true, Corporal, but I appreciate the idea that you're looking after my nephew. Officers like us are full of high courage, but our bodies are inclined to having been dampened a little by a soft, comfortable upbringing. Now, Seb, I know your skills at drawing. I'd like you to ride out with me and do some map-making for me. I've cleared it with your colonel. We may also need another guide. Xolani was born and raised in Natal and knows little about the topography of Zululand. Anyone in mind?'

Seb said, 'Yes, I know a Boer guide, but he's a bit of a maverick.'

'I like mavericks.'

'But, Jack, I'm no map-maker, you know. I can do a good woodpecker or springbok, but as to cartography . . .'

'You're good enough for me. I want three-dimensional landscapes, not flat maps. I had a sergeant once who thought that the world revolved around mapping. Sadly he's no longer with me.'

'Dead?'

'No, worse. They made him a lieutenant. They gave him his own team and let me go to the devil.'

Seb laughed more at his uncle's apparent chagrin than the irony.

'The only trouble is, Jack, I'm in the middle of a murder investigation. At least, I think it's murder – fairly sure. I can't just go wandering off into the bush. I have my job to do.'

'I told you I cleared it with your colonel.'

'But not the general – Lord Chelmsford's expecting me to report on this fairly soon.'

'Are you close to a conclusion?'

'Nowhere near,' replied Seb.

'Then while we're out there, you can run things by me, and I'll give you the benefit of my years of experience. Look, which is more important? Ending this war, or finding a perhaps-murderer?'

Seb said, 'Both are important, you know that, Uncle Jack.'

'Well, which one has the priority? If we don't attend to matters out in the field, we may all be dead and where will your murder investigation be then? Come on, youngster, take me to this Boer and let's be on our way. The sooner we leave, the sooner we get back.'

'You're sure the colonel gave me permission?'

'Absolutely. And what's more I've got you a horse. A very good one. A gift from your decrepit old uncle.'

A horse! That would mean Seb would no longer need to go begging the quartermaster for a mount every time he needed one. He would have his own steed. That was something special. Now Sam would have to learn grooming. Sam hated animals, though. Maybe the boy, Tom, would like to look after the beast? Yes, he would think that a good thing to do, would Tom.

'What is it – mare or stallion?'

'Gelding. A white Arab, like the one Napoleon rode – Marengo.

Not a blemish on his coat. You'd think he'd been dipped in white paint. You don't want a stallion, Seb – they're difficult to manage, unreliable in the field and they chase after mares in season. A gelding's the thing. His name is—'

'Hup!' interrupted Seb. 'My beast, I get to name him.'

Jack grinned. 'Fine. Come on, let's meet the Boer and then we'll collect the mounts.'

Zeldenthuis was in a bar with his cronies. They were making a lot of drinking men's noise, shouting and laughing raucously, though it has to be said Pieter Zeldenthuis himself was not joining in this drunken revelry. He was sitting quietly supping a drink, surveying the scene around him with narrowed eyes. Seb knew that he and Jack had been seen by the Boer the moment they entered the room, though Zeldenthuis gave no indication that he had noticed them.

'That him,' asked Jack, quietly, 'with the red neckerchief?'

'Yes, how did you know?'

'He looks as if he takes life seriously.'

They crossed the dirt floor towards Zeldenthuis, only to find their way suddenly barred by a large boar-shaped man with filthy kid boots and a hat with dirt to match. Strangely the clothes between top and tail were relatively clean, except for some patches of dust. He did not wear a beard like Jack and Seb, and most men of the army, but his chin was covered in thick black bristle. Eyes dull enough for a drunk fixed on Jack, as the man put his legs astride to block their way.

'Ag, no bloody army officers in here, dof!'

Jack did not even break his stride as he kicked away the fellow's right leg and caused him to crash to the floor. On his back, the man tried to sit up, only to find Jack's boot on his chest. His hand went to the knife on his belt, but Jack's other boot came smashing down on the forearm.

'Urrggh, fuck. You bastard, you've broke my arm,' screamed the man.

'I know what it feels like, man,' said Jack in a perfect copy of the fellow's clipped dialect. 'See?' Jack held up his stump. 'But you'll get used to not having it. I did, pretty quickly.'

Some of the other men, whose mouths had dropped wide open,

now started to move forward. One or two had bottles in their hands, others had mugs which could be turned into weapons. Seb's hand drifted down to his sword hilt, only to find thin air. He had forgotten to buckle on his blade this morning. The mob closed in. Suddenly a weapon appeared in Jack's hand. Seb knew what it was: his uncle's favourite firearm. A five-shot Tranter revolver with double triggers, one for cocking, one for firing. Jack covered the advancing men, who were too drunk to realize their lives were in danger.

The scouts, drovers and wagon-drivers were stopped by a shout from the only man still sitting. They stood there and seemed to be in a state of confusion. Their eyes went from the man on the floor, to the two officers, then to the sitting man.

'Back off, you *gesuip* idiots. Can't you see the officer's going to blow your bloody heads off.'

It was Pieter Zeldenthuis who had spoken. He now got up and stepped over the body of the groaning man who was nursing his injured arm. 'Let's go outside,' he said to Seb and Jack, 'before this lot lose their senses again and try to rush you both. They've all had a skinful and they've got about as much caution as a peahen at the moment.'

Outside, Zeldenthuis said, 'I take it you were coming to see me?'

'The major,' said Seb, indicating Jack, 'needs a guide. We're going into Zululand to do some landscape drawing—'

'Mapping,' interrupted Jack.

'Yes, mapping,' continued Seb, having unsuccessfully tried to avoid the word. 'I recommended you as the best guide I know.'

Zeldenthuis smiled. 'Thank you for that recommendation, Ensign. You, I take it, are the mapper.' He turned to Jack. 'This man draws a great buffalo and I should think he draws most things quite well. You made a good choice in him.'

Seb blinked at this unexpected praise from the Boer.

'I know,' replied Jack, 'he's my nephew. My father was an artist. It seems to run in the family.'

Seb thought his uncle was being a bit silly, since he was not from that side of the family. He would have rather, too, that Zeldenthuis had not been made aware of their relationship, but Jack was always open like that. Open in his dealings with ordinary men, while secretive in his dealings with agents and spies. Seb supposed some sort of balance had to be formed in a person's life. Anyway the pair of them were lavishing praise on his expertise with a pencil and brush, and he now had to come up to expectations.

'. . . so,' Jack finished, 'will you do it, Mr Zeldenthuis? I have no authority to order you to come with us, though I could get it if I wanted to – but I'd rather you came as a willing volunteer.'

Zeldenthuis said, 'I thought no one volunteered for anything in the British army?'

'Oh yes, often,' said Jack, smiling, 'I myself once volunteered for the Forlorn Hope. Many do, who wish for promotion.'

'Which is?'

'First into the breach. If you live, you are recognized for the next rank up. Most die, of course, being on the receiving end of a cannonful of grapeshot or canister. Most are cut to pieces within the first few seconds. One or two by a miracle survive, usually with injuries, and are happily one more notch up the ladder as a reward.'

'Injuries?' Zeldenthuis nodded at Jack's missing hand.

'Precisely.'

Zeldenthuis sighed and shook his head.

'You're all bloody mad. All right, when do we start?'

'In one hour,' said Jack. 'I need to arrange for some dragoons to go with us. It'd be foolish to go into Zululand now, while the pot's boiling, without an escort.'

Jack introduced Seb to his white Arab, which was indeed a most beautiful creature. Seb was astonished at his uncle's generosity and thanked him profusely. They stood and admired the beast for a few minutes, with Jack breaking the silence, saying, 'Brave, spirited and intelligent. That's your Arab for you. Any ideas on a name yet?'

'No, I'll let one come to me. In the meantime he's just "Seb's mount", if you don't mind.'

An hour later Major Jack Crossman came for Seb. He was accompanied by Pieter Zeldenthuis and twenty-four troopers from the 1st King's Dragoon Guards. There was no officer with the troopers. Jack explained that a 'friend loaned his men to me and trusts me to return them all undamaged'. They all knew that might not be possible, if they were to come up against a Zulu impi, but Jack always liked to keep his conversations casual and with a lightness of word.

As they rode out, Seb admired the dragoons, who rode heavy horses with the ease of well-trained roughriders. They were wearing scarlet tunics with cobalt-blue collars, cuffs and shoulder straps, fringed with yellow braid. There was a peculiar strangulated raised design on the lower arm of the tunic, which on asking Seb was told was an Austrian knot. They had on blue trousers with a yellow stripe down them and their badge was the Austrian double eagle. They were armed with carbines and heavy swords, with ammunition in pouches on their belts. The rest of their equipment they carried in a small haversack.

Although he only admitted it to himself, Seb was as envious as anyone of the cavalry. Of course everyone admired the light cavalry for their élan and dash, but even the heavy cavalry were one of the first targets of a schoolboy wanting to join the army. Why would you want to go tramping miles over foreign countries by foot when you could canter through the countryside on a horse looking high and splendid in the saddle, then go galloping in a hell-for-leather charge waving a sabre once the fun started? So far as most schoolboys were concerned, there was no choice. You had to be on a steed waving a flashing blade. It was what you trained at the hunt for. Your dreams were full of black panting stallions called Lightning or Thunderbolt, shining with sweat, of which you were the complete and adored master.

Zeldenthuis spoke to Jack Crossman as they came up to the Buffalo River.

'Forgive me, Major,' he said, 'but you look a little long in the tooth for one of your rank. You been passed over?'

Jack raised an eyebrow, but replied honestly, 'Mr Zeldenthuis . . .'

'Pieter – call me Pieter.'

'I prefer Mr Zeldenthuis. It's better we keep a space between us, since I'm leader of this expedition. I began life in the army as a private soldier. When a sergeant I was sidelined into gathering intelligence – a spy, if you like, and a saboteur – and I had a mentor, a sponsor, who pushed me up the ladder. Or to be more accurate pulled me up with him. He's now a general, of course, and deserves it. I, on the other hand, gave only half my life. The other half I felt belonged to my wife and family, and so I did not make the best of opportunities. Some postings I rejected, postings which might have resulted in going higher. There, you have my reasons for being a passed-over major. Now I'm in my fifties and it's doubtful I'll see a colonelcy. It really doesn't matter. I'm a wealthy man, I don't need the money, and I'm doing a job I like – well, a job I'm good at, having done it for so long it's become part of me.'

'You could have purchased a colonelcy, surely?'

'Yes, but I've never believed in that route, otherwise I'd have taken it a great deal earlier in life.'

Zeldenthuis nodded. 'I guess not, since you joined as a private soldier. I have to say, looking at your battered face and broken body, they could have done a bit more for you, since apart from giving half your life, you've thrown in a few body parts as well. You should ask for them back. You could do with a better face, even at your age.'

Jack turned in the saddle and stared at the Boer.

'You have a direct manner of speech, Mr Zeldenthuis, which would offend some of my countrymen. However, to answer your question, you can never expect an organization like the army to feel appreciation or gratitude. It has no soul. Individual men, perhaps, but not the army as an entity. That's the way of the world. I've been lucky to get as far as I have. My commander thought a lot of me. Some soldiers have had cause to curse both the army and their commanders, for not recognizing or rewarding their worth. Wellington, you know, was a particularly ungrateful commander. He fought and won a war with sterling help, whom he promised to advance once it was all over. What did he do?'

'He forgot those who'd gained him his victory?'

'Precisely. He chose to ignore the fact that it takes more than one man to beat a foe, it takes an army. Once they'd got him what he most desired, he abandoned them, most of them. Oh, he had one or two favourites he still looked after – aristocrats, of course, like himself – but the other officers on whom he had relied when times were tough, he conveniently forgot. Some tried to remind him, but never received an answer. He was the most unmitigated snob on the face of the earth, was Wellington. If you didn't own land, and plenty of it, you were nothing. Cost him a victory once, simply because he couldn't lower himself to listen to a junior officer who could have given him information which would have secured that victory. Silly man, really. Very good general, but too puffed up with his own self-importance.'

They rode over the lush grasslands that stretched out from the other side of the river. To Seb, who had entered Zululand before, the clanking and clinking of the dragoons' metalwork sounded like gongs and bullroarers announcing their entry into enemy country. In the distance the mountains squatted like giant toads waiting to swallow anything that came within reach. Dark forests seemed like traps waiting to be sprung. When men go into a place where their enemies lurk ready to leap out on them, everything appears sinister and menacing. Even the gentle grasslands could hide a multitude of warriors armed with rifles, knives and spears. Seb felt sneaking through such a threatening landscape was safer than going in with bells and whistles inviting disaster to fall upon them.

They kept stopping briefly for Seb to sketch his linear maps. He ignored anything beyond two miles on either side of the track they were following, simply noting landmarks and drawing the topography of the line which the main army would follow. Zeldenthuis regarded his efforts with undisguised amusement and Seb knew this was because Boers like him knew every inch of the ground over which they were riding.

However, an army cannot trust its scouts completely, since they might all die in the first battle and then the army is lost. A general needs to know his ground, needs to know his way in and out of a place as vast as Zululand: where the cover is, where the high ground lies, where the rivers run and the trees are gathered. It is more to do with feeling confident than with guiding oneself over foreign ground. The scouts were the orienteers, but the general and his staff needed to know ahead of the march where they were heading and the type of terrain which might swallow them and their troops.

There is nothing worse than an under-confident general who, finding himself in a strange country, engages in blind desperate measures.

Such is the cause of many blunders.

Any game that wandered the grasslands, and there was not a great deal in this part of Zululand, seemed to know they were safe from being shot. Herbivores merely looked up and stared, still chewing the cud, while carnivores trotted on by without a glance in the direction of the red-and-blue-coated bipeds. Animals have this instinctive ability to distinguish between a warrior and a hunter. Warriors need to travel stealthily in enemy country and a rifle shot might prick up ears all the way back to a king in his kraal. So antelopes and deer, warthogs and buffalo, all lifted a lazy head to watch the procession go by. None seemed alarmed by the men in red coats, riding cousins of the zebra. The grass was far more interesting than a herd of humans on horses.

They reached the waters of the White Mfolozi River easily by the late afternoon. Not long afterwards the evening sky was a spectacle of whip-marks of cirrus which turned to raw wounds with the dying sun. Distant dark hills melted into the earth. Crickets, and other noisy nocturnal insects, took over from the cicadas and the rest of the day shift to ensure that the world would not have to suffer peace and quiet. Small mammals that hunted in the twilight and in the darkness emerged from their holes and hiding places to seek their meals. Birds found what roosts the area had to offer, though these were few. There were arguments, of course, about who got to which branch first, and who was entitled to oust another because of superior size or ferociousness. It was not always the biggest who won. A wren will take on anything from a starling to a crow, and in the mammal world a shrew will face down a rat. Even in the animal world there are the small giants.

Major Jack Crossman sought out a suitable campsite, with the river at their back and two outcrops of rock to defend their flanks. Guard duties were assigned by the NCO in charge of the troopers. They lit no fire, for smoke can be smelled from miles away. Biltong was the order of the day, and biscuits, and good clean water.

Zeldenthuis, as was his wont, ate and drank apart from the main body of men. He was joined by Jack's bodyguard, the huge Xolani. The two men seemed to have something in common, for they kept each other's company, mostly in silence it seemed. They were of this land and they were chary of mixing with these foreigners. *My cousin and I are against each other, but my cousin and I together are against the stranger.* An old Arab saying, but it applied here just as well here as in Arabia. Of course, Xolani was also by Jack's side a lot, but his leisure moments found him next to Pieter Zeldenthuis.

Seb managed a word with Zeldenthuis.

'You must not endanger this expedition with your obsession with revenge. That must be put aside, you understand?'

'Obsession, is it? I wondered what it was.'

'Zeldenthuis, I haven't said anything to Major Crossman about it, so I expect you to toe the line here.'

The Boer gave Seb a curt nod then walked away to attend to some domestic duty with his sleeping arrangements. They were around two thousand feet above sea level and the temperatures were mild during the day, dropping at night. The men would sleep without tents, in the open, as best as they could. Without a fire wild animals might venture into the camp so the sentries had to be doubly alert.

That night there was a spectacular dry storm which lit up the horizons all around them. No rain came, but distant thunder smacked the belly out of the sky and lines of forked lightning zapped and crackled their jagged bars from cloud to ground. It was a display that had them all watching in awe and wondering about the puny efforts of mankind to make war. The weapons of nature were far more powerful and took many more lives than those fashioned by humans. Floods, fires, winds, earthquakes, tidal waves. They swept mercilessly over the face of the planet and strained bodies from the mass of population. Happily, this particular storm was just a display of power, not a use of it.

In the morning everyone woke with a start as a cheetah chased a bushbuck close to the camp. With the bushbuck shrieking its head off, no one could get back to sleep. They soon discovered that one of the troopers was blind drunk. When his bottle was unearthed and disposed of he began abusing everyone, including the officers, until his NCO struck him with a log and put him unconscious. They tied him to his mount, face against the horse's mane, and one of his comrades led him by the reins. Once back in Natal he would receive punishment from his colonel. However, Seb warned his NCO that if he continued to endanger the mission he stood in jeopardy of being summarily executed, for out in enemy country they could not spare time, guards or attention on a man determined to cause trouble.

Once they had struck camp, they fed and then started out again, leaving the grassland for bushveld, the open hilly country. Winding over this countryside they stopped every five miles for Seb to do some drawing, moving ever closer to Ulundi, the Zulu capital. These sketches would assist any army that followed with information as to where to locate its forts and which areas were suited to bear the huge wagonloads of supplies that it would need. Thus, they left the banks of the White Mfolozi and struck out southeast for the source of the Mhlatuze, a river that would eventually run close to Eshowe, scene of a battle in the first invasion of Zululand between a Zulu impi and the Coastal Column of the British army.

Their luck could not last, and indeed did not.

'On the hill to the left!' cried Zeldenthuis.

Almost as he spoke half a dozen or so shots came zipping through them, fired from a knoll just ahead. Then around fifty Zulus appeared and began running swiftly down a slope towards them. They were five hundred yards away and closing fast. At an order from the NCO, the dragoons dismounted and formed a line. A volley from their carbines took out several of the front runners amongst the advancing Zulus. They reloaded quickly and gave the oncoming Zulus a second volley, before remounting. There was a ringing in the air as swords were drawn from their scabbards. Jack began a slow trot to meet the enemy, while Zeldenthuis was carefully firing his Mauser from the saddle, sitting up tall in the stirrups. Seb had drawn his sword and was soon up alongside his uncle. The dragoons were now in formation, ready to attack. Without a bugler there was no one to sound the charge, so the order came from the throat of Major Jack Crossman, who like many infantrymen had always wanted to lead a cavalry charge.

Seb, his heart racing and his vision blurred by sweat from his brow, found his way barred by two warriors, one with a magnificent physique, the other rather pudgy around the middle. He went charging between them, the shoulder of his mount bowling the fat one over. The point of his sword caught the other man in the throat and carried him off his feet, the blade lodged in his spinal column. The sword-blade bent heavily with the weight of its victim. The fat man was back up on his feet with a swiftness that belied his shape. As Seb fought to free his sword the fat man's spear-blade passed under his arm, catching in his tunic and taking off a button. Still Seb struggled and was about to abandon his sword as the fat warrior drew back for a second stab. It was never to be delivered, though, for Jack Crossman was there and shot the warrior through the back of the head. The ball came out of the front taking half a face with it and harmlessly struck saddle leather.

The dragoons were riding in amongst the Zulus, thrusting and slashing with their swords. Seb noticed one riderless horse, then saw its trooper lying on the ground with three Zulus puncturing his chest with their iklwas. Seb rode over and scattered them, though without a doubt the trooper was dead. A throwing spear went under his mount's neck and Seb reined in and turned about to make himself a moving target, but fortunately no more missiles came his way.

The whole action lasted only a few minutes before the surviving Zulus disappeared into some long grass. They left seventeen dead warriors behind them. Others would be wounded, but had escaped with their comrades. Three troopers, including the NCO, were wounded and one of these expired within minutes. This did not include the dead trooper who had been unhorsed and stabbed repeatedly. These two dragoons would never see home again.

Of the wounded, one had a flesh wound to his arm. Luckily it did not involve a severed artery and he was temporarily patched up. The other was more serious, having a musket ball in the thigh. He would need the attention of a surgeon fairly quickly, though Jack did not think the leg would need amputating. He tried to reassure the trooper, but the man had seen so many of his comrades lose limbs in the past he had decided to be gloomy about it. Seb knew they had to get this trooper back to camp before he went down with a fever, as so often happened when a man carried metal inside him.

After the skirmish Pieter Zeldenthuis had continued to fire steadily into the grasses with his high-powered Mauser, to discourage any further attacks and in the hope of hitting anyone who lingered in the fringe.

Seb was glad to see his uncle was unhurt, though he had noticed that during the fighting Xolani had been furiously battering any Zulu who came near to Jack with the butt of his musket. Seb wondered what sort of charisma came from Jack Crossman, that he should attract these protectors who were ready to die for him wherever he went. Jack was not especially liked by his own kind, by the officers and class from which he came, yet the wild men of the earth seemed to gravitate towards him and followed him as they might have followed great charismatic generals such as Genghis Khan or Tamburlaine, or indeed the East India Company soldier John Nicholson of the North-West Frontier, whose legendary exploits were legion. Every man in the British army wished to emulate the fearless Nicholson, who was finally killed in the streets of Delhi fighting the Indian Mutiny of 1857.

There was one other loss. The trooper who had been drunk that morning was missing, his horse having bolted once the action had started. Seb doubted they would ever see him again. He felt momentarily guilty at having tied the man to his horse, but on reflection could not think of any other way he could have dealt with him. The trooper had been incapable of riding, being almost insensible with drink, and the patrol had not expected to be attacked with such suddenness. The soldier would wake up and find himself either alone in the wilderness, strapped to his faithful quadruped, or in the hands of an enemy that was not likely to treat him kindly.

'Well done, men,' Jack was saying, 'well fought. Now we need to be somewhere else before we face several regiments of them.'

The dragoons gave him a little cheer, but it was somewhat weak, due to their numbers and also to the fact that they felt anxious to make haste and be on their way out of the area before the twenty-five thousand friends of the fallen warriors decided to exact their revenge. They set off, back towards Landsman's Drift at a lively pace, but not in a panic. The dead troopers were strapped to horses. Zeldenthuis brought up the rear, constantly turning and checking for the enemy.

Seb had to admit the Boer was good at his work, no matter what he thought of his integrity. No one else had noticed the Zulus before the attack and Zeldenthuis's reaction had been swift and decisive. He knew the terrain, he knew the enemy. Seb had witnessed the fact that he could track like a native: indeed, he was native to this land. He could detect the presence of an animal by its scent, tell you what it was and what it was doing. He noticed movements and sounds of birds in the sky, monkeys in the trees, lizards on the ground, and knew what was disturbing them. The Boer did not need to *see* what was going on around him, he could use his other senses to tell him much of what he wanted to know.

Seb was straight out of civilization and had to learn things as he went along. Zeldenthuis was a pioneer, a frontiersman, one of those creatures halfway between a man and a lion.

While he was thinking of beasts, Seb's thoughts turned to his Arab, which had indeed performed with bravery and spirit during the battle. He patted its neck, extremely pleased with it. What a wonderful gift from his uncle. There was no fuss about the creature. No sly meanness or fidgets, or any of those irritating characteristics of some mounts. It simply seemed an extension of Seb himself, which was all a rider could ask for of his companion. So, Napoleon had ridden such a horse, had he? Seb was unaware of that.

Five

The patrol made it back to the Drift without further incident. Jack left after thanking Seb for his part in the foray. He took the landscape sketches with him, saying they would be very useful. 'I'll put in the report on the raid,' he told the ensign. 'Save you having to explain what you were doing out there. I'll go and see the colonel of the dragoons, too, and thank him for his men. Pity we lost a couple. They fought well, though. You can tell an old regiment and the King's Guards is one of the oldest, if not the oldest. Why didn't you go for the cavalry, Seb?'

Seb went red. 'Tried. Failed.'

'Their loss, my boy. You're a good soldier, take it from an old warhorse. You'll go far, if you get the breaks. You need Lady Fortune to give you the opportunities, but when they come, take 'em quickly. I'm told you're doing an excellent job as a policeman too. Don't worry about how the post looks to others. Just keep doing good work, show those who employ you that you'll do any kind of work they want to put on your plate and do it well. The rest will hopefully follow.'

'Thanks, Jack. That means a lot to me.'

Seb then in turn swallowed his pride and went to express his gratitude to Pieter Zeldenthuis for joining them. The Boer nodded curtly, and said, 'Ag, part of the job. I see you've got a new horse, boysie.'

Seb glowed with pleasure.

'Yes, Jack gave him to me. He performed well, you know, during the fight. No panic.'

'Good-looking mount. What do you call him?'

'He hasn't got a name yet.'

'He's a beaut – how about Amasi? That's Xhosa, for a kind of creamy milk they have.'

'Amasi? Yes, nice and easy on the tongue. Very suitable. Thanks. Now, I've got to be going.'

His conversations with this enigmatic Boer always seemed

awkward and unsettling. In fact he had wanted to find the name for his Arab on his own, but had somehow been given it. It would be churlish of him now to change that name, after saying how suitable it sounded. Not very dashing, *milk*. Not like Thunderer or Lightning. Still it was a name from the land in which he found himself at the time, and therefore very appropriate, and it described the Arab very well. He would have fun writing home, asking the family to guess what 'Amasi' meant.

He stabled Amasi and then made his way wearily to his tent, only to be met by Corporal Evans shortly before he reached the area. Evans' eyes were round and expressive, and he mouthed the words 'staff officer' at Seb in a way that was obviously meant to be a warning. Indeed, Seb could see a major pacing near Sam Weary, who was squatting on the ground cleaning boots. Sam looked up at Seb's approach and also made a face, his eyes flicking upwards towards the tall, lean and rather young-looking major.

'Ensign Early?' snapped the officer, as Seb came to him.

Seb saluted. 'Yes, sir. Provost-Marshal.' Seb flicked his sash to draw attention to it. He wondered if this officer had come to report a crime to him. Perhaps a theft? 'What can I do for you?'

Flinty eyes flashed. 'You can start by telling me where the hell you've been these last few days.'

'Sir?' Seb was wondering what business it was of his where he had been. 'I've been assisting a Major Crossman with some mapping of Zululand. Is that of some interest to you?'

'Don't get smart with me, Ensign. You don't have the rank or connections for it. It's of very great *interest* to me, since I'm your commanding officer.'

Seb was astonished. 'You're taking over the 24th?'

'No, of course I'm not taking over the 24th, I'm on the staff as you can plainly see. My name is Major Stringman, I'm the new communications officer, appointed by the general a week ago. General Lord Chelmsford has decided that the office of Provost-Marshal shall come under my wing. In future you will not report directly to him, nor to your regiment's colonel, but to me alone. I shall decide whether you are carrying out your duties and I shall give you your orders. Are we understood?'

Seb swallowed hard. 'I think so, sir.'

'Don't think so. Know so. Now, explain where you've been and how this affects your investigations of crimes. I'm very eager to find the connection between mapping and murder cases. I understand from the general that there's been a duel, someone has been killed, and that you are inquiring as to the identification of the victim and the officer who despatched him.'

Seb swallowed again, mixed feelings of anger and frustration rising in his breast and threatening to get him into trouble.

'There is no connection between my sketching landscapes for Major Crossman of Intelligence, and the case I'm working on.'

The major turned his back on Seb and stared out into Zululand, before turning again and confronting him.

'I thought as much. In future you will confine yourself to the duties of your current post, unless otherwise advised by me. No more swanning about in the bush. You will work, sir, and do the job for which you have been appointed, or you will answer to me. I hate lazy junior officers and I hate even more those who follow their pastimes and hobbies when they should be working. Hunting and fishing and that sort of activity are out, unless you have my express permission . . .'

'Hunting and fishing?' exploded Seb at last. 'I've been out on a very important expedition, Major, one that will benefit the next invasion of Zululand. An expedition on which two men lost their lives. How dare you imply that I've been on some sort of picnic.'

The major visibly straightened. 'Hold your tongue, sir, and listen. You had no authority—'

'I'm afraid I did, sir. Major Crossman cleared it with my commanding officer, so I understand, otherwise I would not have gone.'

'I'm your commanding officer.'

'I didn't know that at the time.'

They stood there and stared at one another. Inside, Seb was seething, ready to explode again. The major, however, looked calm and icy, as if weighing up what punishment to give this upstart ensign. Seb noticed that Major Stringman's nose was very thin, almost knife-thin in fact, and would probably cut cheese without any real difficulty. This feature, coupled with his penetrating eyes was quite disconcerting to the young ensign. Finally, the major spoke again.

'I'm prepared to overlook your negligence of duty in this instance, since as you say you had not been apprised of my appointment. However, in future I expect to be informed of each step of your investigations. You will not go off on any jaunts without my express permission and your work will be closely monitored. If you fail to meet my exacting standards, which are only exacting in that the army expects the best from its officers, then I'm afraid I shall have to relieve you of your post and send you back to your regiment. Clear?'

'Clear,' said Seb, unable to suppress a smile.

'Is that a smirk, sir? Do I see a smirk on your face?' Major Stringman said, incredulously. 'Explain yourself.'

'It's an indication of my inner feelings,' Seb replied. 'You seemed to imply that relieving me of my post, and sending me back to my regiment, would be a *punishment*. Do you believe, sir, that I volunteered for this position in order to get out of the fighting? If so, sir, you are sadly mistaken. Nothing would give me greater pleasure than to return to my regiment, where I feel I belong, to serve alongside my fellow officers in the line.'

The major looked suitably taken aback. 'Then I must ask why you *did* volunteer for the post of Provost-Marshal.'

'It's rather personal.'

'Naturally, any such action would be for personal reasons.'

'All right, I volunteered because my best friend was killed in the post and I wanted to finish the work he started. There was a murder of a captain in the duty officer's quarters . . .'

'I'm familiar with the case.'

'What you may not be familiar with, sir, is the fact that, at the time, only the Provost-Marshal believed it to be murder. Everyone else spoke of it as suicide. I believed in my friend's assessment of the deed and when he died I made it my business to follow up his theory. As it happened, my friend and I were correct and all others were wrong.' Seb paused as the memories of his friendship with Peter flooded back into his consciousness and with them that dreadful feeling of loss. He managed to swallow his emotion and added, 'I knew that if I did not volunteer for the post, the murder case would be dropped in favour of suicide and the murderer would walk free.'

'Very commendable. Very laudable. I accept the explanation, but, Ensign, I have the feeling you are now quite fond of the work you're doing and that as each case is overlapped by the next, your interest switches from the solved case to the unsolved. You enjoy untangling puzzles and confusions. I repeat what I said before. If your work is not up to standard, you will be relieved of your post. I shall expect a report every seventy-two hours on your progress.

'Now, while you've been off gallivanting, another incident has taken place, which needs your attention. An officer has shot one of his men for refusing to obey an order. It seems a fairly straightforward affair to me, but the general would like you to make sure no blame is attached to the officer, who it seemed did his duty.'

'The name and rank of the officer, and his regiment, if you please, sir?'

'Captain William Pickering of the Border Rangers.'

'Sir, can I ask when the incident happened?'

'Yes indeed. It was at Gingindlovu.'

Seb frowned. 'But that battle was back in April.'

'Quite. April the second. And by the way, before we part for the moment, I should like you to know I do not agree with your interpretation of the law regarding deaths at duels.'

'Sir?'

'I understand you informed General Lord Chelmsford that you intended arresting everyone present at the duel, believing all were culpable in the unlawful killing.'

'That's my belief, sir. However, it is up to a trial to rule on whether that is indeed the case. I intend arresting all participants in the duel. The doctor, the seconds and the presiding officer, as well as the man who fired the shot. The court martial will decide who amongst them is guilty or innocent of any charge. If you are about to order me to arrest only the main participant you may take my red sash now, sir.' He almost added, *and find yourself another puppet*, but refrained from that unwise postscript, knowing it would certainly spark a row.

Stringman stared hard at Seb for a full two minutes before saying, 'Carry on, Ensign.'

'Yes, sir.'

With that, the major strode off.

Seb stood there for a few minutes watching the smartly dressed major disappear amongst the tents. His feelings were in turmoil. This was insufferable! To be lectured by a pompous ass of a major, who said he was now his commanding officer? It was infuriating. And the worst part about it was that the major was right. Seb was now fond of his work. He did enjoy unravelling mysteries. Solving conundrums was now in his blood. Yes, he had taken it on for the reasons he had given, to finish Peter's work, but now it was *his* work. However, to do the job under such circumstances, with a priggish major looking over his shoulder and clucking criticism at every move? It was not possible, surely? Would it not be better to resign his post before he was removed from it by Major Stringman? It needed thinking through.

'BIT OF A BUGGER, EH?'

Startled, Seb swung round to find Corporal Evans just six inches from his ear, his deafness controlling his volume.

Seb signed with his fingers, *Do you mean the man, or the situation?*

Both, sir.

'Well, don't voice it out loud, Corporal, or we'll both be out of a job.'

Major Theobald Timothy Stringman was not of the landed gentry. He was one of a new breed of officers who had gone through Sandhurst, had applied himself to the history of military warfare, to tactics and strategies, to all aspects of the army. Due to the fact that his cousin was a very influential politician – connections still counted, even if the purchase of commissions had gone – he had risen very quickly to his rank. He knew he was fortunate in that respect. He was aware of majors like Jack Crossman, who had reached the rank after a long and meritorious career involving many battles and wounds, years of dangerous expeditions. However, he knew his own worth and knew that if he had been forced to take that route, he would have done, and would have been just as successful as the Jack Crossmans.

Ever since he could remember, Theobald Stringman had wanted to go into the army. His father was a Shropshire glove-maker, from Bridgenorth, and the family had always joked that Theo would be the next Shakespeare, William's father being of the same profession. In fact it became apparent that Theo's 'imagination' was severely limited and he had no interest in the arts whatsoever, be it writing, painting, sculpture or dancing. He despised these activities as frivolous. If he was interested in anything at all outside of the military, it was in engines and devices, and his reading went in that direction. His admiration of order and discipline directed him towards a life as a soldier, a profession which he knew would fit him like one of his father's gloves.

Theobald Stringman attended Bridgenorth Grammar School, and was a good student, who excelled in the sport of boxing. Outside the ring he was bullied by older boys because of his insular character. He did not like team games and refused to join in when asked. His boxing skills were no match for six or seven youths two years his senior, who 'taught him not one, but several lessons' with their fists and boots. One of those youths was now a lieutenant on Lord Chelmsford's staff. Stringman's revenge was to completely ignore the man, treat him as if he did not exist, and to cut him dead whenever the opportunity arose. If the lieutenant spoke to him in the course of duty, Stringman walked past without a reply.

Major Stringman had distinguished himself in the Ninth Xhosa War of 1877, which alongside his connections had helped in his promotion from captain to major. The major was brave, steely-minded, ambitious, and as has been said, unimaginative. Imagination was not an absolute requirement of a successful officer, as men like Lieutenant-Colonel Buller had proved, but Major Stringman had one other great failing: he found it difficult to delegate. As one rises in rank in any organization, business or army, one has to broaden one's responsibilities and leave details to those below. A clerk promoted to manager who will not let go of clerkish duties will fail as a manager. Major Stringman did not trust his menials to carry out their duties without examining every tiny aspect of their work. This involved staying up late at night, working through figures others had already worked through. It meant he was inspecting troops who had already been inspected by NCOs or junior officers. It meant picking through minor details which should have been left to men who resented his interference.

Thus, as communications officer, with other responsibilities, Major Stringman was intensely interested in every singularity of the work of those below him, and found it impossible not to interfere.

'Sam, you're one superb cook,' said Seb, licking his fingers. 'What do you say, Evans?'

Evans, sitting opposite his commanding officer, replied, 'If I could do with a lamb what this man does with a spring hare, I'd be the best chef in Wales.'

'Oh, sirs, you must not make a Xhosa man go hot in the face – it is not a nice feeling.'

Sam Weary began to clear up the tin plates and saucepans, keeping down the noise because it was so late at night. Not that the crickets were not sounding like mad machines, or that the dogs were quiet, or that several other unnamed creatures of the night were not making a racket.

Seb made sure Evans could see his mouth, before saying, 'Well now, Corporal, have you had any success with young Tom?' Tom had already gone to bed, but would undoubtedly be listening to the conversations around the campfire.

'Yes, sir,' said the Welshman, managing a reasonable volume for once, 'we did. Tom recognized this doctor. I asked around and found out who he was. He's Surgeon Haggard, of the 91st.'

Seb was buoyed by this news. 'Well done, Corporal. I'll dig him out in the morning. Tom's sure he recognized the doctor from the duel?'

'Yes,' came a sleepy voice from one of the tents. 'Sure as anythink.'

'Excellent.'

Then Tom's voice again. 'I won't 'ave to talk to 'im, will I?'

'No, Tom, I'll do that,' said Seb. 'Your work's done for the moment. Now go to sleep.'

'Yes, sir.'

Six

The night was full of sounds. Apart from the animals, birds and insects, men worked under the jaundiced light of lanterns. The general was eager to get his army to readiness for the next invasion of Zululand. It was rumoured that parliament in Britain was considering sending another commander to replace him. The names of Chelmsford and the High Commissioner, Bartle Frere, were not now being held with any great favour in London. The loss of two thousand men in an utter defeat by a 'bunch of savages' was regarded by the politicians and people at home as scandalous. The South African careers of the two leaders, one in politics the other in the military, hung in the balance and the scales were tipping slowly but definitely towards termination.

Seb rose and dressed, then set out to find his man.

It was not until late in the morning that he ran him down.

'Surgeon Haggard?' The ramshackle barn in which Seb found himself was lined with cots either side on which sick men were lying. It was filled with unpleasant odours that mingled to form a foul stink. Orderlies moved along the rows of patients, some of whom were dying. During the campaign, over a hundred men had already died of disease. Many more had been invalided through accidents. There were two fights going on: one against the Zulus, the other against calamity and illness.

A short, thickset man raised his head from a patient and said, 'Aye?' in an east-coast Scottish accent.

'Ensign Early, Provost-Marshal. Could I speak to you outside?'

'Now?'

'If you please, sir.'

'Well, make it quick, I'm due to cut soon.'

Once outside in the relatively fresh air, Seb took a deep breath and confronted the surgeon.

'You were present at a duel some ten days ago where a man was shot and bled to death.'

Seb knew the value of a blunt statement, not a question, flung straight at the recipient. He was rewarded with a change in colour in the surgeon's face. The surgeon said nothing for the moment, clearly struggling with his reply. Finally, he must have realized that no good was going to come from a denial.

'Yes, unfortunately I was.'

'Then I'm afraid you're under arrest.'

This was, it seemed, quite unexpected.

'Under arrest? I can assure you I did my very best to save the life of the officer. No blame can be attached to my services.'

'You are not being arrested for attending the man, you're being arrested for attending the *meeting*. You were present at an unlawful gathering of officers, two of whom were intent on wounding or killing each other. It is my knowledge that one of the participants in the duel deloped and was then shot down by his opponent. That sounds very like manslaughter or even murder to me, Surgeon Haggard.'

The medical officer's face was now showing anxiety.

'Can you do this? I personally did nothing wrong.'

'You were there. Your voluntary presence indicates that you were in agreement with the purpose of the proceedings.'

'But . . . but I had no idea . . . that is, I was asked – you see, it was not my intention . . .'

'I'm sorry, I'll have to ask you to come with me for questioning, then consider yourself under open arrest. I'm aware surgeons are overworked at the moment and I would hate to rob the surgeon-major of valuable personnel, so I'm not going to confine you. Is there any important duty you have to perform today which will need your presence here? A life-saving operation, perhaps?'

The surgeon replied bitterly, 'I wish there were. Just a moment while I ask one of my colleagues to take over my surgery. It would not do to let another man die of neglect.'

Seb wondered whether the patient would live anyway, since amputations took more lives than they saved.

He took the surgeon to a quiet spot where he knew they would not be disturbed. It was actually under the tree where the duel had taken place. Seb knew that he had pricked the surgeon's conscience and the scene of the crime would work further in that direction. He settled himself on a log and invited the surgeon to do the same. Haggard seemed a little fastidious and scanned his own log for insects before sitting opposite the Provost-Marshal.

'You obviously realize that you're in a great deal of trouble, sir, so I won't spend time warning you about lying. The truth will help your case far more than any attempt to protect those officers who were present at this meeting. I think I'm right in saying that of those officers you have the least to fear, since you might formulate some sort of defence making the presence of someone of your profession necessary.'

'I see what you mean.'

'So,' Seb poised with his pencil above his notebook, 'the names of the duellists?'

Surgeon Haggard's features hardened.

'Despite what ye say, laddie,' he said, his Scottish accent suddenly becoming much broader, 'I can no' give ye those names.'

Seb was disappointed. 'You realize the seriousness of your position?'

'I am bound by an oath.'

At this statement Seb dropped the notebook. He had expected a small battle and protests in the vein that one did not inform on brother officers. But an *oath*? That sounded far more sinister, was obviously far more binding than the loose unspoken code of silence.

'Oh, well,' he said at last, 'if that's the case then we'll just drop the whole investigation. We can't have you breaking an oath, now can we?'

'I see no call for sarcasm,' said the surgeon. 'Clearly you're no' going to drop your investigation.'

'So, having established that fact, are you prepared to come with me to General Lord Chelmsford and repeat your refusal?'

The surgeon's head went down and his headgear fell off, to land on the grassy ground. He was now wringing his hands together as if they were cold, though of course they were not. Then Seb heard the sound of a sob escaping from the man's mouth. He was astonished by this display of emotion. A grown man *crying* because he was being questioned by a very junior officer over an affair that might well end without anything serious happening to someone who had simply been there.

Embarrassed, Seb found himself sounding like his father. 'Pull yourself together, man.'

The surgeon still refused to look up. 'They'll kill me,' he whispered.

'What?' Once again, Seb could not believe what he was hearing. 'Who will kill you? The court martial?'

'No, not that. Them.' A shudder went through the other man and by degrees he seemed to collect himself. He now looked up, into Seb's eyes.

'I've told you all I can tell you. If you have to charge me with aiding and abetting manslaughter, so be it. Charge me.'

Seb picked up his notebook and tapped it with his pencil while he formulated a new attack.

'This oath,' he said at last, 'it's nothing to do with any clan, is it?'

'Clan?' The surgeon looked surprised.

'You're Scottish. You probably belong to a clan, the Haggard clan, or whatever.'

Haggard actually laughed out loud at this.

'You must be a romantic, eh? You've read too much Walter Scott. No, it's nothing to do with me being Scottish. I'm not going to tell what it *is* to do with, so don't waste your words.'

'Are you a member of the Freemasons?'

'No, I'm not.'

'The Hellfire Club?' said Seb, wildly.

The doctor replied, 'I don't know what you're talking about.'

'That club they have in West Wycombe – a Lord Dashwood founded it.'

'Oh – oh, yes, I recall something now. A club founded on immorality, wasn't it? I would have nothing to do with such an establishment, being a good Presbyterian. Listen, before we go through all the secret societies known to you, I have to tell you I'm saying nothing, nothing at all. I won't reveal the names of the duellists, nor their seconds, nor the presiding officer. You may do with me as you wish, I will not, indeed I *cannot* give you the information you require.'

Seb had to call a halt to his questioning. The doctor was beginning to annoy him intensely and he could see he was going to get no further.

'You will answer to this charge later, Doctor, even if we don't find out who the other members of the duel were. And we *will* find out, believe me.'

'I'm sure you'll do your very best, Ensign.'

'It's my job.'

'And mine is saving lives by using my medical skills – which was what I was trying to do on that day.'

'You could have saved a life by reporting the onset of the duel to a greater authority. It could have been stopped before it started. An officer would still be alive. What does your Hippocratic oath say to that, sir? I suppose you can't recall the name of the victim, by the way?'

'Never knew it,' the doctor replied.

Seb shook his head. 'I pity you, sir. You appear to be the pawn of some domineering officer. You may very well be sacrificed like a pawn, in order to save that man's reputation. I hope it's all worth it. You've flung away your integrity and your own reputation to preserve that of another. Don't think the status of someone else is going to protect you. I don't care how powerful he or his father is, you will be court-martialled and the law will punish you for your part. God help you.'

A tone of bitterness at last entered the surgeon's speech.

'I have no choice,' he said. 'No choice at all.'

Seb went straight from this interview to his new commanding officer, Major Stringman. The major was found in the middle of a meal. He told Seb to wait until he had finished eating. Seb was quite willing to wait a half-hour for the major, who eventually came to him.

'Well, what is it?' asked Stringman.

'Sir, you asked me to report to you and that's what I'm doing now. I've discovered the name of the doctor who was present at the duel in which a man died. He is Surgeon Haggard, attached to the 91st. Unfortunately he refuses to give me the names of the others present at the officer's death and says he does not know the name of the victim. It's my recommendation that Surgeon Haggard is court-martialled for the offence. Perhaps the court can prise from him the names of his co-conspirators.'

Major Stringman was as immaculately turned out as he had

been the first time Seb met him, which was remarkable since they were all living in dust, mud and the general filth of a camp where there were too few latrines, too little water for washing in and a great deal of cattle defecating where they stood. It was as if the major were sheathed in a glass case which protected him alone from the squalor and mayhem of camp living.

The major frowned. 'Conspirators?'

'Surgeon Haggard told me he was prevented from giving me the names because he had taken an oath.'

'Ah well,' said the major with a wooden face, 'if the man has taken an oath . . .'

Seb stared at his new superior.

'That was irony, Ensign,' added Stringman, after a few moments of being scrutinized. 'An oath, you say? Intriguing. But I wonder if the general would agree to a court martial? The man is a doctor, who was no doubt on the scene because he'd been asked to assist should either of the combatants be wounded.'

'He had a choice, sir. He could have informed the authorities that there was a duel about to take place.'

'Good point, Ensign. But still, was that his place?'

Seb sighed. 'Sir, if this army is ever going to be policed without prejudice, then we must remain firmly focused on the law. The doctor had a choice. In agreeing to be present at the duel he agreed to be part and parcel of the whole enterprise. It's my belief that this post, the position of Provost-Marshal, cannot retain any credibility if we pick and choose who to prosecute and who not to, simply by following some sort of unwritten gentlemen's code. It matters not whether those present were knights of the realm or kitchen staff. If they were there, by choice, then they were all equally guilty by association. Any one of those officers at the duel could have, should have stepped forward and prevented it happening – doctor, chimney sweep, major-general, whatever.'

'That's your belief, is it?'

'Yes.'

'Then I'll take that to General Lord Chelmsford and you need have no more concern. You will of course continue to investigate around this matter, until we find the perpetrator and his second.'

'Yes, sir.'

'And don't forget that other matter I mentioned to you – the case of the officer executing one of his soldiers.'

'I'll do my best on that front, too, sir.'

'Good, good, and Ensign, try to smarten up a bit, will you? You're a damn disgrace. Trim those side whiskers a little, if you please.'

'Sir.'

Seven

The wind was coming from the east in dust-blinding, sweeping gusts, ripping tents apart and creating absolute mayhem. Where it met a building it screamed around the corners and the eves with a ululating sound reminiscent of a horde of Arab widows bewailing the fate of their menfolk after a terrible battle. There was boxwood in the air, along with clothes and blankets, and other debris. The cattle were distraught, some down on their knees, their eyes wide with panic and their nostrils flaring. Drummer boys were blown off their feet and thrown against sturdier soldiers. Sometimes a spiral of wind tore up a chicken coop or a carefully laid fire and threw the contents in the air. Sharp objects whistled by noses of those trying to keep order in the chaos of the dawn. The air was filled with hats, helmets and caps aplenty. Indeed, on this day in late May the world had gone mad.

'Ne'er cast a clout till may is out,' said the wise Corporal Evans to his closest friend, a Londoner by the name of Donger Scribbs.

'I don't wear no clouts,' said Scribbs, 'an' come June we'll be in Zululand, where it'll be as 'ot as buggery. That's for 'ome, that sayin' is, not for forin climes what ain't got no may bush blossoms.'

Scribbs was a real Cockney, born in the Poultry, which was as close as you could get to St Mary's le Bow without being in Cheapside. The Bow bells used to make his parents' house resonate with their clanging. In fact, just to make sure and stamp his origins on their son, they named him 'Augustine' after bell number seven, much to Augustine's future annoyance, since he was teased by the other children in the street because of his posh moniker. Eventually the kids nicknamed him 'Donger', an appellation which suited him far better than a name derived from that of a Roman emperor or worn by half a dozen fusty old clerics. On Donger's first birthday, in 1856, the bells of St Mary's were ordered to silence because a Mrs Elizabeth Bird, an eccentric neighbour of the Scribbs, feared that the noise might end her life. On his third birthday they sprang to life again and no one was surprised to find that Mrs Bird failed to expire on hearing them.

'Ah, you're not as daft as you look, are you, Donger?' said Evans. 'Most people think that "may" is the month, not the bush.'

'Well, I ain't most people, Taffy, now am I?'

It was true that these two men had sought out each other's company because they were not fools. Though they had come from lower-class families, one from the fields, the other from the streets, the pair owned an intrinsic intelligence which enabled them to gather knowledge without having had a formal education. They both read when they possibly could, picked up information from those who had been to good schools and universities, and were like ferrets after rabbits when they discovered some area of knowledge which had thus far eluded them.

'So, whad'you reckon to this Stringman, eh, Taffy?'

'Got a poker up his arse,' said Evans, staring intently into his comrade's face. 'If he was a ram, we'd get no lambs come spring because his kind is far too finnicky, eh?'

'Know what you mean. Wants perfection in a place where there ain't none. 'Ow does he come to look so spick an' span all the time? Even the flies don't settle on 'im like they do on everyone else. It's uncanny, that's what it is, Taff. 'E's not real.'

A flying kettle struck the side of the tent and punctured it with its spout, before rolling around the peak of the bell and whizzing off to do damage somewhere else.

'Damn,' muttered Evans, 'that hole'll need stitching.'

'Sam will do it, won't 'e?' said Scribbs.

'Sam's a wizard with the cooking pot,' replied the Welshman, 'but not so hot with the needle.'

'Sailors is good with needles.'

This piece of truism from the Cockney needed no affirmation.

A bugle sounded out in the wind somewhere, its notes distorted but easily recognizable by a soldier who had heard the call a hundred times before.

'Duty,' muttered Donger. 'Well, I'll see you later, Taffy.'

'Where're you going?' asked Evans, not having heard the call.

Donger put his fist to his mouth, to simulate a bugler.

'Drill, or somefnk,' he mouthed.

Evans nodded and waved a hand as Donger left the tent.

Shortly afterwards, Evans himself went outside. Out in the natural world it was still blowing a gale. Soldiers were either hunched against the blast in their journeys from one part of the camp to another, or racing after some piece of clothing or equipment which had been whirled from their grasp. Evans, tall and willowy, curved himself forward and walked into the brunt of the gale. As a shepherd in the Welsh hills he was used to inclement weather. There had been times, not many but some, when he had been crouched behind a dry-stone wall clutching a new-born lamb to his breast to prevent it from being snatched away from its mother by a strong wind. Snow, ice, wind, hail – Evans had experienced almost everything the sky could throw at him. So a wind like this was annoying, but not something to get worked up about.

Evans was doing some investigating on his own this morning. His officer had told him about his meeting with Surgeon Haggard. So now they had at least one of the men present at the duel. Evans had decided to take it upon himself to do a little sleuthing. It was his intention to follow Surgeon Haggard, to see who he met up with in the course of his day. The corporal was hoping that the doctor would find it necessary to tell at least one of the others at the duel that he had been discovered and was now under open arrest. Evans eventually found the doctor's tent and sat a bit away from it on a barrel, watching for his suspect to emerge.

The trouble with being a mere corporal was that you were considered universal property. During the three hours that Evans remained on surveillance he was accosted by senior NCOs and officers almost every ten minutes, wanting to know why he was not working, or where his regiment was, or what the devil he thought he was doing, sunning his head when others were so busy. One officer who was having trouble with a wagon load of ammunition yelled for him to come and help his men heave a back wheel out of soft mud. He did this, for he could keep an eye on the doctor's tent at the same time. But then a captain paused on going past him, as he sat smoking his clay pipe on the barrel, and asked him why he was idle when others were working.

'APM, sir,' cried Evans, standing to attention and neatly transferring the pipe to his left hand and then saluting the officer. 'On a mission.'

The officer blinked. 'Don't shout at *me*, Corporal. APM? I fail to understand.'

Evans pointed to the red ribbon on his shoulder.

'Assistant Provost-Marshal, sir. Ex-artillery. Deaf, see, due to the guns. Sorry about that.'

'Right. Deaf, eh?' The captain seemed to be still unsure whether or not he was dealing with a malingerer. 'You seem to hear me well enough and *I'm* not shouting.'

'Read your lips, sir.'

At that very moment the doctor emerged from his tent and began striding off, weaving between working soldiers. Evans watched him out of the corner of his eye, cursing the captain in front of him.

'On a mission, sir,' Evans repeated. 'Please can I go now?'

'You were a moment ago simply lazing around smoking, soldier – correct me if I'm wrong.'

'Wrong, sir. Watching for a party leaving a tent. Party now left the tent. Must follow him. Excuse me, sir. Apologies. Please see Ensign Early if you wish to, sir. Provost-Marshal. Got to go.'

Evans left the spluttering captain and followed rapidly in Haggard's wake.

He proved to be on his way to the camp hospital, which was not good from Evans' point of view. If the doctor was down to perform operations, then it would mean a long period of waiting, and at the end perhaps he would just go back to his quarters. However, luck was with the corporal, for the surgeon stayed only a few minutes inside the hospital, then emerged again, heading in another direction. This time it appeared he was heading for the mess tent for his midday meal and did not emerge for another two hours.

Evans was a patient man. Most shepherds are patient men. It is in the nature of the job. You spent most of the day simply watching sheep and letting the earth turn with you standing on it, carrying you slowly from dawn till dusk. It was not difficult to switch his mind into neutral, slowing down his thoughts, letting them drift around his head. This time he hid in the criss-crossed spars of a water tower, as camouflaged as any zebra or kudu bull whose shape was broken up by the shadows of tree branches. There he stood until the surgeon emerged again. Of course, it could be that the doctor had seen anyone he wanted to see in the mess, but then Evans noticed the man's expression had changed and had taken on a seriousness that had not been there before: a purposeful yet anxious look.

Evans again followed where the doctor led. This time he was taken to the cavalry lines. He saw the doctor stop once or twice, presumably to ask directions, and finally was rewarded with the man approaching a major in the 5th Dragoons, a late-arrival regiment on the African scene. The major looked surprised to see the doctor and for a few moments Evans thought he was going to ignore his visitor. But Haggard seemed insistent and soon they were engaged in what looked like a heated exchange. The doctor consistently slapped the back of his right hand in the palm of his left, as if emphasizing something. The major shook his head several times and finally stalked away from his visitor, not looking back when he was appealed to do so.

Surgeon Haggard stood on the spot for quite a while, amongst the troopers and horses of the 5th, his head hung low. Then with what looked to be low spirits he walked slowly back to his own area of the camp. Evans watched him re-enter the hospital and this time he did not come out before darkness fell. Evans walked thoughtfully back to where Sam was preparing the evening meal.

Eight

On the 1st of April the Prince Imperial of France, Louis Bonaparte, exiled from his own country, had arrived in Natal to become a member of Lord Chelmsford's staff. Louis enjoyed a great deal of support in France and no doubt hoped one day to return in triumph as the next Napoleon. Seb had heard that the prince was an impetuous youth with a great love of soldiering – if he could not have his own army he seemed happy to borrow from the British for a while. Indeed he saw himself as a soldier first and a prince of France second.

He had served his cadetship at the Royal Military Academy, Woolwich – affectionately known as 'The Shop' – where engineers and artillery officers were trained. New cadets were known as 'snookers', the game having been invented by one of their number. Sappers and gunners obviously had to be good students, especially in mathematics and physics. The prince was not famous for his academic prowess, which was sorely lacking, but somehow with help he managed to get through the course, and opted for the artillery.

Seb had seen this smart Frenchie around camp, sometimes riding a grey horse – he knew the gunner-prince was a superb horseman and fencer. He also knew, from his last interview with Lord Chelmsford, that the prince, in his early twenties, was a millstone around the general's neck. He was supposed to be there merely as a spectator and was closely watched to make sure no harm came to him. The majority of the French might not want him as their emperor Napoleon VI (known to the English press as Napoleon III-half) but they would certainly claim him as a son of France and blame the British if anything untoward happened to him in English hands.

The prince was an unwanted monarch, which added responsibility for a general trying to conduct a war which had so far gone badly.

Seb had only spoken to the prince once, when he stopped to view a painting in progress.

'The neck is too long,' said the prince, leaning over Seb's shoulder, 'even for a giraffe.'

Seb, not knowing who the speaker was, but considering him an interfering idiot, told him to mind his own business.

'Charming!' the prince had said, but not with any malice.

It was only later that Mad Henry had said to Seb, 'I say, South-East, that's a bit much, telling French princes to shove it.'

Seb had forgotten the incident. 'What do you mean, Henry?'

'Prince Imperial of France. You told him to bugger off.'

Seb had gone red. 'I did not.'

'Did too. He tried to give you some advice with your painting. You didn't even look at the beggar. Just told him to sling his hook. Not good form, old chap,' Mad Henry said with a little laugh. 'If ever he becomes an emperor he's going to remember you and invade England simply to teach Ensign Early a lesson in manners.'

'Was that him?' Seb had gone into a panic. The son of a school headmaster telling a prince to run off and play somewhere else. 'I didn't know it was him. How was I supposed to know it was him?'

Mad Henry had laughed. 'Oh, don't worry – he thought it was funny. Afterwards, that is. He did ask me "Is it an insult?", but apparently he uses that phrase all the time when he's being chaffed by fellow officers. The French aren't like us. I don't think they ever josh each other in fun, so he's never sure if it's camaraderie or whether he's actually being insulted. I assured him you were just being chummy, though I did add that you were highly sensitive when it came to your art and he said, "Oh, *art*, yes – it makes men stand on their points, doesn't it? I have artist friends who are the same. You can't give them honest criticism. You just have to tell them everything they do is brilliant, even though it looks like someone has sneezed paint over a canvas." '

Seb had suddenly swung back to being incensed. 'He said that? That it looked like I'd sneezed paint on my canvas?'

Mad Henry had placed a hand on Seb's shoulder.

'South-East, my dear boy, do not *fash* yourself, as my Scottish friends say. You paint very well. You're no Constable, of course, but then you surely wouldn't want to be. All those trees. You'd think he'd get tired of trees, wouldn't you? No, your leopards look very cattish and your springboks very springy. I'd buy one if I had the money . . .'

'So, the prince, he's not desperately upset with me?'

'He's not going to challenge you to a duel, which is a good thing, because he's priceless with a sword so you'd be spit-roast if he did. Don't know what he's like with a pistol, of course, but these princely fellows seem to be good at all that sort of thing. Terrible at cards, of course. I fleeced the beggar the other night, without even trying, but expert at killing those who impugn their honour. Chin-chin, old boy, see you around camp, eh?'

Mad Henry left Seb feeling he had been lucky not to have created a mess for himself.

On the 31st of May the army's two divisions were on the move. The 2nd Division, which was to be the main force thrusting into Zululand, was nominally led by Major-General Newdigate, but since Lieutenant-General Lord Chelmsford was accompanying that division the major-general was somewhat hampered in his role as a decision-maker. The 2nd Division would do what Chelmsford wanted it to do. Seb, a long way down the hierarchy of commissioned ranks, would do what he was told by any one of a dozen officers, but especially by Major Stringman, who had visited his tent and told him, 'You will follow me with the 2nd Division. The 1st is of no interest to you.'

So, on the morning of the 2nd of June, Seb, Evans and Sam were camped at a place called Itelezi Hill on the left bank of Blood River, not far from the place where a handful of Boers had defeated a huge Zulu impi using only smooth-bore muskets. On the evening of the 1st of June, though, a dishevelled lieutenant had ridden into camp with the news that the Prince Imperial of France had been killed. The prince had been accompanying a patrol similar to the one Major Jack Crossman had led: a sketching party to map the ground ahead. Everyone was stunned by the news, especially since the other officer with the patrol of under a dozen men had left the prince to fend for himself. Some were calling that officer a coward, others were saying he had had no choice but to ride off and try to rally his men, not realizing the prince was down.

The patrol had apparently stopped by a deep donga, near some deserted native huts, to make coffee. When the time came to mount, a volley of shots came out of some six-foot-tall grasses nearby. Troopers went down. Most of the men managed to mount and ride off, but when a trooper called Grubb had turned to discover who was with him and who had been left behind, he saw the prince attempting his trick of vaulting into the saddle with his horse on the run. Something happened, a piece of leather gave way. The prince was left without his mount and actually fell under the hooves. He rose quickly, turned, and went to draw his sword. The blade was not there, having come out of its scabbard. Then the prince drew his revolver and fired at the oncoming Zulus. The last thing Grubb saw was the prince going down under a welter of hacking spears.

Lieutenant Carey, the British officer in charge of the patrol, had debated whether to go back and look for him, but decided instead to lead the remainder of his men to safety.

The whole camp was stunned by the news.

'Does this mean France will make a war with England?' Sam asked Evans. 'Will they cross the sea to take revenge?'

'I dunno,' replied the Welshman, casually. 'I don't mind so long as they don't come into Wales.'

'Now, now,' Seb had said, overhearing the talk, 'you know you don't mean that, Evans. In answer to your question, Sam, no – the French will not invade us. I suppose they'll make a fuss, but this was an accident.'

'But a royal personage,' said Sam, 'and some say the last of his line.'

Seb mused on this and replied, 'Royal? I would hardly say so. As I understand it, Napoleon Bonaparte was the son of a Corsican lawyer, who was himself anti-French. Hardly a *royal* base for a lineage. And the prince's own mother was actually Spanish, the daughter of an *hidalgo* so I read in the papers. That's a minor Spanish nobleman, Sam.'

'Spanish *and* French,' breathed Sam. 'So Britain will be attacked by Spain and France together?'

Seb gave up. Sam was obviously taken with the idea that a British officer had created a huge faux pas and Britain was going to be punished for it. This was probably wishful thinking on the part of a man whose tribe had been defeated by those same British. No doubt Sam's head held a satisfying picture of Frenchmen and

Spaniards doing to the British what the amaXhosa would like to do to them. Sam was not totally unhappy cleaning the kit of Ensign Early, and cooking for this officer who was not the worst of these redcoat warriors, but he would have been even happier if the roles were reversed and Seb was having to clean *his* stuff.

Still and all, it was another huge disaster in a war that had already created one of the worst disasters ever suffered by a modern army. Isandlwana had badly blotted Lord Chelmsford's copybook. The loss of the Prince Imperial was devastating. It did not matter whether it was the general's fault: he would be blamed for not ensuring the prince's safety. God only knew what would happen to the English lieutenant who had fled the field and left him to his fate. It would have been better to have died by the prince's side. If he was not found guilty of cowardice by a court martial, his career in the army was dead. The cruelty of officers towards one of their own, a man who had not maintained the highest standards of an officer and a gentleman, was a documented fact. Even those who had done no wrong, but simply came from the wrong class, had been hounded into resignation from the service and even suicide.

Thus, the mood around camp was dark and dispirited.

It was in this atmosphere that Seb noticed Major Stringman sitting with Surgeon Haggard outside a tent. The two were drinking and conversing. What astonished Seb was that they seemed to be enjoying a joke together, and were laughing. Seb stood in the moon shadows watching the pair, a lamp smothered in a cloud of insects before them. It seemed a most convivial meeting of two friends. After the pair broke up, the doctor saying goodnight and going off into the darkness, Seb went forward and confronted his commanding officer.

'Sir, good evening.'

The relaxed expression on Major Stringman's face immediately stiffened into a stern mask.

'Ah, Ensign Early. You've come to give me your report?'

'No, sir, I have little to tell you, beyond what I've already imparted in my written report of two days ago.'

'Then what is it? Be brief, I'm about to go and see the general – he's much besieged in spirit and needs the solace of knowing there are loyal officers who will stand by him in these troubled times.'

'I – I could not help noticing you were conversing with one of my witnesses, Surgeon Haggard.'

Major Stringman's expression hardened even further.

'The more I come to know about you, Ensign, the less I like you – you've been spying on me.'

'If I've been watching anyone, sir – and indeed this was an accidental meeting – it would be the doctor, not you. May I ask what you were speaking about? You must know from my earlier report that Surgeon Haggard is under open arrest and is therefore forbidden to discuss the case with anyone but the Provost-Marshal.'

'You are mistaken, sir.'

The words were snapped out, almost in anger.

'Mistaken?' asked Seb. 'About what?'

'Surgeon Haggard. He is no longer under arrest.'

'And how can that be, sir?'

Stringman looked affronted. 'It can be, because I've reversed your decision, Ensign.'

Seb went very quiet for at least two or three minutes, during which the major poured himself another drink. The fact that the major was unsettled, despite his outwardly indignant manner, was evident in the way his hand was shaking. Whether this was anger or some other emotion, Seb was not sure, but certainly the senior officer was not – as was usual – in total command of himself. Normally he was implacable, devoid of any show of inner feelings.

'Sir,' said Seb at last in a rather croaky voice, 'I have to tell you, you are not entitled to reverse my decision. You are the general's communications officer. You are not the Provost-Marshal. That post is my responsibility.'

'How dare you—'

'On what, sir,' interrupted Seb in a higher tone of voice, 'do you base your decision to release Surgeon Haggard from arrest?'

'Ensign Early, I do not know your family background, but an officer and a gentleman does not give his word to others and then break it. It is quite impossible for Surgeon Haggard to reveal the names of others present at the duel, since he gave his word under oath not to do that. Good God, man, can you not *see* that? Such an officer would be a social pariah thereafter. He would never be able to hold up his head again. We can't ask a man to commit social suicide.'

'He will be a social pariah in any case – he was there and is guilty by association of the death of another officer.'

Stringman shook his head. 'That I cannot accept, Ensign. Lord Chelmsford is also of the opinion that you are quite wrong in that assumption. We can only charge the officer who did the shooting, not any others in attendance. Seconds are there merely to see that the rules of duelling are observed. Fair play. It's not their responsibility . . .'

'Sir, it is not unusual for the seconds to also duel, in support of the main duellists, is it not?'

'Well, there are precedents . . .'

'In which case, the seconds at least are heavily involved in the whole action, even if the doctor is not.'

'Will you stop interrupting me, Ensign. I am a senior officer, your commander, and I will not be interrupted every few seconds. Damn it man, this was a duel. Not so long ago men of very high standing were defending their honour in such a way. Yes, duelling is not in the best interests of the service and is now outmoded, but you talk of it as if it were a case of murder.'

'I'm convinced it *was* murder. The dead man deloped before he was shot.'

'You don't know the circumstances.' The major sounded exasperated now. 'You weren't there. Perhaps they were simultaneous, the deloping and the death wound? Perhaps the other officer fired out of nervous tension, not intending to kill his opponent?'

'In which case, everything could be cleared up by knowing the identities of the officers in question.'

Major Stringman's expression suddenly hardened into granite. Seb knew instantly that his protests had gone on too long. The major was seriously out of sorts with him now and he would get nowhere by continuing to insist on the arrest of Surgeon Haggard. But it was already too late. Major Stringman was in the mood for teaching his subordinate a lesson.

The tone was steely from the major.

'Ensign, I have not yet had a report on Captain Pickering.'

Seb blinked, searching for the name in his mind.

'Who, sir?'

'Captain William Pickering, of the Border Rangers – he shot one of his men. Damn it, sir, I gave you the details. Have you done nothing to investigate this matter? It remains open-ended until the Provost-Marshal – I need not remind you, that you hold that post at the moment – has formally interviewed the men involved and closed the matter.'

'I – I would have got round to it, sir.'

'You will get round to it, as you put it, *now*. You will ride to the headquarters of the 1st Division and request permission from Major-General Crealock to interview Captain Pickering.'

Seb was astonished. 'What, now? But we're in Zululand. The invasion has begun. You want me to ride south now on a simple errand which can be dealt with at a more convenient time?'

'Convenient to whom? I am *ordering* you to do so. You will find this Captain Pickering and clear up this outstanding matter. I'm amazed you have not done it before now. I informed you quite a long while ago that the situation was pressing. If there's one thing I can't stand it's lazy officers who procrastinate. Do your duty, sir, or I shall remove you from your post with a severe reprimand.' A smile flickered on the major's face for an instant. 'You might think you want to get back to your regiment, back in the line, but having a blot on your record will ensure that promotion will be withheld for a very long time. I doubt it if you'll even make lieutenant once I've finished with you.'

Seb had to stop himself from leaping on this arrogant man and throttling him. Once he had steadied himself, containing his suppressed fury, he came smartly to attention.

'Yes, sir. You shall have my report as soon as I return.'

Seething with rage, Seb returned to his tent. There he spoke quietly to Sam and Evans. He told Sam to start packing for the three of them, then went and requisitioned another horse. The quartermaster was getting used to this Provost-Marshal taking away his precious horses. Seb himself intended riding Amasi, of course. They would need to ride back to the border and travel down on the far side of the Buffalo. It would be pointless and dangerous to head south straight away, while still in Zululand. If they did they might end up like the Prince Imperial. Seb had considered asking Pieter Zeldenthuis to go with them, but decided that it was not difficult to navigate when all one had to do was keep a river in sight. They set off for the border immediately.

It was Seb's understanding that the 1st Division was camped at a temporary fortification on the banks of the Thekula River, close to the Indian Ocean. However, it was always on the move and could have changed location by the time he and his men reached the coast.

Nine

They crossed the Blood River near Fort Warwick by a pontoon bridge left by the engineers. The crossing was guarded, of course: a company of local militia were there looking bored and listless. The three riders stopped for tea at a stall. Sam went for the refreshments while Seb and Evans rubbed down the horses and gave them a drink. The proprietor of the stall refused to serve 'a bloody ignorant Kaffir' until Sam signed to Evans. The corporal threw down his sweaty rag and picked up his weapon, then went over to the stall owner and offered him a rifle muzzle. A sharp Welsh demand that he 'keep a civil tongue and pour the damn tea' along with the spout of the Martini-Henry in his face persuaded the gentleman to treat Sam with a little more courtesy. Although Seb did not normally favour such behaviour towards civilian businessmen, he did feel that in this instance he was justified in ignoring his corporal's actions.

It was a hot day with the sun slanting down on their backs as they continued their ride southwards between the Buffalo and the Blood. For the most part they followed the Blood River bank until they came to the confluence of the two rivers. Here they crossed the Buffalo into Natal and headed towards Fort Melville, then on to Fort Bromhead, before striking out for Helpmekaar. All over Natal and Zululand, especially in the south along the coast, there were dozens of forts now, mostly named after generals and colonels, but at least two bearing the once-hated appellation 'Napoleon'. Napoleon Hill and Fort Napoleon were of course named after the Prince Imperial, whose sudden death was causing political eruptions on a small distant set of islands where it was said that even Queen Victoria was distraught by the terrible news.

At Helpmekaar they camped outside the fort for the night. It was here that Corporal Evans took off his boots for the first time in three weeks.

'My God, Corporal!' cried Seb. 'Look at the state of your feet!'

Evans looked down at his large appendages. Sam stared at them too. They were black with fungi. One or two blisters had broken and had become infected. To say that they stank would be an understatement. A mangrove swamp's smell was not more offensive.

'Sam cannot sleep in the same tent,' murmured the amaXhosi. 'It is not possible with such a stink.'

'You watch your mouth, Sam,' shouted Evans. 'I can read mumbles as well as words spoke out loud.'

'Evans,' said Seb, 'we have to get those feet treated. Why don't you look after them? You used to be a shepherd, for Heaven's sakes. Didn't you care for your feet then?'

'I didn't have these bloody boots then,' shouted Evans, 'beggin' your pardon, sir.'

It was true that most soldiers had ill-fitting boots, which caused blisters, though removing their footwear might have avoided the worst of fungal rot. Officers had their boots made to fit, at great expense of course, which meant they were less harsh on their skin. Seb realized it was not Evans' fault altogether, though his corporal had to bear some of the blame.

Seb said, 'We have to get them treated. Come with me. No, don't put your boots back on. Walk without them.'

'I'll get jiggers in me toes.'

'No self-respecting jigger is going to bore through that stinking fuzz, believe me.'

So Evans hobbled after his officer, who led him towards a shack on the near side of Helpmekaar fort. On enquiry after a surgeon they were directed to a young woman dressed in a long dark-blue dress and a white cap. She had a band on her arm with the letters S.H. writ bold upon it. Over the dress she wore an apron that had begun life white, but had become stained with blood and other bodily fluids. She smiled as Seb approached her and the ensign's heart melted immediately.

'Are you Miss Janet Wells?' he asked, extending his hand.

The nurse shook it, vigorously. 'Yes, I am, but most of the men simply call me Sister Janet.'

An army officer did not come across many pretty girls on campaign and Seb found himself staring at her.

'And you are, sir?' she said, smiling, seemingly unaware of his rudeness.

'Oh, yes – sorry, ma'am. I am Ensign Sebastian Early, of the 24th.'

'I see you wear an equivalent to my armband?'

'Oh, this? Yes, it means I'm the Provost-Marshal − the army's policeman and detective.'

'It sounds a very important post.'

He shrugged, embarrassed. 'Not really − not as important as someone who cures the sick.' Seb looked around him at the men lying on cots, some on the ground. 'Dysentery mostly, I suppose?'

'And rheumatism,' she replied. 'Marching in tropical rainstorms and through rivers does not do a lot of good to a person.'

'No, I suppose not.'

'Then there're various fevers.'

'Of course.'

'So, Ensign Sebastian Early, are you not well?'

Seb looked surprised. 'Me? Yes, I'm fine.'

'Yet you seek medical help?'

He shook himself, mentally. 'Oh, oh yes − look, it's not me, it's my corporal over there. That lofty awkward-looking soldier standing with his boots in his hands. See the state of his feet? I wondered if you could help him. Clean him up. We're on a mission, you see, to the south, and he won't last long with feet like that. He's an artillery man and used to riding on gun carriages, so his feet are not properly hardened.'

Sister Janet nodded. 'I find it refreshing that an officer is concerned with his men. Not many would accompany their soldiers to the doctor.'

'Well, he's the only one I've got. I used to have a whole company of them − well, not me personally, of course, for there was a captain and some lieutenants, but between us we had a hundred men. He's deaf, too. Corporal Evans I mean, so he needs someone to explain . . .'

He found he was gabbling so he shut up and went to fetch Evans. She found a bowl and to Evans' great embarrassment bathed his feet in something which looked and smelled suspiciously like piss. When he asked, she told him it was diluted ox's urine, which would help rid him of the rotting fungus that was destroying his feet.

'Each evening,' she said, without a blush, 'you must urinate in your boots and let them dry overnight.'

Evans cried, 'I can't do that. It wouldn't be right, eh?'

'You must not be so priggish,' Sister Janet admonished him. 'Ensign, can you ensure he carries out my instructions? The urea will serve to kill the fungus. There's no other effective way of dealing with it, unless you have some native cure.'

'Yes, Sister. I'll see he does what he's told.'

'My mam would have a fit,' grumbled Evans. 'Disgustin', she'd call it.'

'We are not in Britain now, Corporal,' the sister told him. 'This is Africa and there're more things to be wary of here. You are both out riding hard, so I must tell you to drink a lot of water. Many of the deaths here are caused by dehydration. If you start to feel thirsty you have already left it too late. Drink often and regularly as a matter of course and hopefully we need not see each other again.'

'Well, that would be a disappointment, Sister,' said Seb, gallantly, and a little too boldly for good manners, 'for I have enjoyed our meeting beyond anything. I believe you are the most beautiful lady I have met since leaving my home in Shropshire, where even there, I'm certain, there are none to compare with such loveliness.'

'Sir,' she replied, smiling, 'if I had a shilling for every soldier who said something similar to me, I would be a very rich woman. I'm an ordinary girl amongst a great deal of men who are starved of female company. If I were to pass you in the street back in England, you would barely give me a glance, either of you. It's the circumstances that dictate to your feelings, sir, not my looks, which are quite commonplace.'

They protested of course, corporal and ensign together, assuring her that she was a goddess in their eyes.

Sister Janet laughed and then went about her business of assisting the sick and injured.

Once back at the tents, much to the astonishment of Sam Weary, Seb instructed his corporal to pee in his boots.

'Not tonight, I don't have to,' argued Evans. 'I've just been done by Sister Janet.'

'Tonight and every night, until I tell you to stop.'

Evans grumbled and picked up his boots, moving to the edge of the firelight.

'Stop lookin' at me, Sam,' he shouted. 'Can't a man do his business without bein' stared at?'

'Sorry, Corporal,' Sam said, with a little giggle.

Evans turned his back to them and then proceeded to 'do his business' but he could not disguise the noise he made as the pee hit the hard leather inside each boot.

'Just talk amongst yourselves,' he said, loudly. 'You don't have to make a study of a man relievin' hisself.'

The loud laughter told him he was going to suffer quite a bit during this trip to the south of Natal.

That evening the insects were more bothersome than usual, which probably meant that rain was coming. The inside of the tent was black with a thousand species, some of them almost as large as Seb's hand. The three men were sleeping in the same bell, borrowed from a company stationed locally.

Seb wanted to get to the coast as quickly as possible and settle this business with Captain Pickering so that he could return to the 2nd Division before the next attack on the Zulus. He would not feel comfortable, nor would any officer of the regiment, to see battle honours on the colour later if he had not been present at that particular fight, especially since he was in the region and *should* have been there.

Seb walked to the edge of the habitation to view the sunset, leaving his two minions to get the bedding ready for the night.

'I can't sleep with them things buzzing up there,' complained Evans to Sam, talking of the bugs on the ceiling of the tent. 'I'm going to get rid of them, see.'

He took a burning brand from the fire and went inside the tent, intending to sweep the flame under the insects and roast them into oblivion. This he attempted with some success, being rewarded with a sizzling sound and a smell that told of many tiny inciner-ations. Some popped under the flame, some shrivelled, some – like the moths with delicate gossamer wings – flared into small fires themselves. It was these, the fiery ones, that were responsible for the great conflagration. They caused burning holes to appear in the tent, which spread rapidly over the whole cone of the bell and down the sides.

'Hey, ho, hup!' cried Evans, dashing through the doorway and to safety. 'That was quick. Did you see that, Sam? Whoa, look at it go up.' He threw the brand back on the fire quickly. 'It must have been a spark from the fire what did it.'

'How can you say that, Corporal-sir?' said Sam, with round eyes. 'It was your very own firestick that caused this accident.'

'Yes, that's what it is, an accident,' replied Evans. 'An accident no one could prevent.'

Seb saw the fire from five hundred yards away. It filled the skyline with light. He came running back to find that just the charred strips of glowing canvas and bedding remained. Smouldering pieces of blanket wafted in the evening breeze, tumbling over some of the non-combustible materials and objects.

'What happened here?'

'Spark,' muttered Evans, looking warningly out of the corners of his eyes at Sam. 'Flew up from the fire.'

Sam said nothing, busying himself with dragging surviving bits of kit out of reach of the remains of the fire.

'Damn,' said the ensign. 'What bad luck.'

'Terrible luck,' said Evans. 'Me and Sam will sort this out, sir. You go and find some other place to sleep. I'm sure they'll find you a cot, you bein' an officer and all, eh?'

'No, I couldn't do that, Evans. We'll simply sleep on the ground, all three of us. Did you manage to save my helmet?'

'Did you say *helmet*, sir? I thought you did. Good news on that score. I dashed in quick like, before the flames took a proper hold, and grabbed your headgear. Sorry about all this, but there was nothing we could do. It went up like dry tinder, didn't it, Sam?'

Sam was too much a Methodist to lie to his master, but he had no hesitation in telling a partial truth.

'Once it was on fire, boss, there was nothing we could do but watch it burn.'

'I can vouch for that myself,' said Seb. 'One minute it was a tent, the next a ball of flame. However, someone will have to pay the piper – or rather the local quartermaster – and I know who that will be. Sam, how much do I owe you in wages?'

Sam gulped.

Seb grinned. 'Just jesting with you, Sam – it'll be me who'll foot the bill, of course. Now let's clear some spaces around the fire. Have we any blankets left? Just one? Well, Amasi gets that, since it's his anyway. The rest of us will sleep in our clothes.'

'I do that anyway,' said Evans, reading his officer's lips. 'Every night.'

'But this night,' reminded Sam, 'the corporal must not sleep in his boots.'

'He must pee in them,' Seb could not help adding, before he and Sam went into laughter that they tried to swallow, but were unsuccessful.

Ten

They slept in a triangle around the embers of the campfire without a thought for wildlife, whether slithering, crawling or creeping. After so many nights under an African night sky Evans and Seb were inured to those creatures which haunted the nightmares of imaginative people back in Britain. Serpents were real here, and so were huge hairy spiders, so one did not need an imagination. These concerns were so much easier to deal with when they were confronted full on. The only time either man started in alarm these days was when something came upon them suddenly at very close range, like a millipede on a shaving mirror, or an arachnid on a shirt collar.

When they rose they watered the horses and were soon on their way. Seb decided not to report the loss of the tent. It would only involve a lot of shouting and demands for recompense, so he decided to wait until the deed caught up with him and deal with it then. Certainly there was the possibility that it never would reach him, since the army was always on the move, and then there was the probability that he would be killed in battle or eaten away by some African disease by then. A man was here today and gone tomorrow, so why go out of one's way to invite an argument over a piece of canvas?

Towards noon Evans shouted, 'We're driftin' west, sir, I can feel it in my blood.'

Welsh shepherds, it seemed, had built-in navigation devices: compasses of the liver and spleen; universal maps that unfolded within the chambers of the heart; long bones of the arm and leg that doubled as measuring rods.

'You're imagining it, Corporal.'

Sam said, 'I think Evans-corporal is right, boss.'

The ensign could not argue with both men, so he said, 'Mutiny is punishable by death.'

No more was said for a while, until an exasperated Evans cried out, 'We've lost sight of the river.'

'I'm aware of that fact, Corporal,' said Seb, turning so the artillery man could read his lips. 'I want to stop at a farm. We can water the beasts there and replenish our own supplies.'

'If you don't mind me sayin' so, sir . . .'

'Oh, but I do,' muttered Seb.

'. . . there's plenty of farms nearer the river.'

Seb ignored this obvious flaw in his reasoning. He did not add that it was a *particular* farm he had in mind. Unconsciously he had indeed been drifting inland, towards the Donaldson place, where a young woman named Mary lived with her father. The old man was rather irascible and had recently sent a note on a wagon travelling north, the contents of which amounted to a threat to shoot Ensign Sebastian Early if he ever tried to come near his daughter again. Seb had read this note with some annoyance, for Mary was past the age when her father had any hold over her and indeed had encouraged Seb to think she favoured him over other men. Certainly the threat had no power to discourage the young man, who considered it a challenge rather than a deterrent.

Much like his Uncle Jack, Seb was easily enmeshed by pretty females. His recent encounter with Sister Janet was a case in point. Had she shown him the least encouragement he would have ridden out into the wilderness and died for her. At home there was his dead friend's sister, who continued in the mistaken belief that Seb considered her to be the lady of his life, simply because whenever he had spoken to her he had stared into her eyes with rapt adoration. She did not know that rapt adoration was a common expression with Seb when talking to any attractive woman.

In point of fact, this Mary Donaldson had captured his attention more than any other girl. She was lithe and supple in movement, open-hearted, free-speaking; she had sparkling eyes and the softest east-coast Scottish accent that ever fell on a man's ears. Her figure was trim and neat, her skin clear, and her hands looked and felt as soft as the pink underside of a field mushroom, though she had had to work hard on her father's farm. Above all, though, when she first met Seb, and on their only other meeting much later, she treated him as if he were the only man within a thousand miles, and stared into his face with such pleasure and frankness it stirred his feelings into a tidal rush of warm blood.

Towards evening the farmhouse came into view, a ramshackle

one-storey wooden building with mud outhouses that stood like a castle in the fading light of the day.

'There it is,' said Seb, halting Amasi and standing in the stirrups.

Evans was staring at his face and the corporal repeated, 'There *it* is – so we was looking for this farm special, was we?'

'I didn't say that,' Seb replied, turning in his saddle, 'and I'll have you know, Corp—' He said no more because he suddenly spun on the back of his mount and fell heavily to the ground, banging his head on the baked clay. From some distant point the sound of a shot echoed through the twilight. Evans was off his own horse in an instant and had his Martini-Henry in his hands. He levelled the weapon at a copse to the north and fired. Then he reloaded twice more and fired again and again.

In the meantime Sam had slid from the back of the same horse and was helping Seb sit up.

'You are hit, dear sir?' said the amaXhosa. 'Where is the wound?'

Seb, still a little stunned by the impact of his head with the ground, felt his left underarm.

'I don't think it's a bad one, Sam,' he said, a little thickly. 'Have a look, will you?'

Evans continued to fire steadily at the distant copse. Seb could hear the rounds striking leaves and trees in the quiet of the evening. Someone was coming from the farmhouse, running towards them, calling. Eventually Evans stopped firing and helped Sam take off Seb's bloodstained tunic. Underneath they found that the shot had gone right through the fleshy part of Seb's armpit. Once Seb realized it was just a hole and there was no bullet in his body to fester, he felt a lot better. There was pain, but only enough to make his eyes water.

'Oh dear, are you hurt bad?'

Mary Donaldson had arrived. She pushed Sam away and inspected the wound closely. 'It's just a wee hole,' she said, in a relieved tone. 'Thank goodness for that – but who would do such a terrible thing?' She stared through the gloaming at the copse, having seen Evans aiming that way.

'Well,' said Seb, 'how do you do, Mary? I'm happy to see you again. You look well and as beautiful as when we last saw each other.' The polite niceties over, but with no response appearing on the horizon, he added, 'As to who would shoot at me, my first

guess would be your father, since this is his farm and he has threatened to do just that if I try to contact you again.'

'My father?' Mary looked puzzled. 'No, no, not my father. Some
Zulus maybe, come from across the river? Not my father. Come
on, let's get you into the house, soldier, where I can wash the
wound and dress it. You have to be careful in these climes. Cuts
and wounds get infected very quickly. Here, lean on me, your men
will take care of the horses. I'm right fine, to answer your greeting,
and how are you? Och, of course, you're not well at all, are you,
with the wound to your body. Never mind, we'll soon have that
tended to, eh, laddie?'

She put her arm around him and he did indeed lean on her,
though he felt guilty for doing so. He was perfectly able to walk
without any assistance and was not giddy in the least. But the
warmth of her breast through the cotton dress against his side was
worth getting shot for. If he had had to, he would have feigned
dizziness. To be close enough to her to smell her hair and feel her
heart beating alongside his own was almost worth a bullet.

Once in the farmhouse kitchen, Mary took a bowl of hot clean
water and some soap and bathed Seb's injury. Then she put some
ointment on it which stung worse than the original wound and
once again brought water to his eyes. Finally, she insisted on weaving
a bandage elaborately around his chest and shoulder to hold the
pad in place, though the position of the wound made such an
exercise difficult and Mary was no Sister Janet.

Halfway through these ministerings the corporal came into the
house. He took a wooden chair and dumbly sat and watched until
Mary had finished. Then Mary said, 'Who would like a cup of
tea?'

'WHAT?' shouted Evans.

Mary looked at the corporal a little alarmed.

'Deaf,' explained Seb. 'Pay no heed.'

Seb made some signs with his fingers and Evans nodded briskly.

'We'd all like some tea,' said Seb. 'Is it all right if my other man
comes into the kitchen?'

It was not usual for blacks to enter a strange house. Most whites
would have objected strongly to the presence of a black who was
not a house-servant in their kitchen. But Mary was not one of
those immigrants who considered blacks inferior. She had been

partly raised in a wretched croft in the Scottish Highlands where clan elders and others treated her like dirt. Some in her position would have sought an even less fortunate human being on which to take revenge, but Mary was the kind of person who remembered her own misery and would not want to inflict it on another of God's creatures.

'Of course. Would he like tea?'

Afterwards she made all three men, and herself, a meal of eggs and pork. The soldiers and their servant wolfed it down. Mary was more delicate. It was only once the men had their pipes in their mouths and the talk started again that Seb again broached the matter of the would-be assassin.

'Where is your father, by the way? How are you so sure it was not him who shot at me?'

'Because he's in Durban.'

Seb was a little shocked.

'He left you here alone?'

'Not entirely. I'm alone at night, but during the day the workers from the village are here. One of them has a hut not far away. If I needed him I could run to him quite quickly.'

Seb blew out his cheeks. 'All the same, it's very remiss of him. Your father, I mean. Anything could happen.'

She laughed. 'Och, things do happen, naturally – but I can take care of them.'

Sam and Evans then left, stating their intention of going to sleep in one of the barns. Seb was left alone with Mary. In truth he was now feeling a little woozy, the shock of being shot now hitting him. He found himself being assisted to a large double bed in a room at the back of the building. His hostess helped him with the removal of his boots and belt, and one or two other items of clothing, then covered him with some bedclothes.

'You get some rest now, soldier,' she said. 'I'll look in on you later.'

He could not stop his teeth chattering long enough to answer properly. Also his mind was spinning with thoughts. Who was it then who had shot at him, if not Donaldson? He could not think that Zulus would have come this far west of the border – there were several army posts between the river and the farm, besides other farms and dwellings. In any case, whoever had made that shot expected it to be the only one necessary, otherwise there would have been a volley that would have taken all three men out of their saddles. The round had been intended for Seb alone.

Who wanted him dead?

He did manage to sleep, but fitfully, and was later mortified to find Mary Donaldson asleep in the chair by his bed. He woke her and told her to get to her own bed. He regretted disturbing her because instead of obeying his command she forced some medicine down his throat using a mixture of threats and persuasion. He fell asleep again. This time he slept more peacefully, waking when the rays of the early morning sun struck his pillow. When he turned to look towards the unshuttered window, he found Mary stretched out next to him, her lissom pale arm resting lightly on his chest.

She looked like an abandoned angel, lying there with her long fair hair spread over the coverlet, though in truth Seb had been without female company for so long a dowager might have passed as such. However, Mary was indeed a fresh beauty and the sight of her lying there in her thin cotton dress stopped his heart for a few moments. Then he reached out and gently touched her cheek, which caused her to wake with a jump.

'Oh,' she said, 'you're with us.' She slipped from the bed into the chair. 'How's the shoulder?'

He swivelled his left arm gently.

'Stiff,' he admitted, 'but I'm sure that'll pass. The round didn't hit any muscle. Just the flap between my arm and chest.'

'Och, I know,' she said, smiling, 'I dressed it, so I did. Now, will you be staying long, Sebastian? I have plenty of food in the house and you're very welcome to remain as long as you wish – as long as it takes for your wound to heal right.'

He blinked at the use of his first name.

'Well, much as that sounds a most attractive invitation, I have a task to do. Listen,' he paused before going on, 'we didn't . . .'

'Didn't *what*, soldier?'

'I mean – last night, when you came to the bed.'

She laughed. 'What do you think?'

'I believe I was in no fit state,' he replied with some chagrin, 'even if you . . .'

'Even if I had wanted you to? Well, if we're to be absolutely honest with one another, I did want to, which is very bad and fast of me, but sadly the laudanum took you away to dreamland and you only had eyes for the fairies you found there.'

'Oh.' He did not know what to say to this confession and eventually came out with the lame words, 'Laudanum? No wonder my mouth feels so dry.'

After she had left the room, saying she would get breakfast, he kicked himself mentally for not suggesting they take up where she had left off the night before. Sam and Evans would not dare enter the house without being invited, so they would not be interrupted. Then again, the wound and the medicine had combined to draw all the sap out of his limbs and he felt weak and ineffective.

When Evans and Sam were called to breakfast, they asked how he was.

'Well enough to ride, I think.'

'You need to drink plenty of water,' Mary informed him, 'and listen to your men when they say you look tired. Rest as often as you can. What's that smell?'

Mary had tilted her head and sniffed, and was looking very puzzled.

Sam, having bitten into a slice of bread, and was chewing, said with his mouth full, 'It is the corporal's boots, ma'am.'

A sanguine expression came over the face of the artillery man.

Mary raised her eyebrows. 'His boots?'

Again, guilelessly Sam told her, 'He has to make water in his boots every night, ma'am.'

'Does he?' she said, faintly.

'Yes, ma'am. Sister Janet told him to.'

Mary turned to Evans, so that he could see the movements of her mouth. 'Who is Sister Janet? I don't understand. Is this some form of punishment?'

'No, ma'am,' replied the corporal, clearly suffering from excruciating embarrassment, 'it's to stop the fungus growin' between me toes. Sister Janet is a nurse at Helpmekaar, ma'am, and said this was the proper treatment for my complaint.'

'The corporal has foot rot,' Seb said, plainly, 'which is killed by regular doses of urine. Now can we get on with eating? This is surely not a subject for the breakfast table, Evans. I wish you had not brought it up.'

Not wanting the conversation to continue, Evans did not point out that it was Mary who had raised the subject. He would take his revenge on the artlessly honest Sam Weary later, for making him the centre of unwanted attention. Sam could have blamed one of the domestic animals, but no, he had to tell the truth. Well, even though Sam had not meant to harm him, he could not let the Xhosa get away with making him the fool.

The three men were riding out just as the farm workers arrived from the village. Mary stood on the veranda and waved goodbye. Seb, aware of the eyes of his two companions, threw her a casual wave back again.

After a short while, Sam asked, 'Are you going to marry this lady?'

Seb was not pleased with the question.

'That is not a proper question of a servant to ask of his master, Sam.'

Evans, watching Seb closely, said, 'How about if a corporal asks it?'

'Bordering on insolence,' informed Seb, 'so keep your tongue to yourself.'

There was a long period of silence now, then Evans said, 'Still an' all, sir – she's as pretty as a spring lamb.'

'Improper and you know it, Evans. Desist.'

'Yes, sir. Now, about the shooter.'

This was a more comfortable subject for the officer.

'Did you see him?'

'Not as such. Saw the flash of the shot. I didn't get him. After you was taken to the house me and Sam had a quick look in the wood. No sign of any blood. Just the grass where it was trampled down. Rider went north, back towards where we come from. Must 'ave been following us since we set out.'

'You think he might have come from Helpmekaar?'

'Or maybe from further back – from the camp in Zululand?'

Seb mused on this. 'Not Zeldenthuis. If it had been he, I would be dead.'

Evans agreed. 'The Boer can shoot the eye out of a snake at fifty feet.'

'Then we must assume that our investigations are to blame.'

'My way of thinkin', exactly,' agreed the corporal.

'Perhaps riding north was a ruse? What if the assassin did a loop from the south, to fool us?'

'Could be. So the man we're goin' to see down on the coast, he came to us, like?'

'Possibly,' said Seb. 'Even so, I can't imagine a cavalry man going so far as to murder a provost-marshal to escape a court martial over a duel, can you? I mean, it would not only mean the end of his career, it would mean his execution and the ruin of his family name for generations. Killing a man in a duel is one thing, even though technically murder, but deliberately assassinating an officer of the law to avoid discovery and punishment – that would be a most heinous crime.'

'Some men have no conscience, though, do they, sir? They live their lives believin' they're in the right, no matter what they do. I seen a man like that hung once, in Cardiff, and he looked most surprised when he dropped, as if he never thought it would happen in a thousand years. In their heads, they think they're so clever and above it all they can't be touched by ordinary people.'

'I imagine dictators are much like that sort of chap, Evans. Yes, indeed. Well, I hope I'm not being pursued by someone of that ilk, or I fear I'm a gone soldier. That sort of determination is usually only thwarted during or after the act.'

'We will stay next to you, boss,' interrupted Sam, from behind Evans where he was sitting on the rump of the horse. 'The corporal and me will protect and keep you safe from somesuch savages.'

Eleven

They turned north-eastwards on reaching the coast. The Zulus in this area were less effective than those in the north. Chelmsford's victory at the Battle of Gingindlovu had reduced their numbers and desire for battle.

The 1st Division had begun to march on 21 April. The column numbered some seven thousand men, over two-thirds white, the rest black. However, they had not advanced very far from the Thekula, since their commander Major-General Crealock had decided to send advance parties to build each fort, before supplying and occupying them, rather than marching to a spot on the map and erecting a fort in situ.

The arrival of a junior officer in the guise of the Provost-Marshal would not normally have caused much interest amongst the soldiers, but the coastal division was a boring place to be. Progress was slow and tedious, due to lack of oxen and wagons, and the tracks were muddy and foul. There was little or nothing in the way of fighting to be had down in this area of Zululand and men were left with the arduous work of digging out equipment that was stuck in the mud, only escaping it by falling sick with some tropical malaise.

So there was a spark of interest when three riders entered the camp, two wearing the red sashes of army policemen, and one being carried on the rump of an artillery corporal's heavy horse. Soldiers took the opportunity to stop work and watch this trio ride past them much in the same way as road workers in Britain might pause to watch a girl go by or a butterfly flit over ditch weeds. It made for a breather of sorts, attended by mild speculation. Was an arrest about to take place? Or were the provos just coming for a change of scene? Those amongst the watchers who had recently committed a crime wondered if they had been discovered and began forming stories and alibis in their heads, ready for the interrogation. Those who had been good and honest still curled their lips in distaste, for the sight of policemen even to an innocent man is often not one that fills a heart with delight.

Here and there were drummer boys and bugle boys practising their art, probably in order to look busy so that they would not be called upon to put a shoulder behind a bogged-down wagon. Cooks and their assistants too were labouring over tasks which seemed to consist mainly of stirring a cauldron full of greasy grey water, no doubt containing an unrecognizable type of meat. These culinary experts of the veldt were conspicuous by the fact that they were actually dirtier than soldiers digging trenches or dragging equipment through the mud.

Seb noticed that his uncle's regiment, the 88th Connaught Rangers, was in evidence here, along with the 3rd, 60th and 99th. Some 57th were there, and also several auxiliaries and irregulars. He was looking for one auxiliary regiment in particular, the Border Rangers, which had in its ranks the man he had come to interview: Captain William Pickering.

Seb had done some homework earlier in the month and knew that the Border Rangers wore black uniforms with red piping down the outside seams of their trousers, a red loop on the cuffs of their jackets and broad-brimmed hats with red headbands. They carried breach-loading Snider percussion rifles that fired a .557 bullet, an obsolete weapon that was not as effective or accurate as a Martini-Henry, or even a Swinburne-Henry carbine.

Seb reported to Major-General Henry Hope Crealock, informed him why he was there, and was told to get about his business 'without disturbing my operations' too much. The general was heard to ask his adjutant, as Seb walked away, why 'that young ensign' had reported directly to him, rather than to one of his staff officers. The adjutant muttered something that Seb was unable to understand, but was no doubt scathing of junior officers whose appointments gave them the idea they had risen in importance.

Evans and Sam took the horses to water and then set about finding accommodation. Seb sought out one of the surgeons and allowed his underarm to be closely inspected. Mary's blood-caked bandage was removed a little unceremoniously by a soldier with rougher hands than hers, which caused the wound to open again. The surgeon then came forward with his expert opinion and rather gentler manner.

'Who applied the dressing?'

'A young lady.'

'Well, it's better than nothing, but only just – though a difficult position. There does not seem to be any infection, but we'll apply some balm to soothe the soreness. Are you feverish?'

'No,' replied Seb. 'Last night a little, but not this morning.'

'You're a lucky man. This is a bullet wound. Were you shot by Zulus?'

'I don't know,' said Seb. 'Does it matter – medically speaking, I mean?'

'It might, if the shooter dipped the ball in poison before using it. Who knows what those savages do with their ammunition? Still, you don't feel sick, do you? So I imagine it's just an ordinary wound. There are no cloth fibres in there that I can see, either, which is good, medically speaking. You've one or two bruises too. Did you fall heavily?'

'The impact spun me off the back of my mount and I dropped to the ground, hard. I hit my head and stunned myself for a few minutes. Here's the bump.'

Seb showed the doctor a lump on his skull.

'So,' said the surgeon, tying off the bandage, 'he probably thinks you're dead – the man who fired that shot. He's probably congratulating himself. You, on the other hand, may get the chance to get back at him, if the good Lord sees fit to arrange it.'

Thus the wound was dressed again, this time looking less like the rigging of a wrecked vessel after a storm. Seb left the surgeon's tent a little wiser than when he had entered it. Dead. Yes, of course. The assassin would think he had got his man. That might be helpful, if ever Seb came across someone who seemed astonished to see him alive. Of course he could hardly ride into every camp and watch for change of expressions, but the thought was useful.

Now that his wound had been attended to, Seb went on a search of the camp for his prey. After several enquiries he was directed to an area where he did indeed find his man. Unfortunately, Captain Pickering was talking to an officer from the 99th who was well known to Seb. In fact they had been classmates together at Sandhurst. They did not like each other. There was even hate on one side. And the worst part about it was that the officer was not alone. There were others nearby who were in sympathy, who also felt they had cause to hate Sebastian Early.

'Captain Pickering?' said Seb, introducing himself to the man in the black uniform. 'I am Ensign Early, the Provost-Marshal.'

Pickering smiled and extended a hand which was obviously meant to be shaken. Seb shook it, watching the other man out of the corner of his eye. The second officer took a step back and a sneer appeared on his face.

'Early!' said the officer. 'You here?'

'Ensign Greely,' acknowledged Seb. 'Yes, it appears so, doesn't it?'

'Second Lieutenant, if you please,' came back the retort. 'The 99th is not so backward as some regiments. We dispensed with the term *ensign* quite a long while ago, considering it quite antique.'

'Very well, Second Lieutenant Greely. I have no quarrel with that, if that's what you wish to call yourself. For my part I feel that the rank of "ensign" is tried and tested, and has come up trumps time and again.'

'Gentlemen,' murmured the captain standing between them, 'there is obviously some history here which is unknown to me.'

Seb turned to him again. 'I apologize, sir. Can we go somewhere private to talk?'

At that moment two other officers, one a second lieutenant, the other a lieutenant, came and stood by their comrade.

'What we have here,' said the lieutenant, a tallish young man with very large, almost translucently thin ears, 'is a very sly rat who has entered the area without invitation. Is there an exterminator nearby?' He pretended to scour the horizon for this imaginary person. His eyes swung back to Seb again. 'We need someone to get rid of vermin. Our camp has suddenly become infested.'

'I see they're promoting donkeys now,' observed Seb. 'Still, what can one expect of the 99th?'

The lieutenant's eyes flashed and he tried to slap Seb's face, but the ensign avoided the strike.

'Grow up, Downing,' snapped Seb, 'you're in a man's army now.'

The captain could see there was about to be a brawl, in which he would be the senior officer present. He threw an arm around Seb's shoulder and steered him forcefully away from the trio of 99th officers. Seb allowed himself to be walked away, leaving behind three fulminating young men. Once they were out of the area he dropped his hand to his side and said, 'That was quite unpleasant.'

He spoke with a North England accent, possibly acquired in Northumberland. His frame was soldierly, with broad shoulders that stretched the back of his coat taut. The arm around Seb was a strong, firm one. In fact the officer was hard, athletic-looking, and appeared in prime health.

'I'm sorry about that, sir. As you said, history. We were classmates at Sandhurst.'

'I should have thought that a matter for rejoicing, not for a spat.'

'We – we didn't part as friends.'

'I had gathered that.'

Seb stopped and stared into the captain's eyes.

'I suppose I should give you some explanation?'

Pickering nodded. 'If it's at all interesting.'

Seb sighed. 'There were sixty cadets at Sandhurst in our entry and for field exercises we were split into groups of twelve men. Towards passing-out parade, it seemed certain that my particular group would win the award for the best overall performance. We had notched up some impressive results. However, as the day neared, another group, late starters, put a spurt on and almost caught us up. There was a final field exercise. I was chosen as leader. Therefore I had the map and the compass, I was directing my group. I – I deliberately misled them, got them lost. They later realized what I'd done and . . . well, as you can see, they still haven't forgiven me, even though I still bear the scars of the beating they gave me outside the gates of Sandhurst.'

'Yes, it is very interesting – but the reason for the deceit?'

'My friend Peter was the leader of the rival group. He'd had a hard time at Sandhurst. He was not a good student. Not good academically. Had he not led his group to success during that final exercise he would have failed and they would have sent him home in disgrace. I had to make sure that didn't happen.' Seb paused and was silent for a minute or two, but when there was no response from the captain, he added, 'He was my friend from childhood. What else was I to do?'

Pickering said, 'Are you certain you got your group lost on purpose?'

Seb was annoyed. 'I've just said so.'

'Yes, but our minds are friends, sometimes. They help us cover our faults. And we are happy to believe them. Some memories are malleable. We reshape them unconsciously to suit our needs.'

'What do you mean?'

'I mean that occasionally, in retrospect, we embellish our recall with frills that were not actually part of the experience. Is it possible that you *did* make a mistake, an unfortunate but genuine error, and then later added the heroic edge to it, making you saviour of your friend's army career, instead of the fool who lost his way?'

'I'm telling it truthfully, the way I remember it – although . . .'

Pickering smiled. 'Although there *is* doubt in your mind?'

'Well, I'm not here to talk about me,' Seb said, suddenly taking back command of the conversation. 'I'm here to interview you about the death of a private. You reported that it became necessary to execute this soldier during the course of the battle. Can you tell me what happened?'

'I'll try to, though who knows what the unconscious mind . . . ah, I'm jesting, sorry, I know this is a serious business. Private Brandon refused to obey an order to take his place in the square. I gave the order clearly, three times, yet he remained firm and obstinate, refusing to move from behind a wagon. Other men had formed up and the assistance in the line of every soldier was vital to our success. Private Brandon was displaying cowardice in the heat of the battle. I couldn't allow such a situation to continue, since I was afraid it would affect others and make them question my orders too. I had my revolver in my hand. I gave him one last order and said that I would shoot him dead if he did not obey it – he refused. I shot him through the heart.'

Seb took out his notepad and a pencil and scribbled on the blank page.

'This was on the 1st of April – at Gingindlovu?'

'Yes, around 6 a.m. we were called to arms. A large impi was seen approaching our position by the picquets. We were in a square and they – the enemy's left horn – came at us from a north-easterly point first of all, attacking the north face of the square. It was a classic Zulu attack and soon the right horn of the buffalo attacked our west face, and the rear of the square. My men were on the west face, under the direct command of Lieutenant Ruiker. Once I had dealt with the craven Brandon, I joined my lieutenant in the line.'

Seb continued scribbling. 'I understand the Zulus were driven off, by heavy rifle fire and the Gatling gun.'

'They ran back and hid in the long grasses, firing at us from that position.'

'And after that?'

'The general – Lord Chelmsford, that is – sent out the mounted troops who drove the Zulus down to the river and cut them to pieces. We all had Isandlwana uppermost in our minds at that moment. There was the smell of revenge in the air.'

'Well,' said Seb, closing his notepad, 'it all seems quite straight-forward to me. So in all, Private Brandon was given the order three times? Then you felt you had run out of . . .'

'Patience, yes.'

Seb said, 'I was going to say *time*, but it's of no real matter. One more thing, Captain. Did you know Private Brandon personally? I mean, apart from the fact that he was a soldier in your company?'

For the first time, Seb saw the captain's face twitch.

'What do you mean?'

'Oh, well, was he an old soldier who'd followed you from regiment to regiment? Some do that, grow fond of their commanders and request transfers if their officer changes regiments.'

'I have not been an officer in another regiment – this is my first command.'

'An auxiliary regiment?'

'I was an ordinary soldier in the regular army, in China and India, but when I joined the Border Rangers they offered me a lieutenancy, due to my past military experience. You can tell I'm not high-born, from the way I talk and from my accent. I'm the son of a Durham baker and am up from the ranks. I'm proud of that fact, Ensign Early. No leg-up from Daddy. No influential friends. Just me, on my own ability.'

'In point of fact, you strike me as an educated man. I'm surprised to learn you're not.'

'Self-taught.'

'Really? And as to pulling yourself up by your own bootstraps, my uncle would approve of that. He too made his way up through the ranks, though he came from an aristocratic family.'

'I would be honoured to shake his hand.'

'You might indeed see him around. Major Crossman, of the

88th. Now, can you answer the question of motive? Why would an experienced soldier – I understand Brandon, like you, had several years of service under his belt – why would he refuse to obey such an order? You were not, after all, sending him out on a suicide mission. He was just taking his place in the line, as he must have done a hundred times before. Was he of a rebellious nature?'

'You mean was he a difficult soldier? Not especially. He complained about many things, from the food to lack of equipment, but then they all do that, don't they? I don't recall him ever refusing to obey an order before this incident. Oh sure, he's been surly in the past, on occasion, belligerent, but then again, many soldiers have their personal grouses and dig in their heels when they feel they're not being treated fairly. One thing I remember him saying prior to his refusal to join the line: "I've had enough." ' Pickering paused and looked thoughtful, before adding, 'Perhaps that was it? Perhaps he'd reached the end of his tether, wherever that was, and wasn't prepared to go any further, do anything more for the army? Every man has his own individual limit, a point which when it's reached causes something in his head to snap. Most never get there, thank God, but one or two are less fortunate.' Another pause, then, 'Will that be all then, Ensign? I have my duties.'

'Yes, sir, thank you for your time.'

A hand was thrust out. Seb shook it for the second time. It was difficult not to like this captain of auxiliaries, though Seb was aware that a dark side must have been lurking beneath his surface openness. You did not shoot and kill a fellow soldier, albeit a member of the rank and file, without suffering some kind of torment, surely? Doubts of the legitimacy of the act must creep in. Guilty feelings when one thought of the man's relations back home. A wife and children, perhaps? No man of honest demeanour could execute a fellow soldier and leave his soul unscathed.

Pickering said, 'I'm glad to have met you, I just wish it had been under different circumstances. I hope this rotten business is now over and done with. This is something I'm definitely not proud of and it's left a very bad taste. I had to do it. It had to be done. But I hope there's never a repeat.'

The captain began to walk away, when Seb said, 'Oh, I'll need to interview your lieutenant – what was his name? Ruiker?'

'Yes, Ruiker, but you'll be disappointed. He was killed in the battle. Fell at my side with a musket ball lodged in his head. Sorry.' With that the captain continued on his walk.

Seb then went to join Sam and Corporal Evans, circumnavigating the part of the camp where he might run into the 99th. He did not want to see Greely, Downing and Pomeroy again.

Evans had found them a spot a little up from the river, beneath some large fulsome trees.

'How'd you get on, sir?' shouted Evans. 'Get your interview all right?'

Seb signed him to stop talking and use his hands.

Yes, I did – how about you?

There was an understanding between the Provost-Marshal and his assistant, that while one was investigating commissioned officers, the other would do likewise with the rank and file.

I saw some of the Border Ranger boys, yes. Had a nice chat with them.

Seb signed, *My man told me that Private Brandon just snapped. Wouldn't go into the line.*

I was told he stayed by a wagon and the officer went to get him.

Sounds like the two versions agree.

Sounds like, sir.

Did they hear the officer order the man to join the line? Did they hear a refusal?

They were too far away to hear most of what went on. Said they kept their voices low.

'That's strange,' Seb mused out loud. 'An altercation like that? Why would they keep their voices low? Perhaps they might speak evenly, not shouting, but deliberately whispering?'

Well, that's what I was told.

Seb thought about this for a while, then remembered some actual words had been passed on to him.

Did they hear the words, 'I've had enough'?

Ah, that's a good one, eh? Evans signed. *What my men said they heard was, 'It's not enough.'*

Twelve

Seb puzzled over those words for the next twelve hours, when he revisited Pickering and put the change to him. The Border Ranger captain assured Seb that the words were 'I've had enough' and that his soldiers must have misheard.

'After all,' Pickering said, 'I was standing right next to the man. The line was many yards away and there was a great deal of noise, as you can imagine. A battle was in progress. The Zulus are not quiet during battles and we had bugles, drums and guns going ten to the dozen. How any of them heard anything is a miracle.'

This sounded quite reasonable to Seb, so he pursued it no further, only thanking Pickering for his time. He walked through the thriving camp, with men busy on all sides and staring at him enviously, since he obviously had time to spare. In fact he was doing his job. He was thinking. Much of his work was a mental exercise, going over and over scenarios in his mind, trying to find pieces of the jigsaw to fit those he already had. The sound of cattle, spades, hammers, loud voices, these did not bother him when he was working. An army man gets used to a background noise that others who rely on thinking for their work would find intolerable.

Seb naturally went to interview the men Evans had spoken to and found them suspicious of their officer. In their own words, two of them said there had been a strange kind of relationship between Pickering and Brandon.

'Can't put me finger on it, 'xactly,' said one soldier, 'but you knew they was not strangers to one another.'

The soldiers were emphatic about the last words spoken by Brandon.

Further enquiries around camp added nothing substantial to the information Seb had already gathered and once more he felt frustrated by the job. An answer to a problem always seemed just out of reach, on the tip of one's mind-tongue, on the edge of a dream. You could almost reach out and touch it, but not quite. Answers are elusive things, that hide behind invisible barriers of the brain.

Just before the three left the 1st Division's camp, Corporal Evans, accompanied by the redoubtable Sam, met again for a few drinks with some of Pickering's company. Liberal doses of free gin and rum are of course highly instrumental in recovering lost memories and loosening knotted tongues. Using Sam as his ears as usual, with Sam signing to him, Evans discovered one more titbit involving Brandon and Pickering, which he passed on to Seb. The soldier had told Evans:

'While we was on the march, before the war was started, we passed another regiment. The 58th it was. One of their men must've known Bill Brandon, 'cause he yelled to him, somethin' like, "Where've you bin, matey?" Brandon ignored 'im, but looked across, quick like, at the captain. The man in the 58th was told to shut 'is gob by 'is Colour and we marched off in different directions, so nothin' came of it at all, but I could see both Bill and the captain was rattled a little by the encounter.'

Seb congratulated Evans and Sam on this discovery. He felt he at last had something he could use. The 58th were with the 2nd Division, who were probably now well on their way to Ulundi. It was time to ride back to the main column and investigate further.

The horses were fetched, Evans and Sam mounted one, and Seb was on Amasi. They rode west into Natal for a short way. However, when they reached a grove of trees some three hundred yards from camp, they were suddenly accosted by three figures, who stepped out into their path.

'Greely, Downing and Pomeroy,' said Seb.

Pomeroy came forward and grasped Amasi's bridle.

'Nice mount, Early. Yours?'

'A gift, Pomeroy. Now, be a sensible chap and let go, so we can be on our way. This isn't Sandhurst and you can't give the Provost-Marshal a drubbing — it would be a court-martial offence.'

'Oh,' called Greely, 'we weren't thinking of scragging you. Something a bit more serious than that.'

'We drew lots,' said Downing, 'and Pomeroy won.'

Pomeroy sneered. 'We need twenty yards of cold earth between us, Early — you know the form.'

'Ah, like that is it?' said Seb, grimly. 'I do indeed know the form. Where's the killing ground? I take it you've paced it out already? And the weapons?'

'Primed and ready,' replied Pomeroy, 'behind that clump of trees.'

Evans now spurred his mount forward so suddenly that Sam fell off the back and landed on his bottom in the dust.

'Now, now, sirs,' cried Evans, having gathered the gist of the agreement from reading Pomeroy's lips. 'We can't have any of that here. This officer is going about his lawful business, see, and though I'm just a corporal, I won't stand by and let a duel take place before my very eyes. I would be held accomplice to the crime. The Provost-Marshal himself knows that.' He unslung his Martini-Henry. 'There's one up the spout and I'll shoot any man, officer or not, who tries to force a duel.'

Greely sighed. 'Early, get your man on board, will you?'

Seb turned to his corporal.

'Evans, this is not quite what you think – just bear with us for thirty minutes.'

'I'm not going let them shoot you, see?'

'They won't.'

'Nor you shoot them, sir.'

'I promise not to kill anyone today.'

Seb walked Amasi forward, to go round the grove, saying, 'So you chose by lot? It just happened that it's Pomeroy, who has the shoulders of Hercules, who's won the lottery?'

Downing replied, hotly, 'It was done fairly, Early. I would give my right arm for the chance to be in Pomeroy's place, believe me.'

'Except that without your right arm, you'd be pretty useless in a duel of this kind, eh?' said Seb. 'Come on, let's get it over with. You know what happened last time. I did bowl for Shropshire, you know. You do know that?'

'As if we cared,' snarled Greely through gritted teeth.

Evans followed on his mount, with Sam trotting alongside, complaining bitterly, 'Corporal-sir, please give me warning next time. I have a very sore tail now and several days' riding ahead.'

Evans wasn't looking at the amaXhosi, though, so he failed to hear and Sam got no answer.

On the far side of the trees were two baskets, approximately twenty yards apart: the length between the two batsmen's creases on a cricket pitch. In the baskets were large hard potatoes, eighteen of them in all – or three overs. This was how duels were settled at Sandhurst during Seb's time there. The two opponents would take turns to 'bowl' potatoes at each other, aiming specifically for the vulnerable parts of the body. A potato was not a bullet, but nonetheless it could cause quite a painful bruise if accurately tossed and with some strength.

Both men stripped to the waist. Pomeroy was indeed an athletic, muscular figure, with broad shoulders and thick biceps. Seb had never fought a potato duel with him, but he guessed Pomeroy was a sportsman.

'Are you sure you drew lots?' asked Seb again. 'I'd rather fight Donkey Downing.'

'Well, you can't,' snapped Greely, 'you've got Pomeroy and I hope he gives you a pasting, you swine.'

Pomeroy was staring at Seb's bandaged shoulder. 'What's the matter with your arm?' he asked.

'My master has been wounded,' cried Sam Weary, from the edge of the trees. 'The ensign has been shot just two days since.'

Pomeroy looked at his two comrades.

'I can't fight a cripple,' he snorted. 'There's no honour in that.'

Seb said, 'Think nothing of it, Pomeroy – it's the left shoulder and I bowl with my right. Only a scratch, anyway.'

His opponent stared at him keenly, then nodded.

'If you say so.'

'Let's get to it, then,' said Seb. 'I have some riding to do.'

Pomeroy was indeed a sportsman. His first potato struck Seb in the chest and almost knocked him off his feet. A blue bruise quickly revealed itself. Seb missed with his first, but his second bowl caught Pomeroy on the cheek, causing him to stagger from his upright position. (The rules required that the 'batsman' simply stand erect and full front on, to receive the 'ball'.) The two men continued to hurl missiles at each other, some of which broke on impact, others causing superficial damage to flesh and bone. A nasty full toss caught Seb on the top of the head and stunned him for a few moments, and a straight-armed fast bowl struck Pomeroy on the knee making him yell and go down. All in all, Seb was glad when their baskets were empty. Pomeroy had raised enough bruises to give him trouble for a week. He hoped he had done the same, but was especially gratified to have taken out one of Pomeroy's front teeth, knowing that the lieutenant was vain about his looks. Seb had ruined the Greek god's handsome visage temporarily at least.

Seb put on his shirt and coat, with Sam's help, then placed his helmet carefully on his head, trying to avoid the lump above his ear. In the end he had to wear it askew. It must have looked a little comical but he preferred to look silly rather than suffer the band grinding his bump.

He mounted Amasi and settled himself in the saddle, knowing the injuries he had received were going to make for a very uncomfortable ride. Then he turned to the three officers who were silently watching him.

'Good day to you, gentlemen,' Seb said, stiffly. 'Until we meet again?'

'My turn next time, Early,' answered Greely.

'A pleasure,' said Seb, coolly. Then he gave them a grin. 'Sandhurst has a long arm, does it not? Reaching down to the feet of Africa. Well done, Pomeroy. Sorry about the tooth. Well, not really, but you know what I mean. Gentlemen?'

He saluted them and received theirs in return, though the faces wore grim expressions. Then he walked his horse forward, with Evans and Sam following him on theirs.

'What I mean,' bellowed Evans, after an hour's silent riding, 'is what schoolroom do they make officers in? Like a load of kids, if you ask me.'

He came up alongside Seb to read his reply from his mouth.

'No one's asking you, Corporal, and you're getting dangerously close to insubordination. We may be out in the wilderness, but I'm still your commanding officer.'

'Huh!' came the reply from the unimpressed Welsh NCO. 'I wonder if *your* commandin' officer would approve of such rompings.'

'Tradition,' said Seb. 'You wouldn't understand.'

'Sir,' Evans came back, 'don't tell a Welshman he doesn't understand tradition. We've got it all in the valleys, in the mountains. What've you English got, apart from a few nancy dancers with bells on their socks? Nothin', so far as I can see.'

'We have many fine traditions in England, thank you very much, Corporal.'

'Such as?'

'Henley Regatta. Epsom Derby. Smithfield meat market. Hundreds.'

'That's not tradition. Not like our male choirs or Eisteddfod.'

'How long's the Eisteddfod been going?'

Evans said proudly, 'Since the twelfth century.'

'About the same time as Smithfield.'

'Eh? Oh, sir,' cried Evans, almost knocking Sam off the horse when he jerked backwards at this remark, 'you're not seriously comparin' a meat market with a festival of Welsh culture?'

Seb smiled to himself, deigning to answer, knowing he had wounded his corporal deeply.

Thirteen

The ride back to the 2nd Division was uneventful, even the trek east across Zululand, where Seb followed the trail of men coming and going back and forth to Natal. Not only was there a visible groove in the landscape left behind the British army, there was litter, debris and a string of couriers, conveyers of replacement equipment, sick and injured men, and disillusioned hangers-on who were no longer interested in hanging on.

The division had advanced into enemy territory but not very far. This was of course due to the usual problems of moving hundreds of wagons across rough country. The sixteen oxen yoked in pairs to draw each one of these giant ships of the veldt over rocky ground, mud, streams and grasslands needed to be hardy beasts. Their life was one long happy round of immensely difficult work, dragging wagons across country that would have destroyed a heavy horse within an hour.

Local Africans walked alongside, encouraging the beasts forward with shouts and deft flicks of their long whips. It was said many of these skilled *voorloopers* could take a fly off an ox's nose without causing the animal any pain. All along the line, but in much lesser numbers, were 'conductors', who managed the slow-moving column of wagons, which kept the army moving at its snail's pace of only a few miles a day.

Wagons broke down and more had to be sent for, so continuous traffic was in progress all the way back to Natal. This was not so much an army on the march, as an army on the stroll. A good walking pace is five miles an hour. Soldiers had to heave wagons out of the mud, cut dead oxen from their traces, pick up dropped equipment and haul their boots out of sucking ground; they could have advanced faster in their sleep. It was a creeping army, strung out for miles and miles, the noise of whose thousands of clattering pots and pans scattered the game of the veldt on all sides.

The division's crawling march had taken them from Fort Whitehead situated between the Buffalo and Blood rivers deeper into Zululand. Now the division was in the process of building yet another fort, which Lord Chelmsford had named Fort Newdigate, after the major-general who commanded his 2nd Division.

Fort Newdigate lay in a south-easterly direction from Fort Whitehead and was still in a feverish state of construction.

Nominally independent of the 2nd Division was the Flying Column, under the command of Brigadier-General Evelyn Wood. This consisted of cavalry – 17th Lancers and the 1st King's Dragoon Guards – and infantry regiments. However, despite its title it neither flew nor was really a separate column. It dragged itself along not far from the main column, expecting to join it when it became necessary to attack the Zulu army.

Lord Chelmsford had ordered that dogs were not to be taken on the invasion of Zululand, but the operative word was *taken*. Dogs will follow where food goes and, inexplicably, they refused to obey the orders of this general who was not their master. Fleet of foot, they will accompany any army in the belief that war is a game, no doubt started for their benefit. They increased the chaos and noise of the march by racing ahead of the column, then when they realized no one was with them, charging back again. Their yelping and barking added to the cacophony of snorting oxen, clashing metal equipment and bawling NCOs. No wonder the Zulus thought they were being invaded by 'wizards'. Only creatures of dark evil regions needed to herald their invasion with such an unholy racket.

Seb arrived in camp in the very late afternoon, just as the column was stopping for the night. He went first to find a surgeon to re-dress his wound, which seemed to be healing without any serious infection. When he removed his tunic and shirt the surgeon was astonished to find his patient covered in black bruises. Seb's explanation, that he had been playing cricket, was met with a frown of disbelief.

'What were you using for a ball? A rock?'

'Potatoes,' replied Seb, 'though the bowler would have been happier with rocks.'

The doctor raised an eyebrow but probably felt that further questioning would only deepen the mystery. Balm was applied to Seb's bruises as his wound was cleaned and bandaged.

Afterwards, he went looking for Major Stringman, to give his report on the mission.

Stringman was watching a company of the 2nd/21st at target practice. The Martini–Henry was an extremely efficient weapon and could achieve a rapid-fire rate of twenty rounds a minute in expert hands. However, the army discouraged such a high rate of fire, believing it wasted ammunition, even when the order had been given for independent over volley fire. Slow and accurate was considered preferable to fast and wild. Four or five rounds a minute was more the norm for a good rifleman under extreme duress, but often less than that.

'Ready!' came the cry.

The soldiers loaded their weapons.

'Present!'

There were three long moments, then the riflemen opened fire at their targets, some empty bottles two hundred yards to their front. No order to fire had been given. A soldier took that order as given on the command of 'present', and timed his squeezing of the trigger by three slow beats from that point.

White smoke rose from the rifles, drifting upwards in veils to obscure the late-afternoon light, as many of the target bottles were shattered. Seb knew the men enjoyed this kind of practice, rather than shooting at paper. There was something primally satisfying about watching a bottle explode into glittering fragments.

'Sir?' said Seb, grabbing the major's attention by saluting. 'I'm back.'

Stringman, hands clasped behind his back, immaculate in his uniform as usual, stared down at the shorter ensign with a wooden expression.

'You look extremely dishevelled, Ensign Early,' was his first comment. 'An officer in the post of Provost-Marshal should present himself with some smartness – and – and *dignity*.'

'Yes, sir. I was however wounded on the way to the 1st Division, hence the lumpiness of my dress.'

The eyebrows of his commander rose a fraction.

'Wounded?'

'In the shoulder, sir. An assassin.'

Stringman blinked at that last word.

'And,' he said, after a few moments, 'who would want to assassinate *you*? You're hardly the Sultan of Turkey, now are you?'

'I've been considering that carefully, sir, as you can well imagine. I can only come up with one answer which satisfies my reasoning. I believe it to be one of the officers involved in the duel I'm investigating.'

The eyes of the other officer widened.

'Am I hearing right? You're accusing brother officers of an *assassination* attempt? Who do you think they are? Barbary pirates? These are gentlemen of Her Majesty's armed forces. We do not recruit Dyak bandits or Syrian raiders into the army of our empire, Ensign Early, no matter how good they might be at fighting. We recruit *gentlemen*, for the most part landowning, but at a push the lowly sons of schoolteachers . . .' this was a direct jibe at Seb's father's occupation, and he flushed in anger '. . . so I think not. I think not. You will have to look for your assassin elsewhere. If anyone shot at you, it was no doubt a stray Zulu looking for an inattentive target.'

'You cannot know that, sir,' said Seb, bristling, 'and I take exception to the word *inattentive*.'

'Do you? Take it up with the Board of Governors,' replied the major, sarcastically. 'Now, you have your report – in writing?'

'In writing, no. I came to give you my oral report.'

'Ah, now this is the sort of – ' there was a crash of fire, as the next volley destroyed a batch of bottles – 'sloppiness I've come to expect from you, Ensign. It won't do. However, now that you're here,' he looked Seb up and down, 'unkempt and – wounded – you may as well tell me of the success or otherwise of your mission, which I hope at least has closed the pages on Captain Pickering's act.'

'Not exactly closed, sir. There were some anomalies.'

'Anomalies,' repeated the officer, with a long exaggerated sigh.

'Sir, the statement Captain Pickering gave me, as to the last words of the deceased Brandon, did not totally match the reports of others.'

'Did not totally match.'

'No, sir.'

The pair of them stood there, each waiting for the other to speak. It was Stringman who eventually said in an exasperated tone, 'Well, are you going to tell me what were the private's last words?'

'According to the reports they were, *It's not enough*.'

'And according to Captain Pickering?'

'*I've had enough*.'

'And your inference from the difference?'

Seb swallowed. 'I don't know.'

'You don't know.'

'Sir,' said Seb, with a sudden flash of anger, 'I wish you would not keep repeating my words in that weary voice. I think there's enough of a difference between those two versions to cause considerable unease. I intend following up my interviews with the Border Rangers with an interview here, and if you don't like it, take it up with the Board of Governors.'

A look of astonishment came over Major Stringman's face.

'Ensign?' he cried in a shrill voice.

'Merely repeating *your* words, back to *you*,' replied Seb. 'Now, sir, I am exhausted from my ride. I need to wash and – and sort myself out.'

'Sort your . . . 'The major stopped himself in time, and continued with, 'Let me get this straight, you're accusing the cavalry of an attempt on your life, an assassination attempt, and Captain Pickering of the Border Rangers of – of some crime, we're not sure what, but it's quite heinous.'

'I'm not sure I'd put it quite like that, sir, but something of that nature.'

The major breathed heavily down his thin nose.

'Ensign, you are walking a very dangerous line.'

'I am the Provost-Marshal, sir. It's my duty to walk where a criminal case takes me. If I spend my time cowering in a corner, biting my nails and wondering if I have the courage to interview a senior rank, and if I end up suspicious of his version of the truth wondering whether I'll do anything about it, I will not be doing that duty. I must take every small piece of evidence and look at it carefully, turning it over and over, until I'm satisfied where it fits in the jigsaw puzzle.' Seb suddenly decided he liked that analogy. 'Yes, for that's what it is, a jigsaw puzzle, for me to complete.'

The two men parted without another word.

Seb went to find his men.

The engineers and their unwilling helpers were working even

as the gloaming swept across the plains of Africa. Two square redoubts some fifty yards apart had been set up. They consisted of dry-stone walls protected by trenches six foot deep. The wagons were positioned to form an arrowhead between the two redoubts, closed at the rear by more dry-stone walls. In true military style the wagons were all facing the same way and the oxen traces were extended outwards, laid out on the plain, to form net-like obstructions to any attacking force of Zulus, whose ankles would become entangled in them before they reached the wagons. The cattle were allowed to roam and graze beyond these traces, guarded by sentries.

Lord Chelmsford was making sure that there would be no second Isandlwana. No repeat of a battle which saw the massacre of almost two thousand soldiers bearing modern weapons, and from which only seventy-six colonials and British soldiers and a small unknown number of native troops, escaped with their lives. Such a defeat by a force armed mainly with primitive weapons could never, ever be allowed to happen again. The general who permitted such a dreadful failure to repeat itself would be a ruined man fit only for an ignominious old age divorced from society.

However, so far as Fort Newdigate was concerned, not all the troops could be camped within it, but it was a stronghold within whose walls they could muster if an attack took place. A defensive area that could hold out against even a determined impi, similar to the post at Rorke's Drift, where a mere hundred men had defended themselves successfully against several thousand determined Zulus.

Sam and Evans had erected the tent and as usual the efficient Xhosa had supper on the boil. A small unknown mammal, caught by the deft hands of Corporal Evans, was in the pot. It might have been some kind of rat, but by the time it reached Seb's plate it would only be recognizable as cooked meat and would be shovelled down the young man's throat without a second thought.

Under the lamplight, Seb took out his notebook. He turned to the page on which he had been working during the interview with Captain Pickering, but there were no words there. No notes of the interview that had taken place. Instead there was a sketched portrait of Pickering himself. It was a good one, for Seb was an excellent artist, but the ensign wondered if a photograph might be better. He sent Sam out to find where the photographer Jack

Spense was camped. Sam returned and then led Seb to where Jack was working on some plates.

'I could have found this place by the smell of your chemicals,' said Seb to Jack, wrinkling his nose. 'How you can work with that stuff all day and every day beats me.'

'Does make the eyes water a bit,' replied Jack, 'but you get used to it. What can I do for you, young South-East? Dead bodies for me to photograph? Hanged men?'

'No, I want you to study this picture and tell me if you have a photograph of him.'

Seb produced his drawing. Jack shrugged.

'Heck, who can tell? I take pictures of hundreds of men. Some of them in groups. Would you like to look through my folio and see for yourself? You might be lucky. Is it one of the men in the duel you told me about?'

'No, this is another case.'

Sheaves of photographs later, Seb had come up with nothing. He had been poring over group pictures with Jack's magnifying glass, trying to find one of Pickering, without success. His eyes were sore with straining against the lamplight.

'So, as far as you know, Jack, you have no photograph of the Border Rangers?'

'I have plenty of colonial troops, but I don't recall ever taking one of that lot. Look, Seb, that drawing is almost as good as any picture I could take. Can't you work with that?'

'Looks like I'm going to have to. Have you any squareface amongst those chemicals?' he asked, enquiring about the local gin. 'I have a fancy to get a little foxed tonight.'

'Certainly,' replied his friend, 'I wouldn't mind getting somewhat disguised myself.'

The pair sat together until the late hours, discussing among other things the times they had got drunk with their late friend Peter, shot down by accident in a street in Ladysmith. Seb had to wipe away a tear or two, for he tended to get maudlin with a few gins under his belt, but for the most part the two men had a pleasant evening out there in the middle of the Empire of the Zulus, the land of the African King Cetshwayo, a place of wild animals, wild people, wild rivers, and wild, wild dreams.

Fourteen

The following morning Seb woke with a bad head and was snappy with his men. Evans eventually got fed up with it and gave his commanding officer some good advice as to what he could do with his head. In order to save himself from being accused of insolence, the advice was given in Welsh, which of course could have been Chinese as far as Seb was concerned. The ensign knew that Evans was being insubordinate and he told him if he did not use English he would jump on him anyway.

'I thought you was learnin' Welsh, sir?' said the innocent-looking corporal. 'You said you was.'

'I haven't yet got around to obscenities,' snarled Seb, 'but when I do, you'd better watch out, Corporal.'

'Oh, I don't think there's anything like that in Welsh,' replied Evans. 'We're a nice race of people, we are. Not at all like some nationalities.'

Once he had indeed soaked his head in a bucket of water, which was actually what the corporal had been recommending, albeit accompanied by a swear word or two, Seb felt a lot better. He dressed himself in a fresh smart uniform, having three sets in the trunk being carried in one of the wagons, and marched off towards the tents of the 58th.

The wound in his shoulder seemed now to require only change of pad and though still a little stiff-skinned he had healed quite well.

As he strode along he wished he could come across Major Stringman, for he knew that apart from the smudge on his helmet, which had rejected all attempts at removal, he looked the soldier from head to toe. No such encounter occurred, however, and by the time he reached the 58th's lines he had a thin layer of dust over him, having walked past crews of men digging, rock-piling and shaking Africa out of various pieces of canvas.

The whole fort and surrounds were busy. Cattlemen were herding their beasts to water and to food, fussing over the traces, walloping the coverings which protected their loads to get rid of small beasts and dirt. Wheels were being greased on limbers, carts and wagons. Military exercises were being carried out by those not employed in manual labour. Tents were being taken down, tents were being erected, tents were being stowed, tents were being unpacked. Sergeants and corporals were bawling at men, at dogs, at oxen, at really at anything that moved except those magnificent and privileged creatures who wore officers' insignia. Other soldiers were gathering knotted grass for the cooking fires or engaged in one of the other multitude of tasks in an army fort.

The army does not like an idle man, unless he stands rigidly to attention outside a sentry box with a glassy look in his eyes.

Out in the greater world there was also noise and movement. Birds were perched or flew above, some of them with splendid, impressive wingspans, others sporting brilliant colours. Beasts roamed the horizon as silhouettes. The sun blazed down on red-ochre earth, verdant green grasslands and shining silver waters. Africa had on her fancy pants and was strutting the stage for the benefit of all.

The swift were out there: horned, lean and streaky. The strong were amongst them: muscled and spiked, bearing mouthfuls of fangs. The wily, the lumbering, the slithery, the loping, the crawling, the hopping, the darting, the leaping, the flashing, the diving, the lurking, the swinging. They were all out there somewhere, little pieces of a mobile scene on a vaulted, breathtakingly vast, clear landscape. It reached into Seb's soul and gave it a twist, giving him the feeling that the Creator had not only produced a masterpiece here, He had also taken the time to put a young impressionable man in the centre of it, to appreciate its wonders.

On reaching the 58th, Seb went up to a bored-looking lieutenant with prominent teeth.

'Provost-Marshal,' said Seb, flicking his red sash. 'All right if I pin this up somewhere where everyone can see it?' He produced his picture of Captain Pickering.

Underneath the likeness was written:

DO YOU KNOW THIS MAN?

IF YOU DO IT IS YOUR DUTY TO REPORT TO THE PROVOST-MARSHAL.

The lieutenant nodded at the poster.

'You think that'll bring 'em in? "Your duty"? They'll run a mile first.'

'Well, what was I supposed to put?' asked Seb, looking doubt-fully at his own handiwork. 'I mean, I can't offer a reward. That wouldn't be acceptable to my commanding officer.'

'You could imply it,' said the toothy lieutenant, stifling a yawn.

'How?'

'Oh, I don't know, something like AND LEARN SOMETHING TO YOUR ADVANTAGE.'

'You think that might do it?'

'No,' admitted the lieutenant, 'but it stands a better chance than DUTY, which frightens away the best of them.'

Seb was not sure. In the end he changed the poster to read DO YOU KNOW THIS MAN? REPORT TO THE PROVOST-MARSHAL. After all they would not come to see him if they had nothing to say.

'Can I pin it to the flagpole?' he asked.

'Certainly not,' said the lieutenant, spraying spittle everywhere. 'The very idea.'

'Well, where?'

The lieutenant pointed languidly. 'Stick it on that post over there, by the latrines – they all have to shed their loads, you know.'

'Thank you for that thought, Lieutenant,' said Seb, heading towards the pits where the men defecated. It stank of course, to the very heavens, and was infested with swarms of flies. Whether anyone would linger long enough to read a poster was anyone's guess, but Seb saw the logic. At some time during the next twenty-four hours all the men of the 58th would pass the post which now bore the notice. Some of course would run past it, in a great panic, Africa being a place that loosened the bowels with remark-able swiftness and frequency.

Seb then went back to his tent, where breakfast was waiting. Once the meal was over, he began to write a letter home. He knew it could not be sent for some time, and indeed would take a few weeks to reach his father, but the thoughts of a soldier on campaign needed to be put on paper while they were fresh, for remarkable things happened every day and the new ones tended to push out the old before they could be properly recorded. Not only were there astonishing facts about life in a foreign clime, and

feats of an army at war to recount, but also the everyday life of a
soldier on the march. All these would be of interest to his parents
and siblings, not to mention neighbours, those at church on Sunday,
and casual visitors to the house.

He did not mention his wound, so as not to worry his mother,
though he dearly wished he could write about the incident to his
father. Putting them down on paper, in words, somehow made the
events clearer and Seb was still pondering the mystery of the assassination attempt, if that was what it was. He did, however, mention
Mary Donaldson, for he wanted word to get back to Peter's sister,
who had the idea that she was waiting for Seb to propose marriage
to her – so he thought. If he put in a letter that he had met a
very attractive female, who had captured his attention, Peter's sister
might – in a pique – suddenly marry the Reverend Alfred
Fletchingham Wingate, the young curate who had been dangling
after her since Seb had left.

That would be a good thing, the ensign thought.

Once the letter was written, in which he asked to be remembered not only to his own family but to Peter's as well, he took
out his painting materials and went some way off to make a repre-
sentation of Fort Newdigate to include with the letter, so that they
could see back home how comfortable was the hinterland of Zulu
country. The colours flowed from his brush and he was quite
pleased with the result, returning to his tent at noon.

Major Stringman was there, with Evans standing nearby, rolling
his eyes from behind the field officer's back.

'You pinned the portrait of an *officer* to the latrines of common
soldiers?' cried the major, his eyes popping with fury.

'A colonial in an auxiliary regiment,' said Seb. 'Not one of Her
Majesty's commissioned officers.'

'Is he British?'

'By birth, I would say, yes.'

'You amaze me, Ensign.'

'Thank you, sir. I do my best.'

A sharp intake of breath told Seb that his light jesting was
increasing the damage done by his pinning of the notice to the
latrine post.

Stringman said evenly, 'I meant of course that you amaze me
by your stupidity.'

Seb was jolted into anger himself.

'Be careful, sir. I will not tolerate that word, even from a senior officer, especially within hearing of the rank and file, who need to respect their officers if they are to follow them into battle. I am not stupid. I'm trying to do my job, my duty, by the best means available to me. I believe a murder has been committed and it's difficult enough sorting through the evidence, or lack of it, without having to brook insults from my commanding officer. You will retract that word, if you please.'

'Will I?'

'If you do not, I will go to the general, whose patronage I enjoy.'

This outright lie was instantly swallowed by the major, who was always impressed by the great and good of the army. Seb had not said *which* general, but the major assumed it was Lieutenant-General Lord Chelmsford, though even Major-General Newdigate was someone to whom Stringman felt deferential. He managed to produce a wry expression, saying, 'I thought for a moment, Ensign, that you were about to challenge me to a duel.'

'Sir, you know that's against the law, otherwise I would most certainly have sought satisfaction.'

'Ensign Early, you will revisit the line of the 58th and remove that portrait from its current position . . .'

At that very moment a soldier came marching up to the pair, with Evans ogling in the background, and came to attention to salute them.

'Sorry to interrupt the officers, sir – sirs – but I got to be back in ten minutes for parade.' He then turned his full attention to Seb, staring at his red sash. 'Sir, I seen the man on that poster you put up and have come to report, as ordered.'

A great feeling of well-being flowed through Seb's form.

'And you are?'

'Private Wilson, sir, of the 58th.'

'Speak your piece, Private,' said Major Stringman. 'We're all friends here.'

'Well, I just wanted you to know I recognized the picture.'

'Captain Pickering,' said Stringman, and Seb wanted to strangle the major.

'Please, sir,' he said, turning to his commanding officer, 'if you don't mind, I will conduct the interview. These – these things,' he was aware of the soldier standing there, 'need a certain delicacy of handling in order to extract the most enlightening information.'

'What?' snapped the major.

'In short, sir, you are blundering forth, revealing things I would rather have kept from the – the, er, interviewee.'

Before the major could interrupt again, Seb returned to Private Wilson.

'Did you recognize that man as Pickering?'

'No, sir, I din't. I know him as Corporal Swale, from when I was in India. Him and Private Thackery deserted, runnin' off into the Afghan mountains.' The private then revealed his reasons for turning informant. 'Lost me me stripes they did. I was the Colour on duty that night, see. I took the blame for them bast— for them running off.'

Seb stared at the soldier with an intensity that clearly began to disturb both the private and the major. It appeared to them that the ensign might be about to have a fit. The soldier had obviously seen the same light in the eyes of Indian sepoys, just before they ran amuck with a knife or hatchet. He took a step back and glanced at the senior officer, as if to say, 'Do I have to do something about this?'

The cause was partly to do with Seb's family history. Just before he left the household to join the army, his father took him into the parlour and gave him a lecture. The culmination of that lecture formed the essence of the advice the older man had to offer his son. 'Sebastian,' he had said, 'you will find as you go through life that you will have what I call the *incandescent moment*, when God or Nature will reveal to you some wonder, some hidden secret of which you were not previously aware. Indeed I have been fortunate to have several of these intense and profound moments during my own lifetime. Do not ask me where they come from or when they will come, you will know when you experience one.'

Now Seb's father's incandescent moments, as he had gone on to try to explain, came about when some natural phenomenon occurred, and it usually involved light. Once it was a sunrise over the standing stones at Avebury, a blinding scarlet dawn that struck like a dagger. Another time it was an altar window in a church, when the evening light caught the bright-yellow gold of St George's sword. During these experiences, which lasted but a fleeting second each time, his father's jaw dropped open and he felt the wind of heaven rush through him, stirring his blood and bones.

Seb, too, found he had such moments, incandescent in their revelations. But his were to do with his work, when suddenly the case he was working on opened like a crack in creation, and gave him the answer he was looking for.

Major Stringman brought his attention back to the real world.

'Ensign, are you feeling well?'

Seb snapped to.

'Yes, sir. Perfectly.'

'Then why are you looking at the private as if he was the Messiah returned?'

'Sorry, sir, I just realized why Captain Pickering – or Swale – killed Private Brandon.'

'All right, Private, you can go,' said Stringman to the soldier. 'Let me just say that maligning the reputation of an officer is a serious offence, the punishment for which is extremely severe. Go away and think on this before the Provost-Marshal calls on you again . . .'

'Sir,' snapped Seb, 'I wish you would not interfere with my work. Wilson, thank you for coming to see me . . .'

Private Wilson was, however, already on his way back to his roll-call parade. Seb wondered how much harm the senior officer had done. He would need Wilson later, to give evidence at the court martial of this deserter – and murderer.

'Well,' said the major, 'am I to be privy to this astounding realization?'

'Sir,' replied Seb, 'it doesn't take a great deal of reasoning to see what has happened here. I believe the captain was being black-mailed. Private Brandon was probably the other deserter, Thackery. Swale and Thackery ran off into the Afghan hills. They become adventurers for a time and were fortunate enough to survive their life on the run. Somehow they made their way to South Africa, probably working their passage on a cargo ship. Here they looked for work, but actually there's only one kind of work they're suited, for – the army. Thus they re-enlisted, this time in a colonial regi-ment. One of them was more favoured than the other and rose through the ranks to become a captain. Once that status was been reached, he had a great deal to lose. The other, jealous of his comrade's good fortune and having a lot less to lose, decided to blackmail the new captain, threatening to reveal the truth unless he was paid to keep his mouth shut.

'*It's not enough.* Those were the words that Brandon – or Thackery – used. He believed he was not getting enough money from his former friend. So Pickering – or Swale – shot him, and made it look as if it was expedient, punitive justice handed out to a coward on the battlefield.'

Seb was breathless after he finished. Major Stringman's lips were pursed. The ensign expected no less, for he believed the major was very hard, if not impossible, to convince when it came to circumstantial evidence. What the major probably required was a finger pointing down from the clouds and the Almighty's words, 'He did it!'

'Of course,' Seb said, as more sober thoughts followed his incandescent moment, 'it will be extremely difficult to prove.'

'Impossible, I would say,' replied the major, 'but if this Wilson is correct, we shall get the fellow for desertion and put him away for a long time, if not hang him.'

Seb felt that his enthusiasm had at last rubbed off on the other man.

'Indeed. I have found that compromise is often the best the path to follow.'

'The end result,' said the field officer, 'is much the same.'

'Yes, sir.'

'Well done, Ensign. Carry on.'

With that Major Stringman marched away, towards the tent where the staff officers gathered in hugger-mugger, their secrets coughed into their collars so that no ordinary mortal might know what his fate might be in this ill-judged war. This tent was where the grey warlords debated, gave their general advice, took their orders and handed them down to those who had to carry them out. This was the tent where men's souls were of no account and the only concern was a thing called *victory*.

Fifteen

The next morning, out of the tall windswept golden grass which spread over the wide plain and covered it in waves like the sea, came a contingent of Zulus. They approached the fort under a flag of truce. They had brought the Prince Imperial's sword from King Cetshwayo, who said in his message that he highly regretted the death of the noble Frenchman and that it was a mistake. Cetshwayo also asked for peace and sent a number of other items – Martini-Henry rifles captured at Isandlwana – and gifts – ivory and cattle. Major Jack Crossman, the intelligence officer nominally a member of the 88th Connaught Rangers, was with Lord Chelmsford when the Zulus were giving their talk to the general. Uncle Jack later spoke to Seb about what had happened.

'The general has rejected any idea of a peaceful end to this war,' said Jack, the weariness showing on his scarred features. 'Isandlwana needs to be thoroughly avenged.'

'Is that what wars are about?' said Seb. 'Revenge?'

Jack sucked on his long-stemmed chibouque pipe, filling the air around his head with smoke.

'Some are,' he said. 'Also, Chelmsford has heard that General Wolseley is on his way to take over from him.'

'Wolseley? *Our Only General.*' Seb was quoting the press. Sir Garnet Wolseley was the darling of the British press and many regarded him as the best general in the British army. No doubt after the tragedy at Isandlwana the government had to be seen to be doing something and sending Wolseley was obviously the answer. He had led several successful campaigns, including the Red River Expedition in Canada. His march there was considered by many to have been among the most arduous in history. Over a thousand men had to transport all their ordnance and stores over hundreds of miles of wilderness in appalling conditions, including high summer temperatures, while beleaguered by mosquitoes and flies.

Wolseley had also fought in the Crimean War, then in Burma,

but most importantly he had been in Africa, up on the Gold Coast just five years earlier, leading British troops against the powerful Ashanti kingdom, whose main economy had been the slave trade and the subjugation of neighbouring tribes.

'That's the man,' said Jack. 'So, as you can imagine Lord Chelmsford is not going to sit on his backside and wait for Wolseley to come and snatch away any glory that's to be had from this war. We'll be on the march very soon.'

Seb might have reminded his uncle that there had already been a good deal of glory, in that eleven Victoria Crosses had been awarded for the action at Rorke's Drift, and there had been other individual VCs handed out for several other battles during the war, plus talk that a number of Distinguished Conduct Medals were being considered.

There was glory around, if one could gather it in. Unfortunately for Seb, though he was at Rorke's Drift, he had to leave immediately afterwards and was not listed as taking part in the action. The doctor, Reynolds, had mentioned to others that he thought that he had spoken with an ensign at the Drift, but this was dismissed as a 'heat of the battle' momentary fantastical glitch of the brain.

'So, we will march on to Ulundi, no matter what Cetshwayo does?'

'I'm certain of it. Lord Chelmsford plans to link up with the Flying Column tomorrow, then we'll move up for the attack, before the Ashanti Ring gets wind of what's happening.'

Seb was momentarily puzzled. 'Ashanti Ring?'

'Wolseley's secret society, formed during the Ashanti wars. We have two of his coven here at least. Brigadier-General Wood and Major Buller. Maybe others. Glyn was here too, wasn't he? There's ten or more officers who served with Wolseley up on the Gold Coast and it's rumoured they took an oath of allegiance to him. You know, Seb, that the loyalty of the British soldier is supposedly firstly to the monarch, but in fact as everyone knows, a soldier's prime loyalty is to his regiment. I'm sure the Queen sees that as a good thing, since the regiment as a whole serves her body, mind and spirit, and she loses nothing by the quibble. For us soldiers, though, we look upon the regiment as our family and we know that if we do our duty by it, the regiment will see us through adversity. We are a band of brothers and brothers look after one another.

Brothers come first and others come after. We each look to our regimental colour, that piece of cloth bearing our victories and battle honours, which gives us an intense pride in ourselves and our regiment. We swear by our regiment while fighting for the Queen.

'Wolseley, however, had men from several different regiments looking to him as if he was a reincarnation of Alexander the Great or Julius Caesar. They formed this ring, which swore an oath of loyalty not to the Queen, not to the regiment, but to General Wolseley himself. A network of what he considered were able officers drew in a tight circle around him. He tries to take all of them with him on his campaigns and they consider themselves special because of it. I suspect promotions come their way through him, or the thing wouldn't work. Officers of calibre need rewards. One or two of the ring I do not rate very highly. Buller, for instance, is a fine-looking man, brave as any lion, and the troops admire him, but he drinks far too much and lacks the necessary intellect for great leadership. He's a rhino, rather than a big cat, and charges in without any real idea of the end game.'

Seb was astonished by these revelations. 'It all sounds a bit dark and sinister to me – oaths and blood-brothers, that sort of thing.'

'Well, there you have it, this is the man who Lord Chelmsford is trying to avoid. The general believes Wolseley will steal his glory and my thinking is, he *will*, if he catches up with us and takes over. Chelmsford will have nothing but Isandlwana to look back on in this campaign if he does not get his victory at Ulundi. Not much to go home with, is it, a major catastrophe, the worst defeat of a modern army by a foe bearing primitive weapons? Chelmsford needs this battle to save his reputation and his life in the army. He has to outrun Wolseley.'

'And we're lucky if we make five miles a day.'

'Precisely. Oh, by the way, Seb, your friend Major Stringman did well, didn't he?'

Seb straightened his back, surprised. 'He did? That is, he's not my friend, exactly – he's my commanding officer.'

'I heard him telling everyone how he solved the murder of a soldier in the Border Rangers. A patrol has been sent down to arrest a Captain Pickering with the 1st Division.'

Seb almost exploded with indignation and wrath.

'*He* solved . . . ? That bastard . . .'

Jack frowned. 'Now, Seb – your commanding officer!'

'Major Stringman,' spluttered Seb, 'did everything to *prevent* the solving of that crime. Major Stringman is a liar and a blackguard, and I will . . . I will . . .'

'You'll what, young Sebastian? Now don't go doing anything foolish, simply because you're in a froth. Cool down, think rationally. The man is a major and you're an ensign. Stolen your glory, has he?'

'Rebuked me for what I did, now claims *he* did it!'

'Well, don't do anything rash. He sounds the sort of officer who'll turn any accusation you make against you. Remember, revenge is a dish best served cold. Think it through, deliver it after planning.'

'Just so long as I get to serve it,' muttered Seb, narrowing his eyes and clenching his fist. 'He can't get away with this.'

Jack left him fuming. Later Seb dropped in on another Jack, namely his photographer friend. Jack Spense was knowledgeable about all sorts of things that left an ordinary soldier uninterested. He wrote out a list of names on a piece of paper and handed it to Seb. It read:

<u>Ashanti Ring</u>
Garnet Wolseley
John Carstairs McNeill
Hugh McCalmont
Redvers Henry Buller
Henry Brackenbury
William Francis Butler
John Plumptre Carr Glyn
Baker Creed Russell
Henry Evelyn Wood
John Frederick Maurice
George Pomeroy Colley

'They range from generals down to captains. I trust you'll keep that to yourself, Seb,' said Jack. 'I can't afford to upset any generals, if I want to be allowed to follow the army into desperate places.'

'Just interested, Jack,' came the reply. 'Purely academic.'

★   ★   ★

Donger Scribbs licked his fingers and threw away the leg of some unidentifiable bird of Zululand. He then took a long draught of water from a kettle. Finally he broke a twig from a bush and used it to pry out any meat stuck between his teeth. All this had been carried out under the close scrutiny of Corporal Evans, who was waiting for Donger to complete the sentence he had begun before picking up the roasted drumstick. Donger turned his face to his friend, so that the Welshman could read his lips.

'. . . so what I mean is, whatever I eat or drink, wherever I goes after this bloody farce of a campaign, I ain't never goin' to get the taste of African dust out of me mouth. Y'know?' He licked his lips and spat. 'It's got a rare taste, this dust. And it's got a perfick way of introducin' itself to every crease of a man's anatomy. It gets under yer 'elmet, up yer nose, in the crease of yer backside, 'tween yer toes, everybloodywhere. Turns yer hair to tangled straw. Once it's in the 'ollows of yer body the sweat turns it to paste, then it bakes hard and makes plugs, so you can't breathe, piss, hear no command, open yer eyes wider than a slit, or diddle with yer toes. This is what war's about, ain't it? War in foreign climes.'

Evans nodded solemnly. 'The heat. It never lets up, does it?'

'The dust, the heat. Then there's the bloody smell. A sort of musty, musky stink like no other I've ever sniffed. If you was to bake a dead dog in an oven, along with a pair of shoes throwed away by some tramp what's worn 'em for a dozen years wivout takin' 'em off, add a handful of burned gunpowder, you'd only come close to it.'

'Yes, the dust, the heat, the smell.'

Donger waved his hand in front of his face.

'And don't forget the flies, an' all his uncles and cousins, never lettin' up, no matter what time of day.'

Evans said, 'Who could forget the flies?'

Donger looked out over the flowing grasslands.

'We're just lucky there ain't many big savage beasts out there. Lucky if we sees an antelope, eh? In India we was took by tigers and stamped on by elephants. They've got 'em here o' course, the big ones, but we don't see 'em much, do we. What we see is the little beasties. Them that bite and sting. Jiggers, scorpions, mosquitoes. Eh?'

Evans felt he ought to contribute to this list of problems which plagued the white man in Africa.

'And the disease. There's plenty of that, eh?'

'Oh yes, plenty of that 'ere, Taffy – but you got that every-where, ain't you? In London they was goin' down like skittles wiv the typhus. Came up out of the drains smellin' like death, it did, and death it left behind it, sure enough. No, Africa ain't the only place where you gets sick. You can do that in Southend-on-Sea, mate.'

A loud series of explosions made Donger jump, while Evans still sat placidly drinking his tea.

'What's up, Donger?' asked the Welshman.

'Gunnery practice. You can't 'ear it, can you?'

'I felt the vibrations, like.'

'Well, it's got me heart doin' a tattoo. Why don't they warn you? Wouldn't take much, would it? A bugle call? No sense of decorum, the army. Where's that black o' yourn? Ain't seen 'im since he gave us that bird a 'alf-hour ago. You trust 'im, do yer?'

'Didn't at first, see. Him being a Kaffir. But Sam, he's like one of the family now. They're the same as us, really, when you get to know them.'

'Well, I wun't trust a single one of 'em.'

'Donger, you wouldn't trust your own brother.'

Donger Scribbs smiled at this. 'Too true. That's the way I was brung up. Watch your back or you'll lose the collar off yer own shirt. You mean to say he's not stole off you?'

'Not a farthing.'

'Hard to believe. They don't 'ave the same conscience as us. It's in their nature to take things what don't belong to 'em. In their eyes everythink is common property. I'm not sayin' they can help it. They can't. It's just in their nature.'

'Sam's a Christian. He knows the Ten Commandments.'

Donger nodded, gravely. 'A Christian thief – they're the worst kind. Steal yer soul, they will, and give it to the Devil.'

'PRIVATE SCRIBBS!'

Donger jumped for the second time in only a few minutes. He leapt to his feet at the yell, which was very close to his ear. A sergeant had crept up on him and had taken great delight in fright-ening the life out of him.

'On parade, Scribbs,' growled the sergeant. 'Sorry to break up the tea party.'

'Yeah, I'm sure you are,' muttered Donger. He picked up his Martini-Henry, put on his helmet, and nodded to Evans. 'See you later, Taffy. Save me one o' them biscuits that there Sam bakes.'

'Will do, Donger.'

With that the Londoner strolled after the sergeant to where his company was forming up for drill.

Sixteen

Seb woke with the smell of wood smoke curling around his brain. Sam was cooking breakfast and singing softly: an amaXhosa song with a lot of clicks in the words. It sounded a sad melody and this suited the mood Seb had woken with. Jack Spense had shown the young Provost-Marshal photographs of the battlefield at Isandlwana. Rotting bodies were everywhere. Rags hung from corpses and looked to be fluttering in the wind. Equipment lay scattered over the landscape forming a wide area of debris. It was an awful scene for a young officer of Her Majesty's army to behold. Still, even now, Seb could not believe that his regiment had been slaughtered by primitive warriors.

He thought back to that day when he was riding towards Rorke's Drift and looked over his shoulder and found himself witnessing an incredible scene. A black swarm was engulfing the camp where he had left his friends and comrades. Soldiers were being put to the spear, disembowelled, beaten to death with clubs. A small boy was running towards him, tears streaking his terrified face, his arms and legs windmilling in survival mode. Two thousand highly trained soldiers were being overrun by twenty-five thousand highly trained warriors. Soldiers who were doomed to bloody and savage deaths. All this happened only a few months previously, in January. It was now only June and the emotional wounds were still raw.

He lay there for a long while, his thoughts becoming ever more depressing, then suddenly the mood changed to anger. Who did these people think they were? This was the British army they were dealing with, not some poor backward nation. They needed to be taught a sharp lesson and Seb felt an urgent need to administer it. He knew that Major Buller – he of the Ashanti Ring – was riding out today with the Frontier Light Horse. He rose with a determined feeling in his breast, dressed himself quickly in his uniform, bellowed an order at Corporal Evans concerning his horse, ate a very swift breakfast – much to the indignation of his black servant, who had spent a great deal of love and affection on the cooking of it – and rode out to the Flying Column to seek permission to join Buller's troop. The major shrugged his shoulders and said he could not care less if the infantry ensign came with them, so long as he did not get in the way and was not a drag on his cavalry. Seb slightly resented that remark, since he knew Buller's regiment was the 60th Rifles and the major was therefore a foot soldier himself.

The Frontier Light horse had, after all, been originally raised by a Lt Carrington of Seb's own regiment, the 1/24th, though now under new command. They were, according to a newspaper correspondent, a rough lot of men, having been recruited from 'discharged common soldiers' and 'varsity men, unfrocked clergymen and sailers, cockneys, yokels and cashiered officers'. Unusually, they grouped their troops by the colour of their horses. A troop rode bays, B troop chestnuts, C troop greys. They had fought at Hlobane and Khambula and so far the men with the red bands around their wide-brimmed hats had acquitted themselves creditably.

Action!

It would fire the blood of any young officer. He was riding with the Frontier Light Horse. It was a heady business. They cantered several miles before coming across some Zulu kraals. Buller ordered his men to set fire to them. Then they took their horses down a slope to a valley with a river running through it. It was a bright morning, with the sun lancing off the water, and the troopers naturally felt light-hearted. The scene even lifted Seb's spirits. There were yellow-flowering shrubs on the slopes and a light-green covering to the valley below. The river itself was not deep and the men could see fish amongst the bottom stones, flashing silver as they darted back and forth. Once the force had dismounted on the other side of the water, one of the men attempted to catch a fish with his bare hands, as one would tickle a trout, but to the amusement of his friends he was unsuccessful.

'I could do this, once upon a time,' he argued. 'Today is too much of a hurry-up for hand-fishing.'

A frowning Major Redvers Henry Buller, hero of Hlobane and other wars and recent engagements, drew the attention of his men to a large force of Zulus not far away.

'Keep your mind on your job,' he warned, the dust in his throat giving him a hoarse tone. 'I want no stupid errors here today.

Sergeant, get the horse-holders to lead the mounts to a safer area. The rest of you, find cover and fire on the enemy, if it please you.'

His politeness was of the sarcastic variety.

Within minutes the troopers were raining fire on the Zulus, who immediately scattered and hid in the brush. Soon the enemy were sending as much as they were receiving and Seb had to leave his first position and find a rock which was better at stopping bullets than tall grass. Zulus were much better at blending in with the landscape than the soldiers in their red or blue coats and the enemy made difficult targets. Their darker skins were a natural camouflage in the shadows of shrubs and the drifting smoke of working rifles. They squirmed their way around to the flank of the troopers and suddenly opened up with devastating firepower, probably with Martini-Henrys from Isandlwana.

'Fall back!' cried Buller. 'You, Ensign, get out of there. Do you want to get left behind?'

Seb followed the men as they backed away. Volunteer cavalrymen are not great fighters on foot and Seb could sense a feeling of unsteadiness amongst the local troopers, who looked around for the mounts. They were insecure without horse flesh between their thighs, being far happier on four legs than on two. However, another force had arrived: the 17th Lancers and the 1st King's Dragoon Guards, led by no less than a general. Seb did not know who he was, but he guessed it was probably Major-General Marshal. A display of charges followed, as the dragoons rode along the banks of the river and the lancers went hurtling through the grasses with their lances before them, trying to flush out any quarry which might be hidden there.

This rather gallant but relatively useless exercise drew the attention of the Zulu marksmen, who began to take dragoons out of their saddles with well-aimed shots. One senior officer, a colonel, dismounted his troop to return fire only to have one of his lieutenants shot dead before his eyes. Seb was now aware that, as is ever usual, the situation was not under the control of the British. The enemy had a distinct advantage in their own territory and they were making the most of it. Men were going down under the withering fire from the rocky crevices and boulder-strewn slopes above. They had allowed the Zulus to gain the high ground, a fundamental error which even the most inexperienced general knew to be idiotic, and the dark shapes of the enemy darted from rock to rock along the ridges, following the cavalrymen below and picking them off with ease.

Seb was almost hit several times and he began to curse his morning fervour for battle experience. He had forgotten how difficult it was for cavalry, this fighting on a harsh, jagged African landscape. The ground was rough and seamed, deadly for a fast-moving horse, covered with stones and pits, cracks and antheaps, and not the sort of level pastureland that a quadruped enjoys. Galloping was out of the question. Even a fast trot was dangerous. The column wound its way along the valley at first, then in more open country, but nowhere was without its ridges and outcrops so successfully employed by the Zulus who raced easily on two legs between cover. Once more the British army had been humiliated by delighted tribesmen, whose nimble feet, dark forms and swift actions made them superior fighters in their own country.

Seb and his cavalry friends limped into Fort Newdigate, now built and containing big brass as well as junior officers, and began counting the dead and wounded. Seb was only halfway through his account of the day, speaking with Jack Spense, when the alarm was raised and the camp was in a quiet panic yet again. It was not quiet for long, as the uneasiness spread and men began to shoot at shadows, even opening up with artillery fire at one point. It took at least an hour for the camp to settle down again afterwards, as skirmishers were sent out in the moonlight looking for Zulus that were not there.

Shaken, and in a bad mood, Seb went to look for Major Stringman. He found him flitting around the staff tent, looking a very busy bee.

'Might I have a word with you, sir?' said Seb. 'In private.'

Stringman eyed his subordinate with obvious distaste.

'Now? Is it important?'

'Yes it is. I wouldn't bother you otherwise.'

Stringman looked about him as if exasperated by this irritating ensign who required his immediate attention, but then said, 'Oh very well.' Then to another field officer, he called, 'James, tell the general I'll be a moment, will you? Apparently this officer can't function without my supervision.'

The pair then stepped away from the tents.

Seb was seething, but managed to keep his anger contained.

'I understand that a patrol has been sent to arrest Captain Pickering.'

'Correct. Under my orders. Now is that all?'

'I also understand you are claiming the credit for solving the murder?'

Major Stringman looked uncomfortable and went red in the face, but said nothing in reply.

Seb said, 'Let me apprise you of what occurred here, sir. I told you I had solved the case and you poo-pooed my findings. In fact you attempted to interfere with my investigation by ordering me to remove the picture of Captain Pickering . . .'

'That was not the way to go about things, Ensign,' shouted Stringman, now very agitated. 'You cannot display portraits of serving officers, simply because you have an idea they might be involved in wrongdoing.'

'Sir, that method brought the results which you are claiming are your own work. You, sir, are a blackguard and a disgrace to your uniform. I would like you to remove that uniform tonight and meet me somewhere, a place of your choice, so that I can have satisfaction. There will be no weapons involved. I'm not going to break the law for the likes of you – but I think I'm entitled to a little Queensbury justice.'

'How dare you!' shrieked the major. 'Threatening me with violence. Insulting me to my face. I am your senior officer . . .'

'Sir, you do not act like an officer, let alone a senior one. My challenge is there. Are you a gentleman, sir, or not?'

A shudder went through the incensed major. He stared in fury at the ensign before him for a good minute, before replying.

'You, boy, are a worm. I shall tread on you before too long.'

With that, he whirled and would have marched back to the staff tent, if his way had not been blocked by someone who had come out of the darkness to stand behind him. That someone was a lieutenant wearing a top hat and smoking a chibouque. The lieutenant's uniform was embellished by a blue silk scarf which was tied around his waist and which hung to his right side with flair. On facing each other the lieutenant lifted his top hat as if saluting a woman.

'Worm?' said Mad Henry, after removing the pipe from between his lips. 'I should say, sir, that *you* are the worm. Refusing to accept a bout of fisticuffs? My word, do you mind if I go in your stead? I think I could take young South-East here,' said Henry, using Seb's nickname. 'I really do. He's solid looking, good pair of shoulders and a deep chest, but I think I'm quicker.' Henry did a shuffle in the dust. 'Yes, definitely quicker. I strike like a snake. You could come and watch if you like, sir, and decide for yourself who is the better.'

'Get out of my way,' growled the major, clearly upset that this lieutenant might have heard the whole of the conversation which had just passed.

'Please?' added Henry.

'Bah!' shouted Stringman, and passed around the flamboyant lieutenant to stride away towards the staff tent.

Once he had gone, Henry said, 'I don't like that man very much – he has no sense of humour.'

'Yes,' replied Seb, 'you're quite right about that. How are you, Henry? Haven't seen you in an age.'

'Oh, fair to middling, fair to middling.' Mad Henry sighed. 'You know I miss my railway station.'

It was well known that the baron, when at home in his country seat, would don the uniform of a railway guard, march down to the station, and spend the day happily whistling and flag-waving the trains in and out. The regular staff had given up trying to get rid of him and just let him get on with it, hoping that the next day their local nobleman would decide to go hunting or fishing instead. However, since Henry was destitute and owed many creditors a great deal of money he did not have, his country seat would not see him for many a year. There was a horde of tipstaffs waiting for Baron Henry Wycliffe to set foot on English soil again, so that they could pounce on him.

'I'm sure you do,' said Seb. 'An admirable hobby.'

'Indeed it is – but to get back to that fellow we've just seen humphing off in high dudgeon. Not a nice chap, you know. Too full of himself. And I heard what passed between you. Claimed credit for your work, did he? Typical senior officer, eh? We fight the battles, they get praise and the rewards. Hey!' He whipped the pipe out of his mouth again. 'What about we go and give old Chelmsford an apple-pie bed? Maybe stick a snake in there, for good measure?'

Seb laughed. 'Not a good idea, Henry. They'd court-martial you for that.'

'Hmm. Oh well, we'll keep that one in abeyance. But that fellow Stringman? We'll think of something special for *him*. You wait. It'll come to me in the middle of the night. In the meantime, look after yourself, South-East. The army won't.'

With that, Henry faded away into the darkness.

Seb watched his friend walk away. What a strange man Henry was, and came from a strange family. His sister, according to Henry himself, collected picture frames. She hung them on the walls of the family mansion. Only the wallpaper was visible as the scene in the frame: no actual pictures or paintings. Henry's sister was not interested in watercolours, oils, or anything of that sort. She liked frames. Carved frames, plain wooden frames, elaborate gold frames, silver frames, even frames sculpted from stone, but the pictures, if there were any when the item was purchased, were always removed. Some said she had thrown away a fortune in valuable paintings that were of no consequence to her. A strange woman with a strange brother.

Seb went back to his own tent, where he found Sam and Corporal Evans sitting by a small campfire.

'Men,' he said.

'Sir,' they replied in unison.

Seb sat down, wearily. He had seen soldiers die today, taken out of their saddles. He had almost been killed himself, though that was the lot of a soldier. 'Almost' was not dead. Men almost died crossing the street in London after a good breakfast. Still, a close encounter, with all the chaos that went with such encounters on the battlefield, was enough to make a man revise his philosophy on life. Lying under his blanket that night would bring reflective thoughts on the subject of what was important and what was not. There was a good officer lying in state tonight, who had eaten a breakfast that morning. Seb hoped it had been a good one.

'I would like eggs and pork bacon for breakfast tomorrow, Sam, if you have them?'

Sam's black face, shining in the firelight, creased in a smile.

'Oh, yes, boss. I've got 'em.'

'Good, thank you. Evans, anything to report?'

'What?' yelled Evans.

Seb winced and signed, *I said, anything to report?*

Oh yes, signed Evans, *I've got a good thing going.*

And this good thing going, is what?

5th Dragoons.

Apart from the 17th Lancers and the 1st King's Dragoon Guards, and of course the volunteer cavalry regiments, there was a squadron of the 5th Dragoons attached to the column.

What about them? signed Seb.

Evans signed a name, which Seb could not interpret.

Spell it.

Evans signed *Private* then spelled *Gupta.*

An Indian name?

Yes, sir. Bengal. Joined our real army a year ago, after doing something in the way of a hero in India.

They took him in the Queen's army?

Yes.

And what is his significance?

'He tried to kill you,' shouted Evans.

Seventeen

Lieutenant Frederick John Cokayne Frith, the one officer killed in the fight that day, was buried that night on the banks of a Zululand river. Choirs of frogs and crickets sang him to his final resting place. The wind rustling in the reeds, the wings of angels unfolding, were his orisons. Seb, though exhausted, went to the funeral. Under the starlight the chaplain read a suitable passage from the Bible and one of the lieutenant's friends delivered an impromptu eulogy, which was quite moving and emotional. No one mentioned that it was probably an error of judgement that had hastened his death – not his mistake, but that of others – but errors of this kind are inevitable in war. Snap decisions have to be made and even when hours or days of planning have gone into an operation, things always go wrong.

After the funeral everyone drifted off, either to their duties, or to bed. Thousands of snuffling, grunting oxen; thousands of snoring humans; unnumbered lowing cattle and horses; these sound effects did not make for a peaceful night at Fort Newdigate in the heart of Zululand, but certainly the departed Lieutenant Frith would sleep soundly.

Seb did sleep a little, and woke with the memory of Evans' information at the front of his brain.

He tried to kill you.

Seb was going to have to interview this soldier before possibly having him court-martialled for attempting to murder an officer.

Sam delivered the egg and bacon breakfast, along with some delicious redbush tea and unleavened bread. Afterwards, refreshed and ready to take on the world, Seb spoke with his corporal. He faced him square on, so that Evans could read his lips.

'So, Private Gupta tried to kill me?'

'That's what he told me, sir.'

'Why?'

'I think you should ask 'im yourself. You can speak nice an' quiet with him, like, whereas you've got to shout at me, eh?'

'All right. But I hope he realizes he's going to hang for his admission?'

'No,' replied Evans, emphatically.

Seb jerked upright. 'What do you mean, *no*?'

'I mean, sir, I promised him nothin' would happen to him if he confessed up to you. He came to me in good faith and I told him anything he said would be confidential, like.'

'What are you, Evans, a Catholic priest?'

Evans grinned. 'I wouldn't be in this bloody man's army if I was, now would I, sir? I'd be sittin' on a silk cushion and eating bloody grapes.'

'You'd also be trying to explain to your mother why you left the chapel for Rome. Now, seriously, Evans, you promised this Indian that he would not be prosecuted for his crime. You know you can't do that?'

Evans took on his ex-shepherd look, which was to say a superior expression. 'Sir, what's our job, may I ask?'

'Solving serious crimes for General Chelmsford.'

'Right. An' what tools do we have for that work?'

Seb frowned. He could of course have shouted at Evans and told him to shut up, but the pair had long since gone past the ordinary association between officer and ranker. Theirs was the forbidden relationship of a commissioned officer on familiar terms with his rank-and-file subordinate. They were not friends, though even that level of contact was not *far* away, but they were confidants and held close acquaintance with one another. So the conversation they were having, which would have been frowned upon by Seb's astonished colleagues, was not terminated by a haughty order for Evans to 'remember his place'.

'We have the might and right of the army behind us.'

'Yes, sir, and guile?'

'Guile?' Seb frowned, but replied, 'If necessary.'

'You'll admit, then, that we have to use all the means at our disposal to solve these here crimes, eh?'

'In certain circumstances, I suppose.'

'Well then, in order to get information I had to give a promise, which I know you won't break, of immunity from justice. Otherwise, I wouldn't have got it. The information. Sorry, sir, but you've got to let 'im go, this Gupta, so's we can solve this crime. How's the shoulder, by the way?'

Seb rubbed the place where he had been wounded.

'Not so . . . but look, Evans. Are you saying it was this Private Gupta who shot me?'

'I'm not sayin' nothing, sir, till you promise no punishment for the man. I need your assurance on that. I give my word to him. I'm a man of honour, for all that. *Anrhydedd ymhlith bugeiliaid*, as my old dad would say, bless him.'

'And that means?'

'Oh, I thought you was learnin' Welsh, sir?' said Evans, innocently. 'Bit advanced for you, that one, eh? It means "honour among shepherds".'

Through his uncle Seb learned that the rumour was definitely no longer just gossip, but true. General Chelmsford had been superseded: General Wolseley had taken over command of the army. However, General Wolseley was not at Fort Newdigate, just a hop, skip and jump away from the Royal Kraal at Ulundi. Apparently Lord Chelmsford had not been told officially that he been replaced, but had learned it in a message from his brother. There were just forty miles to what everyone knew to be the final battleground of this unfortunate war. Lord Chelmsford was not going to roll over and submit to someone taking over a campaign he had planned and put into execution after surmounting enormous difficulties. This was Chelmsford's war and he was going to finish it.

In the south, the 1st Division under Major-General Crealock had not made the progress everyone had hoped for. Officers were now beginning to make fun of the men of the division, calling them 'Crealock's Crawlers'. Army officers are not far away from schoolboys when it comes to putting down their rivals. In truth everyone knew that General Crealock had a much more difficult job when it came to transportation, since General Chelmsford had commandeered all the best beasts and wagons, leaving the shabby ones for Crealock.

Once Chelmsford knew Wolseley was on his tail, he gave orders to move forward with all speed to Ulundi. It was like telling the

tortoise to dash ahead of the hare. There was no perceptible difference in pace, but there was a feeling of urgency in every breast,
and on the face of each soldier was a determined expression. There
was the idea of speed in every mind, but in fact the army plodded
along as usual.

During one of the breaks in the march, Seb sent Evans for
Private Gupta, who came looking furtively over his shoulder.

Evans said as quietly as was possible for a man of his deafness,
'Tell the officer what you know, Guppy.'

Seb took the man well away from any ears and began his
interview.

'Private Gupta, you are in the 5th Dragoons?'

'Yes, sir. I was happy to be in the 2nd Bengal Light Cavalry in
my own homeland, but am now proud to be in Her Majesty's
army.'

'I am told by my corporal that you tried to kill me. Was it you
who followed me south and shot me in the shoulder?'

Private Gupta's face fell and he looked down at the ground. He
mumbled, 'Yes, sir, it was I.'

'You know I could hang you for this crime?'

The head came up. 'Of course, sir. Gupta deserves his punishment. Will you hang me here, sir? Or shall Gupta fight his last
battle? Perhaps he will die in the big fight and there would be no
need to bother the Provost-Marshal to hang him.'

This acceptance of the inevitable which men from the East had
running through their veins had always fascinated Seb. They seemed
to go to their fate without a murmur of dissent. It was what made
them such wonderful material for soldiers. If your number was up,
you were going to die, and there was nothing you could do to
avert it. So why not march to that death in battle cheerfully, without
a grumble on your lips, and do the best you can right up to the
moment of truth. A British soldier required courage to do his duty.
An Indian soldier, albeit just as brave, needed nothing more than
his stoic acceptance of fate.

Seb sighed, before answering, 'I am not going to hang you,
Gupta. But I do need to know who sent you to do this deed.'

'He will kill me, sir, if he finds out I have betrayed him.'

'Probably he may try to kill you, since he is a murderer, and
one more won't make much difference to him, but there is no

betrayal here, Gupta. I'm told by my corporal you were ordered to kill me. In which case you had very little choice in the matter. The right thing to have done would have been to come to me and tell me what you had been ordered to do. However, I accept that you are a foreigner in the British army and are in a very difficult position. You do not fit and therefore you're probably put upon by the NCOs and officers. No doubt the other troopers tease you just for being an Indian.'

'Yes, sir, a little – but Gupta does not mind.'

'I'm just trying to establish that as an Indian in the British army you're particularly vulnerable and open to abuse, which is why this officer – it was an officer, was it not? – chose to order you to do the assassination.'

Gupta's head wobbled from side to side in that submissive way that Hindus use when being polite.

'Sir, you must know this. The major is of the understanding that I am a Hindu, which is correct, sir. And he is finding out of me that I am a follower of Shiva. Let me tell you, sir, that we worship three big gods, though there are many, many little ones. These three are Brahma, Vishnu and Shiva. Brahma created the world, so his job is done and mostly we do not pray to him very much. Vishnu makes the world work properly and protects us, so we follow him very much. Shiva, sir, as you know, is called the destroyer-god, because he—'

'Destroys?' Seb did not know that, but he was not going to confess his ignorance to the private.

'Yes, sir, exactly, sir,' replied Gupta, enthusiastically. 'But, sir, Shiva only destroys the bad people, and bad things, not the good. This the major did not know. The major thinks because I am a follower of Shiva I am a destroyer. No, this is not correct. If I kill a good man, then Shiva would not be happy with me. So this is why the major choose me to shoot you. Because he thinks I am doing my duty to my god.'

'Now, Private Gupta, you must tell me the name of the major who forced this action upon you.'

'Yes, sir, it is Major Bradford Lunt.'

At last! A name.

'And do you know why he wanted me killed?'

'Yes, sir. He told me he fight an honourable duel with an officer who insult his family and you wish to hang him for this proper act.'

'Let me tell you, Private Gupta, that it was not an "honourable" duel and that Major Lunt killed a man in cold blood. So you need have no fear that you have betrayed an honourable man. Thank you for coming to me. I am aware you risk your life in doing so. When this affair has been settled I shall do my utmost to have you promoted to corporal. Would that please you?'

'Very much, sir. And Gupta is sorry for the shoulder. He – he could have hit the heart, but at the last minute his spirit failed him and his aim was turned just a little.'

Seb suppressed a smile. 'Well, let me say I'm happy to be sitting here and glad that your spirit failed you.'

Once Private Gupta had left, Seb thought about what had passed between them. He had a name now, but there was no sense in rushing in, marching up with an armed guard and arresting Major Lunt. He would simply deny everything and it would be the word of a British officer against an Indian private. No contest. It would end up with Gupta being court-martialled for defaming an officer of Queen Victoria's army. Other officers would close ranks around the major, support him to the death. Even if they disagreed with what he had done, they would never allow an Indian to send one of their own to the firing squad or gallows.

Hard evidence was required before Seb could move on Lunt. Evidence that did not depend on the testimony of a foreigner, for unfortunately and contrary to the laws of nature, foreigners – Africans, Indians, whatever – were all born liars in the eyes of many British aristocrats. As indeed were common lower-class British soldiers out of the slums of London and Glasgow. Somehow truth-telling was a gift of class and privilege. If you were poor and in need you connived as a matter of course because that was a way of life with the underclass, to whom truth was a stranger. And if you were born in Calcutta, Singapore, Malaysia or Zululand, mendacity was as natural to you as eating and drinking, whether you were a cleaner of toilets or the sultan of a large state. You lied because you were a wily man of the East, who saw no wrong in twisting the truth.

So, what to do now? Interview the surgeon again? Haggard. Seb took out his notebook and studied a scribbled copy of the last interview. Something stood out from that talk. The word *oath*. The back of Seb's neck prickled. He found himself experiencing one of his incandescent moments. Oath. Uncle Jack had used that word when speaking of the Ashanti Ring. Officers had taken an oath of loyalty to Wolseley, rather than to the regiment or the queen.

Yes, it was time to interview Surgeon Haggard again.

Eighteen

The march through Zululand continued at its snail's pace. Fort Marshall was established, then Fort Evelyn. Seb tried surreptitiously to get a good look at his suspect, Major Bradford Lunt. It was not easy because the major knew who his enemy was and if he noticed the Provost-Marshal taking an interest in him he would know he had been betrayed. So Seb had to be particularly careful, using field glasses from behind a redoubt.

What he saw was a tall, lean man with broad shoulders who possessed a surprisingly handsome face, though with a backward-sloping forehead topped by a widow's peak. He was young for a major, perhaps in his mid-twenties, and seemed to smile readily when speaking with his fellow officers. He had blond hair, a straight nose, even teeth and a careless pose, displaying all the élan expected of a cavalry officer. He rode well and no doubt was quite the hero of his men. There was nothing about him, physically or charac-teristically, which indicated that under that smart uniform, beneath that young breast, beat the dark heart of a corrupt and flawed officer.

'I shall have you,' whispered Seb to himself. 'I shall have you though you look like the Archangel Michael himself on a mission from God.'

Seb could not forget, while viewing this aberration of a man, that the fellow had ordered a subordinate to assassinate him. A soldier may look the thing, even act the thing, but in the end need not be the thing. Lunt was a thug in a righteous warrior's clothing and Seb was determined that he would not get away with his crimes. Somehow Seb was going to make him pay.

The army was now closing in on the Royal Kraal at Ulundi. The excitement amongst the soldiers was intense. However, the 1/24th Regiment, they who had been massacred at Isandlwana, heard on the grapevine that they would be held in reserve. It was in effect a new regiment, the dead having been replaced by fresh soldiers from Britain, and therefore inexperienced. As a regiment they craved revenge and those few who had survived that slaughter, mostly because elsewhere at the time, were desperate to teach Cetshwayo a lesson, but Lord Chelmsford had decided that the 1/24th would not fight unless it was absolutely necessary.

Seb woke on the 3rd of July 1879 and suddenly on a whim permitted Sam to trim his facial hair before shaking hands with the day. The sentries had been jumpy again last night, but no alarm had been given, and there was not the debacle that had occurred a few days earlier, when the camp had been roused and men had panicked and shot at shadows. Seb inspected himself in the mirror, noted the hollow cheeks and slightly sunken eyes, and decided that although his mother would be anxious if she were there to see him, he was going not too badly when compared with many others. Quite a few men had been ravaged by dysentery and typhoid or some unknown, or even known, tropical disease. Others had poor feet, sores on their legs, gum disease, heat stroke. Several had died on the march.

'Compared with a corpse,' he told his mirror image, 'you don't look half bad, old chum.'

Once he had fed on Sam's pancakes, he gathered his small regiment of two about him.

'Sam, Evans,' he said, 'you both know what Haggard looks like. We have to scour the camp for him. No enquiries, if you please. If he knows we're after him, or Major Lunt is aware of our interest, then he'll disappear.'

Evans, studying his officer's lips closely, asked, 'Where would he go to, out here?'

'There are ten thousand men in this army – he'd find somewhere to hide, believe me, Corporal.'

Evans then added, 'It'll be some task, if we can't ask.'

'That's true, but I would like you, Corporal, to get your friend Donger to help, and I shall ask the scout Pieter Zeldenthuis to assist. Right, off you go, there's a lot of faces to look at. Let's see if we can track him down by lunchtime today.'

Seb first looked for the Boer tracker and found him easily enough, where the scouts had corralled their horses.

'Here's your little friend,' said one of the Boers, in his clipped English accent, 'come to arrest you again.'

Pieter was carving himself a piece of meat from the leg of a shot and cooked gazelle. He looked up with a wary expression on his face.

'Don't worry, this is a social call,' Seb said, anticipating some acid remark from his acquaintance. 'I'm not here to arrest you.'

'Ag, you're damn right you're not,' came the reply. 'So, to what do we owe the pleasure, Provo?'

'A favour.'

'Another one? When do I get one back?'

'I hope the occasion arises,' replied Seb. 'Nothing would please me more.'

'Even though I murder innocent Zulus.'

Seb coloured, remembering Pieter's vendetta with a certain Zulu chief, the man who had killed his father. 'Let's forget about that, shall we?' he said.

'Very big of you, rooinek.'

'I haven't the time to stand around arguing with you – are you going to help me or not?'

Pieter nodded, chewing on a piece of meat. 'I usually do get you out of trouble, don't I?'

The entertainment for the other grinning scouts was over and Seb took the Boer aside to explain what he wanted.

'I'm looking for a man,' Seb said, 'who looks like this . . .' and he produced a sketch he had done that morning.

Pieter glanced at the drawing, asking, 'Is that accurate?'

'Pretty much. The man's a surgeon with the 91st, but doctors are here, there and everywhere in an army on the march. They tend not to stick with their regiments. I need to find him without asking for him or letting him know I want him.'

Pieter squatted on his haunches, inviting Seb to do the same. Seb went down knowing he could only hold that pose for about ten minutes before his joints ached so much they would force him to his feet. The blacks could do it, and the Boer scouts, but not the British. It was not a natural position for an Englishman's body. When you have had to sit bolt upright at a dining table for your whole childhood, squatting is the least favourable posture.

'So, what's the story on this sawbones?'

Seb drew in his breath, before answering. 'There's something pretty dark going on. This general that's superseding Lord

Chelmsford? Wolseley? A secret society formed round him, after the Ashanti wars in the north of Africa. Officers who had been with him on other campaigns, especially the big march in Canada, became members of a ring . . .'

'Not so secret, ag? You know about it.'

'Well, it's an open secret. No one would dare to call it official, because it flies straight in the face of all the British soldier stands for – loyalty to his regiment, loyalty to his Queen. Here we have a senior officer, a general, who seems to demand loyalty to himself first, then the traditional regiment and Queen. Can you see how dangerous that might be? Colonists might laugh at the purchase system in the British army – officers buying their commissions – but as I've explained to you before, it's a safeguard against revolution. No senior officer would want to overthrow a government which is protecting his own status and position in society, his wealth and estates, and even if he did he would not be able to mobilize soldiers whose first loyalty is to the Queen.'

'You just said his first loyalty is to his regiment.'

'Regiment, yes – not the regimental *commander* – and the regiment's loyalty is to the Queen, so it's all one.'

'Go on.'

Seb warmed to his theme. 'Well, it seems we now have a general who has officers under him who have taken an oath. *An oath of loyalty to him as a man.* Now I'm not saying for a moment General Wolseley would exercise that power and attempt a coup, making himself the first dictator since Cromwell . . . all right, that's stretching it a bit, but Cromwell was not universally liked. Ask any Irishman. What I'm trying to say is, if Wolseley was a man seeking ultimate power then he would have the machinery to make an attempt at obtaining it.' Seb paused, before saying, 'I've never been overly concerned about secret societies, though they don't interest me personally. The Masons, the Buffaloes, that kind of thing. But when it's a group in the military, formed out of commissioned officers, it becomes something else. There is a sinister weight to it. My God, an *oath*, Pieter. Do you see what I mean?'

The Boer nodded. 'I can see why it worries you.'

Seb continued. 'I think a man has been murdered because he threatened to uncover such a clique. I am determined to bring those who murdered him to justice. The first step is to find the

man I have sketched for you, Surgeon Haggard, and frighten the
life out of him. Now, will you help? You have some of the sharpest
eyes in this man's army. Lend me those eyes for a day.'

The Boer nodded and followed Seb.

Thus four men scoured the camp, searching amongst thousands
of soldiers for that one face. Of course, they could narrow that
search somewhat. There were places where they were most likely
to find Doctor Haggard.

It was indeed Pieter Zeldenthuis who found the surgeon, who
happened to be doctoring a horse not a human. The next step was
to get the surgeon out of the camp. This was done by Evans, who
went in wild-eyed to almost drag the surgeon from the camp,
proclaiming that a fellow soldier, 'A picquet, sir,' had stepped on a
three-inch thorn and was writhing in agony behind an outcrop.
When Haggard got there, however, with Evans herding him from
behind, he found a tribesman, an ensign and a mean-looking scout
waiting for him.

'Och, what's this?' said the surgeon, frowning. 'I was told . . .
this man here . . .' Then he noticed the red sash on Seb's
shoulder. 'Ah, I know you. This will be reported, sir, I warn you.
You have no right to take me away from duties under false
pretences. We have had our discussion, Ensign. You have learned
all you are going to . . .'

'Get off the horse,' said the Boer in a dangerous voice, 'before
I yank you off.'

The doctor looked highly indignant, but on viewing the other
grim faces did as he was told.

'If you think to intimidate me, Ensign Early, you'll find me an
obdurate man.'

Sam had made a fire and was now adding more wood to it,
though it was low and contained. As the darkness fell over the
scene the fire's light made the faces around it seem more sinister.
The surgeon noticed that the black man had a long-bladed knife
in his belt. The tall corporal was staring intently into his face. The
ensign had an expression as hard as rock on his, and the scout with
the dangerous eyes looked coiled and ready to strike at any moment.
The surgeon's confidence left him as his indignation trickled away
and a real fear took its place.

What were these men going to do to him? Should he shout

for assistance? Surely there was someone within earshot who would come to his aid? Yet he and the corporal had ridden quite a way out into the bush. Perhaps not. Perhaps he should just brave it out. They surely would not dare to torture him, not unless they murdered him afterwards. No, the Provost-Marshal would not stoop to such a heinous crime as torture, no matter how desperate he was for information.

'You had best let me ride out of here now,' Haggard stated. 'I am prepared to let this stupid exercise pass without further comment, but I insist on being allowed to return to camp this instant.'

'Forget it,' growled the Boer. 'You're not going anywhere. Sit down, shut up and listen.'

The ensign now spoke to him.

'You are a member of Lunt's Ring, are you not?'

Haggard's head jerked back at these words, which had surprised and chilled him to the marrow of his bones.

'Lunt? Not Lunt.'

'Who, then? Give me the officer's name.'

'I shall not. I refuse . . .'

The ensign's eyes bore into him. The doctor's unease increased. How much did this provo know?

'I'm sure you must be aware that Major Lunt attempted to have me assassinated,' said the Provost-Marshal. 'If he does not hang for the murder of the unknown officer, he will certainly be held to account for *that* crime.'

Haggard swallowed hard. What was this? A lie? Would Lunt actually have a fellow officer murdered in cold blood? Yes, yes, that was possible. Lunt would do anything to protect himself.

How did I get myself into this mess, thought the surgeon. *I'm a doctor, not a warrior. I save lives, not take them. That fool Lunt will drag me down with him into the pit. What shall I do? What shall I do?*

The ensign now peeled back his coat collar and shirt, and showed the surgeon the healed wound in his shoulder.

'You can see this was caused by a bullet? Major Lunt sent someone after me, when I went on a mission. Ordered him to kill me in cold blood. That man has admitted his crime to me and stands ready to testify against this despicable officer. You, sir, will go down with him, believe me. I know you to be a member of a ring, whether headed by Lunt or some other officer.'

Haggard said, desperately, 'I'm sure no officer of the Queen would fall so low as to . . .'

The corporal, his eyes staring intently into the surgeon's face, now spoke in a very loud voice. 'I was there, sir. My officer was shot by an assassin, see? I was the one who found the man who shot him. He was ordered to by this Major Lunt. Said so, plain as could be. They're going to hang you out to dry, sir, beggin' your pardon. Wouldn't be at all surprised if they was to blame you for all of it, see what I mean? You can't trust murderers, sir. They'll pull you down with 'em and even if they can't get you to take the whole blame, they like company when they're bein' fitted with a rope round their necks.'

The surgeon looked round, into the darkness.

'Dinna shout, man.'

'I wasn't shoutin',' shouted Evans. 'Not so's you know it.'

'You need to tell us now, Surgeon Haggard, all you know,' said the Provost-Marshal, quietly. 'You may be able to walk away from this, if not with your reputation, at least with your freedom. I shall stand up for you, and praise your assistance, when the time comes. And the time will come, whether or not you help us here. If you do not speak now, I shall do my damnedest to see you imprisoned for a long time.'

Seb was aware that he had the man now, back on his heels. In the firelight he could see the sweat trickling down the surgeon's face. The man was wringing his hands. The truth was coming. Seb glanced at Pieter, who gave him a slight nod.

'If Lunt finds out I spoke . . .' began the surgeon.

'Not until the trial,' promised Seb. 'Not until he can no longer reach you.'

Surgeon Haggard licked his lips, before beginning.

'It was in India,' he said. 'There were seven of us, officers from different regiments, attending a function being held by a local nawab. Despite that the Indians did not imbibe alcohol, they had laid on plenty for us, and most of us were drunk when we left the nawab's palace. It was late at night and we were passing a large house in the forest, all in riotous mood, being very loud and boisterous, when a woman came out of the house and remonstrated with us. Lunt dismounted, laughed in her face, then – then grabbed her and fondled her breasts. He – he was – it was the drink, I suppose.'

There was a long pause as Haggard wrung his hands again. He continued with, 'I do have fierce regrets you know. I am contrite.' He stared into the ring of faces around the fire. 'I am not a man without principles, without integrity.' He stopped again, staring into the flames. Seb quietly urged him to go on.

Haggard did so, a little hoarsely.

'A man, an Indian, came out of the house – her father, I think. He had a club in his hand. He hit Major Lunt across the shoulders, to get him away from his daughter. Lunt drew his sword and ran the man through. Then as the woman screamed, he – he put her to the sword as well.' Haggard swallowed again, before continuing. 'It probably wouldn't have mattered much if the pair had emerged from a hovel, but the house – it was a large, not quite a palace, but certainly a hunting lodge. The clothing they had on, the murdered pair, was made of rich cloth. We knew then that the man we had killed was not a peasant, but probably a *malik* or a *zamindar*. A chief of some kind, an important man. If it was discovered that army officers had done this thing . . . well, I need not say more. It was not a time in India when one could simply do as one wished because one was white. It was certain there would have been some sort of retaliation. An uprising, possibly, which would have resulted in more deaths. The authorities would have been incensed. Lunt is not the sort of man who takes to being disciplined. None of those officers present, with the exception of one man, wanted this incident to come out.'

There was a shocked silence around the fire. Sam had been adding a twig to the flames, but was frozen. Even Pieter Zeldenthuis, who had seen and experienced much in the way of atrocities, looked somewhat stunned.

'A British officer did this?' whispered Seb.

The surgeon nodded. 'Aye, they were a wild bunch of officers, hell-bent on riotous behaviour. There had been incidents before, though none of them as monstrous as this. Anyway, we left the corpses just outside their house, to look as if they had been fending off badmashes, or dacoits, intent on robbing them. Indeed, later we heard that a couple had been killed defending their home against robbers.

'Now, Lunt was not the senior officer amongst us. There was a colonel – I'm not going to give you his name, he's dead now, killed in a battle in Burma. It was he who suggested we form a ring, like Wolseley's Ring, to protect everyone present at the killing. One or two officers were still carrying wine with them. Lunt put his sword above a jug and ran two fingers down the blade, so that the blood from his victims went into the wine. Then we stood in a circle, took a swallow from the blood-wine, and made a dark oath. The oath was to remain loyal to the colonel, to Lunt, to each other. I was on the very fringe of this group, I hardly knew them but just happened to be with them that fateful night. I was drawn into this hideous oath-taking, partly because I was highly intoxicated, and partly through fear of the other officers forming the ring. These are not excuses. I was wrong and I'm sure I shall be punished for my stupidity.

'However, one man, a lieutenant, refused to join with them in this depraved and scabrous scheme. He mounted his horse and rode off into the night. I heard the next day that his regiment had left that morning and he was out of the reach of those who wished to do him harm. He did not surface again until he rode into Landman's Drift one evening. Lunt immediately challenged him to a duel. The lieutenant refused, but was dragged from his bed at dawn and taken to the spot where the duel was to take place. The young lieutenant deloped, leaving Lunt uncontested. Major Lunt shot him dead without, it appeared to me, any shame or compassion.'

Haggard expelled his breath deeply, as if ridding himself of all the bad air in his body, before saying in haunted tones, 'There you have it, the whole. But know this, Provost-Marshal, I will not testify. I just canna. It is beyond my capabilities. I am mentally exhausted by the whole affair. I am at the end of my tether and shall go mad before you get me to stand up as a witness. You will have to do it without me.'

'What was the name of the lieutenant who rode away?'

'That I do not know.'

Pieter Zeldenthuis said, 'You surely *do* know.'

The surgeon lifted his face again.

'No, I swear. I told you, I was on the very edge of that group of men. I did not know all their names. Since that terrible night I've avoided members of the ring as much as possible, though Lunt sent for me the morning of the duel and made sure that only those in the know were present. We were to be the only witnesses of the affair . . .'

Seb said, 'You will be astonished to hear then that there were at least a dozen other witnesses who saw the whole thing.'

Haggard looked suitably shocked. 'No!'

'Yes.'

'I tell you, I was there,' the surgeon said, now with some anger in his voice. 'There was no one else present. All around us was open space.'

'But you did not look up.'

'Up? Up where?'

'The duel was fought under a large wide-boughed tree. In the branches of that tree was a crowd of youngsters. Somehow, earlier, they had scented a duel. Drummer boys, local youths, wagon-drivers' sons, they're like a swarm of mice in a military camp. They run around almost unnoticed, listening, watching. They pick up things that most adults would not hear or pay much attention to, hints of things that interest them, like boxing matches behind the latrines, supposedly secret expeditions into enemy territory – and duels. They're very good at discovering what they want to know. Shrewd little devils with eyes like eagles', ears like an elephant's. Not much passes them by. This one certainly didn't. They saw the whole thing, were able to recognize you, Doctor, and put me on to you. Oh yes, a dozen witnesses, at least.'

The surgeon's face registered dismay.

'They saw me there. They can place me there.'

'I know one boy who is certain.'

'Oh my God.'

Nineteen

Seb let the surgeon go back to the camp. The scenario had now been fleshed out in full. He had been apprised of the facts behind the unknown lieutenant's murder. It was now up to him to bring the killers to justice. He thanked the others, especially Pieter Zeldenthuis, who was nothing to do with the whole affair but had added his intimidating presence to the group.

The Boer said to him, 'Ag, I don't envy you, bru. It'll be difficult, prosecuting a cavalry major in your army. Not something I'd want to do. A bit like going for a member of your family. Some newspaper's going to get hold of this – it's dirty and it's nasty – all very newsworthy. You'll do your job, but you won't be thanked for it. Lord Chelmsford and the staff? They'll hate you for dragging the army's name through the mud. Most of 'em will think you should have left well enough alone.'

Seb sighed. 'I know, but what is one to do? The man's a murderer. It's a dark and messy business. I can't let it lie, can I? And I'm not going to leave it at Lunt. I want the others too. They're all culpable, all as guilty as he is for assisting him. The army will hate me even more for my insistence on group guilt. I have to, though. I am the law. I am justice here. No one else will take the responsibility.'

The Boer's hand fell on his shoulder.

'Good luck, bru. I mean it. I admire you. You're a tenacious littler bugger, ain't you?'

Actually Seb was feeling despair at his role.

'They give you a job,' he said, 'then they do their best to stop you doing it. Well, if they just wanted a figurehead they chose the wrong man. My father instilled me with principles and I'm not going to compromise those principles for the sake of an army's good name. I want my father to speak my name with pride.'

Pieter smiled. 'Good for you,' he said.

Seb went back to his tent with Evans and Sam. Sam kept mumbling comforting words, congratulating his boss on his success with the witness, but Evans seemed withdrawn and unusually quiet.

Was he also concerned by the gravity and depravity of this affair? This was his army too. Evans might only be one of the rank and file, but soldiers were proud of their regiments and proud of their campaigns. He would not want his campaign to be besmirched by something as sordid as this. Dark, secret societies in this man's army? Unthinkable. Yet here it was. A hellfire club within the ranks of senior officers. Men of honour. Men of standing. A group of despicable cowardly murderers.

Seb somehow fell asleep close to dawn and was woken by the bugles it seemed only a few minutes later, though in truth he had had around two hours' sleep. He stumbled out of his tent and gratefully accepted a mug of tea from Sam, who never seemed to sleep at all. However, before he could wash and trim his beard, a figure strode towards him out of the morning light, looking to be full of righteous wrath. Major Stringman had a piece of paper in his hand, which he waved at Seb. As usual the major seemed to be in a state of high fury with his subordinate.

'Ensign Early! You are aware what you have done?'

Seb buttoned his coat against the dawn's coolness.

'Sir,' he replied wearily, 'I'm sure you're going to tell me.'

'A man − a *good* officer − has committed suicide because of you,' spat the major. 'Shot himself not an hour ago.'

Hope sprang to Seb's beleaguered mind. Surely this was Lunt? Surgeon Haggard had told him of the interview and he had decided the game was up and took the honourable way out? O blessed day.

'Not because of me, sir,' said Seb. 'I encouraged no man to take his own life.'

'Read this!' Major Stringman thrust the piece of paper under Seb's nose dramatically.

Seb took the note and read it in the first of the sun's rays.

'Forgive me, my dear Margaret, my beloved wife. I can no longer live with this guilt. Last night the Provost-Marshal extracted a confession from me and you will probably hear all sorts of bad things said about your husband. Please remember this. I love you, I have always loved you, you are the most precious and valuable experience of my life. I was dragged into this terrible affair against my wishes, against my will, but had not the strength to resist. I personally did nothing wrong, but I am weak and allowed others so to do. That is my crime and I can no longer live with it. Give my fondest love to our children. I hope and pray the Provost-Marshal will manage this affair with compassion and allow you, my darling, to keep your head up high and my family to be untouched by scandal. God have mercy on my soul.'

It was signed, 'Your Own Robert'.

Seb was aghast. 'He shot himself?'

'Because of you, Ensign!'

Seb looked up, angry yet again with this stupid major.

'Not because of me. Because of what he had kept secret from others and because of his involvement in a heinous crime. Can you not read, you fool? He talks of confessing to a crime. He killed himself because he could not live with that fact.' Seb was almost shouting now. 'I am a policeman, sir. I am an officer of the law. I cannot allow a man to go free of involvement in a transgression simply because he might have the weakness to commit suicide. Good God, sir, when will you realize that I have a job to do. A very unpleasant job which is made worse by officers of your stamp. Instead of berating me every five minutes you should be giving me encouragement and assistance.'

Stringman's eyes were bulging, as they had done in previous encounters such as this, but before he could start yelling at Seb, and threatening all kinds of punishment for calling him a fool, a voice behind him said, 'He's right, you know.'

The major whirled, to find Lieutenant Henry Wycliffe, Baron of Stantonhope, looking with mild eyes into his face.

'I beg your pardon, sir?'

'And well you may, but better,' said Mad Henry, pointing with his pipe, 'to beg the ensign's pardon.' Henry was wearing a yellow Chinese-silk dressing gown embroidered with green dragons flying through puffy green clouds. On his head was a nightcap that flopped over his left ear. His feet were slippered in yellow velvet. 'The young pip is trying to do his best for you and all you give him is criticism. My pa always taught me that for every piece of criticism you offer a man, you should add three pieces of praise. Doing a good job, this lad, under difficult circumstances. Yes, he's right, you should be assisting him, not making life difficult.'

'I would ask you to mind your own business, Lieutenant,' replied Stringman, with less vehemence than he would normally speak to one of that rank, due to Mad Henry's civilian status. You do not yell at barons, even if they are a couple of rungs lower down the military hierarchy and on the run from an army of creditors. Men like Stringman were afraid of the aristocracy, not for what they did but for what they were. He was in awe of the mystique of the nobility. Yet he still sought to protect his own status as well as he could. 'This is police business, sir, and you would do well to keep out of it.'

'Major, as I understand it, police business is the business of *all* of us. We must all seek to keep the law. It's how we maintain stability in the fragile theatre of war. Why, if we did not, we would descend into anarchy, and if there's one thing that upsets the apple cart, sir, it's anarchy.' His eyes misted over a little, before he added, 'And chaos. Chaos is just as bad, in my opinion.' He moved his face closer to the major's. 'Some people think me insane,' said Mad Henry, 'but my kind of lunacy is not of the anarchistic, chaotic sort. I like order. That's why I help the guards on my railway station at home, so that the trains go out on time. The strict adherence to a timetable is a necessary thing for the orderly running of the railways, Major. Order, sir. That's why I joined the army. To be in an ordered environment. And if the law is flouted, we have disorder. That's all I have to say.'

He jammed the pipe back in his mouth and stepped away from the major's personal space.

Stringman could think of nothing more to do or say, and flung his arms in the air, before snatching the suicide note out of Seb's hand and marching away towards the staff quarters.

'That man,' said Mad Henry, puffing away, 'will explode one of these days, South-East, you mark my words. He will blow up like an over-fuelled steam engine. I hope I'm there to see it. It'll be an interesting spectacle, I'm sure.'

'Henry, thank you.'

'What for?'

'For intervening. I shouldn't have called him a fool.'

'Poo! The man *is* a fool.'

'But he's also a major, and my commanding officer.'

'More reason to learn that he's a fool. Not that he'll believe it. He still thinks he's the brightest star in the firmament, which makes him an ever *bigger* fool. Oh, well, have a good morning. I shan't ask you what that was all about. That's police business, and no business of mine. Toodle-pip, young rooster.'

Mad Henry strode away in his fine nightwear, unconscious of the stares that followed him.

Corporal Evans had risen even earlier than his commanding officer. His silence after the interrogation the previous evening had not been because he was concerned about the good name of the army, as Seb had imagined, but because he had experienced his own incandescent moment. An idea had come to him during the interview of Surgeon Haggard. Evans had always been a deep thinker. A shepherd had little else to do while tending his flock. You watched your sheep, yes, with an eagle eye, but you also had the other one on the drifting clouds, the green valleys of Wales, the mountains and the dancing brooks. Even if there were other people around, burly Welshmen building the dry-stone walls with expert hands, or English gentlemen climbing the grey peaks, past the dew ponds and rock stacks, you could still lose yourself in your head. There were vast moors inside the head of Evans, great mountain fastnesses, which had the potential for endless exploration. Every small dell was worth investigating, every peat hag and water channel worth studying.

Evans was making his way through the troops towards the quartermaster's area. The postal service in the army was a haphazard affair and mail came by various couriers, not always for the specific reason of delivering letters and parcels. A delivery of ammunition or food stores might also bring with it a bundle of letters for the soldiers on the front line. So, like the office of Provost-Marshal, someone was assigned to the task of sorting through the mail when it came, and getting it to the intended addressees.

In the case of Lord Chelmsford's army, it was a harassed sergeant attached to the quartermaster's domain, who had to put up with complaints about which he could do nothing and was pestered night and day by young men whose wives and girlfriends were not missing them enough to write frequently. Sergeant Thompson was a nervous, worried-looking man at the best of times, but on mail duty he had the demeanour of a harvest mouse during the reaping of the corn. On the approach of a tall corporal with a determined expression his general fears rose within him.

'You're goin' to bother me, ain't you, Corp?'

'Speak into my face, if you please, Sergeant, I'm deaf.'

This was going to be worse than normal, thought Thompson. A bloody Welshman. Welshmen got up his bugle. Scotsmen got up his bugle too. And the Irish. They all had this grievance against Englishmen that they did not make any effort to hide. It was all about past battles between Celts and Anglo-Saxons. The Celts were always noble warriors, dreadfully wronged, in those battles. The English were always dastardly invaders winning their wars by foul means.

'What do you want, Owain Glyndwr?' he shouted at the corporal. 'There ain't no mail today.'

The corporal ignored the snipe and asked him if he had any letters for a lieutenant which had not been collected.

'Why?' he demanded. 'You ain't no lieutenant.'

The corporal drew himself up a few inches higher.

'I am the Assistant Provost-Marshal,' he said loudly. 'I'm investigatin' a case. That's what this red ribbon is for, see? To tell you what I am and what I do. Now spill.'

Thompson eyed the faded bit of red cloth dubiously, but decided he had heard of the fact of men being designated army provos.

'What regiment?' he yelled an inch away from the corporal's nose. 'The lieutenant?'

'Don't know. Just get your letters, them as what haven't been claimed, and we'll look through 'em.'

The sergeant stared at the corporal, thinking, This fellah's a bit above hisself – I might just tell 'im to stick his head in a water butt, but then decided that the only way he was going to get rid of the gangling Welshman was to do as he asked. He went to his tent and collected a large bundle of letters and undid the string that tied them.

'Lieutenant Frith?' asked the sergeant, holding up two letters that had arrived yesterday.

'Nah, that's him who was killed by the Zulus.'

'Oh yes,' said the sergeant. 'I've writ *Deceased* on the back.'

There were one or two more, with the same word on the envelope, and then finally a batch of five letters for a Lieutenant David Shepherd.

'How long have you had these?' asked the corporal.

The sergeant studied the envelopes. 'Seems I might 'ave had 'em since we set out from Landsman's. See here, I writ the date on one of 'em in pencil, though it's rubbed off a bit. He must have bin sent somewhere else. Maybe to the 1st Division, eh, down south? He ain't dead, otherwise I would've bin told straight off. They always tell me the names of the dead. I've got a long list of dead uns. Here, I'll show—'

'Got you!' cried the corporal, in a voice of triumph, snatching up the letters.

'What?' said the sergeant, alarmed by this sudden yell and backing away. 'I ain't done nothin' I 'aven't bin told to do.'

'No, not you,' shouted the corporal. 'I've got 'is name at last. Thank you, Sergeant. You've assisted in the solvin' of a major crime. You might even get mentioned in dispatches.'

Thompson was hopeful. 'Will I?'

'No, you silly arse, but thanks anyways. Can I take these letters to my officer? He'll see they get sent back to them as sent them.'

'Well, they're my responsibility. I dunno . . .'

But the corporal was gone, striding away through the lines of tents, clutching the batch of Lieutenant David Shepherd's mail.

'Well done, Corporal. Well done, indeed!' said Seb, after he had read through the letters. 'I'm sure this is our murder victim. Why didn't we think of that earlier? To look through the mail for letters that hadn't been collected? I didn't ask you to do it earlier, did I?'

'No, sir, you didn't,' confirmed Evans. 'This was my idea.'

'Yes, sorry. I'm just surprised at my own ineptitude. I should have . . . well, never mind. You thought of it and it's done. Lieutenant David Shepherd, eh? Poor man, to get on the wrong side of our Major Lunt.'

'What do the letters say, sir?'

'Nothing that helps us, I'm afraid. There's no mention of Lunt or any other officer. All five letters are from Shepherd's sister, Jeanette, who simply passes on news of the family to him. At some time I shall have to go and see the colonel and he'll have to write to Miss Shepherd and give her the sad news of her brother's death. What the colonel will tell her, I don't know. But I can't do anything at the moment to jeopardize our investigation. We need to nail Major Lunt to the cross, first.'

Evans looked disapprovingly at his officer.

'He ain't Jesus, he's the opposite.'

'Corporal, thousands of criminals were crucified by the Romans, not just one man.'

'I know, but when you say it like that . . .'

'I take your point. It was meant otherwise. Put it down to my classical education. I was just being clever.'

'So, where does that leave us, sir? With this Lunt, I mean?'

Seb considered the question very carefully before replying.

'Well, we've lost our star witness in Surgeon Haggard.'

'Took the coward's way out,' said Evans.

'I'm never sure of that, since it must take some kind of courage to end your own life, though it leaves a great mess of feelings behind amongst the loved ones. Lunt will deny everything, of course, and we have no more names. I could confront him with Lieutenant Shepherd, but I don't think that'll work either. I think we have to bide our time, Evans – Evans, look at my mouth, you're not listening – I think we have to wait until we get back to Landsman's Drift. Hopefully Tom will recognize him as the man who shot his opponent in the duel. Then we can round up a few more of the boys who witnessed the murder. A court might not take much notice of one boy, but surely several? Even then a clever defence might get him off. Still, that's not my worry. My job is to catch the killer and I know who he is and I know where to find him. What's more I have the motive for the murder. I will bring him to book, Evans.'

'Yes, sir, we'll get him.'

Suddenly there was a great yell from one of the tents where the staff were quartered. Seb and others ran to the spot to find out what was causing such bedlam, thinking that perhaps Zulu warriors had crept into camp and attacked. What they found was indeed an attack of a kind, but not by Zulus, by frogs.

Major Stringman, dressed only in his underwear, was staggering around the flagpole trying to wrench green mottled frogs from his face. There were several of the creatures, gripping his ears, his eyelids, his lips, his nose, and removing them appeared to be a painful business. Seb inspected one that was tossed his way and saw that it was a ghost frog, a species which was confined almost exclusively to the streams and rivers of the Drakensbergs. It was known for its tenacious grip, with its suckered feet but more especially with its mouth, which it needed to cling on to rocks in the fast-flowing waterways. Several of these local amphibians were gripping a distressed army major, clearly intending to hold on as long as possible and with the utmost obstinacy.

For a good few minutes the distressed major pulled frogs from his face while a crowd gathered and roared with laughter. Finally the last amphibian was torn from his left eyelid, leaving a red mark where its mouth had been, and Theobald Timothy Stringman was left with just the raucous hilarity of the audience to deal with. Since there were officers amongst them, some of them of senior rank to himself, he could hardly yell at them and tell them to go to the devil. Instead he fumed, staring at faces distorted with humour, looking for a scapegoat. Seb quickly ducked behind a man wearing a gaudy pelisse, who was hooting at the top of his voice, and crying, 'Let's hear it for the ghost frogs!'

Finally, Stringman gave a sound like a sob, turned, and stalked back to his tent, disappearing inside to mocking applause.

The man who had hidden Seb from the major now turned and saw him. It was of course Mad Henry.

Henry took a puff on his pipe, winked at Seb, and whispered, 'Told you I'd get him. Came to me in the middle of the night, like I thought it would. Woke up in a bit of sweaty funk after dreaming of ghosts. Dream of the beggars quite a lot, as it happens. Mostly the spirits of dead comrades. Then it came to me! Ghost frogs. A whole bucketful of them, eh? Your man got 'em for me. It's that Stringman fellow's own fault. Man's creature of habit. Goes for a nap at exactly the same time every day. Bound to get taken advantage of when you do that. Wouldn't you say? Toodle-pip, young rooster.'

With that Mad Henry strolled away, the clouds of smoke from his Meerschaum pipe wafting yellow in the air above his head.

Seb went back to his own tent with misgivings stirring in his breast. He called Evans to attend him. Evans vehemently denied collecting frogs for Mad Henry. Thus it had to be Sam Weary, the Xhosa, who was clinking silver coins in the pocket of his threadbare trousers when Seb asked him to come over.

'Did you collect frogs for Lieutenant Wycliffe?' Seb asked Sam in a severe tone.

'Yes, boss.'

'Well done,' said Seb, breaking into a grin. 'Now go and wash your hands. I'm told those little beasts can have toxic skins. I don't want the taste of frog in my supper tonight. Even if it's not there, I shall probably think it is, so go and have a good scrub.'

'Yes, boss,' replied Sam, smiling, still clinking his precious pieces of silver. 'A good scrub! You have fine language, boss. I like that word, *scrub*. It is good and strong. Scrrub. Scrrrub. Yes, sir, I will scrub away like anything, you will see me shine like boots.'

Twenty

Seb's regiment was not part of the front line. They had, as promised, been left in reserve. But since he was not of their number while he was Provost-Marshal, he sought permission and was granted leave to join the Frontier Light Horse. The cavalry had crossed the White Mfolozi River earlier and were on the Mahlabatini plain. They had already met with some resistance. Zulu snipers had been waiting in the rocks on the far side of the river and had been about to open fire on Buller's men, when Baker's Horse circled behind them and sent them scattering. Around fifty Zulus fled while troopers shot at them, killing several. To Seb it was a bit like a turkey shoot and he had a distaste of firing at the back of a man, though he knew there was good reason for it. Those men were obviously the enemy's crack shots and to get rid of them now would save the lives of soldiers later.

There was another attached officer riding alongside Seb with Major Buller's troopers. He learned this was Captain Lord William Leslie de la Poer Beresford of the 9th Lancers over from India. A long and powerful aristocratic name that intimidated the ensign somewhat, when he had to reply simply, 'Ensign Early. Your servant, sir. Provost-Marshal for Lord Chelmsford's army.' Beresford told Seb he had asked permission of the Viceroy of India to sail to Africa to fight the Zulu. Seb was all for doing his job as a soldier, but he did not understand officers who chased after wars, simply to do a little more killing. Beresford was a big-game hunter too, so perhaps he saw humans in the same light? 'Provost-Marshal, eh?' said Captain Lord de la Poer Beresford. 'Sounds an awful job. What do you do? Arrest people?' Seb replied, 'I solve murders. I'm rather good at it.' Beresford raised his eyebrows, as if to say, every man for his own interest.

After the skirmish, Buller ordered the Frontier Light Horse, the Transvaal Rangers and Whalley's Natal Light Horse to advance on Ulundi. Seb rode Amasi through the long grasses towards the dark kraals in the distance. The horse was delighted to be out and about again, the wind in his nostrils, a rider on his back. He was not one of those mounts who resent those they carry. Amasi liked the company of his owner. You could see it in the toss of his head when Seb whispered in his ear and in the lightness of his step when gently urged to change direction. He liked nothing better than sharing the wilderness with his rider and though he enjoyed a good gallop, was just as happy with a walk, trot or canter. The smells were strong out here, though, of fires and cooking, and strips of meat drying on poles, and the sweat of men. Amasi knew there was going to be fighting too. Its scent was also in the air.

The excitement and battle anxiety were building in Ensign Early's chest. Seb was conscious of the discomfort of the heat of the day, of the clouds of insects which Amasi's hooves created from the grass, of the giant African sun that climbed steadily above the horizon. Senses live and acute, he was also aware of small clumps of Zulus, including women and children, that scrambled out of the way on the approach of the horsemen. They looked both terrified and slightly bewildered.

When Seb looked for the Zulu army, though, there was none ahead.

Perhaps an impi was hiding in the grasses? Perhaps they were thousands strong, ready to shock the white invaders by rising up suddenly and letting out their chilling, haunting, deep-throated war cry? They had done as much at Isandlwana, appearing out of a shallow hollow on the landscape, almost out of nowhere, to swarm forth and overwhelm their enemy. It was possible that they might do the same again. For all the soldiers knew, they might be surrounded. These warriors of the Zulu nation had built an empire on their ability to make war. They were not simple primitives who had no idea of strategy or tactics. There were able generals amongst them. Men who knew the value of surprise, of overwhelming numbers. Battle-hardened leaders of battle-hardened men. It did not do to underestimate the Zulu, despite their lack of heavy weapons. Isandlwana had taught Seb and the other soldiers of the Queen that much at least.

His fears were not imaginary. A minute later there came a massive volley of shots from the surrounding grasses as thousands of Zulus rose up in concert with that terrible war cry on their lips. Ahead of Seb a trooper spun in his saddle, his horse bolted, and the man flopped to the ground stone dead. Seb drew his sword and shouted, 'Here they come!' It was an unnecessary cry: everyone around him was aware of the enemy. There were more shots and Seb saw several troopers drop from their saddles. Now near the rear of the column, he was unable to assist those who had been wounded, but other officers and men managed to pick up some of the troopers who had been unhorsed. The dead remained.

There was now a gallop back to the river before a horde of bloodthirsty Zulus, desperate to wash their spears in the blood of British soldiers. On reaching the river and looking behind him, Seb saw his erstwhile companion Beresford trying to persuade a dazed unhorsed soldier to climb up behind him. The Zulus were closing on the pair very fast and though the soldier managed to mount, he seemed to pass out and pull Beresford from the saddle with him. This dangerous event occurred at least twice more, until eventually Beresford and his soldier reached the water's edge, both without further wounds.

The cavalry crossed the shallows of the river and then swiftly dismounted to fire at the Zulus who were crowded on the opposite bank. The enemy returned the fire with enthusiasm. Seb saw one large, courageous warrior, his black skin shining in the bright sunlight, wading into the shallows to get a better aim. He was an easy target and went down in a blizzard of British bullets, staining the water red. After this, the fighting ceased as both armies watched his head-feathers part from his hair and drift downstream on the current.

That night, under a full moon, Seb reflected on the day's events. The 5th Dragoons had not taken part in the foray over the river. Seb desperately hoped now that Major Lunt would not be killed in the coming battle. He wanted him to face his accusers and to account for his crimes. In the normal way of things, he would rather a criminal was killed in battle to save his family back home from suffering. After all, they were not responsible for the crime, yet often they were the ones who bore the brunt of the condemnation. In this case, however, Seb felt an example had to be made. This fraternity of military thugs had to be broken up and that would not happen without a trial where everything came out into the open. If Lunt were to fall in battle, some other officer might take over the pack.

His musings were interrupted by Major Stringman.

'I hope you've had time to reflect on your mistakes, Ensign.'

Seb stared with dislike into the moonlit face of this unlikeable man.

'We all make mistakes, sir. However, I collect you mean Surgeon Haggard? That was unfortunate, but the officer brought it upon himself when he aligned himself with criminals.'

Stringman blew out his cheeks before saying, 'Criminals?'

'Sir, once this war is over I intend prosecuting a senior officer, bringing him to justice, and I beg you will not interfere. I know his name, I know his regiment, I know all about him. He will be brought before his peers and made to account for his actions.'

A shake of the head, before, 'It does not do to bring disgrace upon a regiment. These things are best done quietly. I take it you are referring to the officer who shot another in a duel? You will inform me of the name of this individual and I shall decide on the best course of action, once I have interviewed him.'

Seb looked up balefully at his commanding officer.

'I must remind you, sir, that it is I who am Provost-Marshal, and not you.'

'Yes, you are, but you are subject to my supervision.'

'No, I am not, for that would compromise my office.'

Stringman frowned. 'How so?'

'What if *you* were the one I was after?'

This rocked the major back on his heels.

'That is not the case, Ensign.'

'It *could* be, that's the point.'

'I shall get General Lord Chelmsford to order you to release this officer's name and then you'll have to comply.'

'Not necessarily.'

Stringman's eyes widened. 'You would defy an order from your general? Then you would end up in prison yourself.'

Seb smiled, ruefully. 'That would be ironic, wouldn't it. No, firstly I don't believe the general would give me such an order, not after I explained the circumstances to him. Secondly, what I said to you, applies to anyone, general or private. I am the law here. There is no other. All men are subject to the law, whatever their rank. If I believe it to be in the interest of justice to retain information, not even a general can force me to reveal it. I'm a junior officer, the most junior one can get, but my office is unique and powerful. For once, sir, go back to your tent and reflect on your position. If you should force me to bungle this case, your name will be all over the front page of the *Thunderer*. You might even be subject to a court martial yourself.

'This war is already unpopular back in England. We know that from the newspapers and letters. It was begun by an ambitious politician and our general, and the government in Britain is highly displeased with what we've done here. There may be further shocks to come. It would be wise of all of us to keep our heads down for a while. That doesn't include allowing murderers to get away with their crime. It does include bringing such a crime to a satisfactory conclusion. Now does that make any sense to you, or are you still determined to interfere?'

Major Stringman stared down at this presumptuous ensign before turning on his heel and walking away.

The rest of the night hours were mainly sleepless. The British army had left one of their troopers alive in the hands of the Zulu. The warriors had given him to their women and he was tortured throughout the dark hours, his screams reaching the ears of his countrymen. Few could sleep through that sound. Many of his comrades wanted to rush to his aid, charge across the river in the darkness and put his tormentors to the sword, but of course they were restrained. They were members of a disciplined army and subject to the orders of their general, who was no doubt as upset as any to hear terror and pain coming from the mouth of one of his soldiers, but knew that any attack at night was folly.

Early on the morning of the 4th July the soldiers of Lord Chelmsford's army were going about their pre-battle rituals. Any man facing the strong possibility of imminent death experiences an immediate rise in superstition. Perhaps he survived the last battle because he put on his boots in a certain order: the right boot first, then the left? Or perhaps it was because he folded his blanket in a certain way, or trimmed his moustache, or saddled his horse at precisely five of the clock? Or was it that letter he carried from Sophie, in his pocket? Or the cigar case given him by his brother, Sam? Or the cross and chain he wore that his mother insisted on him taking with him to Africa? It was not your skill in battle

which kept you alive, not when you were one in a thousand in a
line of ducks standing there almost motionless, waiting to be shot.
It was God or Lady Luck. Many prayed, of course, even though
they were possibly atheists before joining the army. Most went
through as many as a dozen rituals. A great many men did both.
Even Seb had his private rituals and private prayers. In his head
he scorned the idea of the supernatural watching over him, but
his heart was fearful and like many, many soldiers he said, 'Oh,
what's the harm in it all, if it makes me feel better?' And so did
them anyway, even if he thought it foolish.

General Lord Chelmsford crossed the White Mfolozi River to
a plain abutting the Zulu capital, Ulundi. The general was accompanied by five thousand men, six batteries and a cavalry regiment.
He had left the baggage train in Fort Nolela, on the other side of
the river, and he ordered the forming of a square. Each wall of
the square was four men deep and some had thought they ought
to begin digging trenches, having done so at every stop on the
way from Landman's Drift, but Chelmsford was finished building
forts. He wanted a battle and he wanted it today. They were here
at last, facing the Royal Kraal of Cetshwayo, and things would be
settled before noon. Chelmsford had heard that Wolseley had joined
the 1st Division and was closing on him. Luckily Crealock's column
was creeping very, very slowly northwards to Ulundi, and was
nowhere in sight. It was Chelmsford's last chance to crush the
Zulus before he was relieved of his command and the war passed
into other hands.

Seb left Amasi with the baggage train and joined the monstrous
square that soon began to move like an ungainly geometrically-
shaped beast up a long slope in the direction of Ulundi. The cavalry
charged ahead, firing kraals and attacking any Zulus they found.
Then suddenly, like dark ghosts emerging from the ground, Zulu
regiments rose silently from the tall grasses on either side of the
slope. They stood up in their thousands, their shining black bodies
presenting a dazzling sight in the morning sun. They then began
to move into some sort of formation, though Seb was unsure what
that might be. All he could see were these massed movements of
men, drifting back and forth. It was an eerie few minutes and Seb's
heart was in his throat. He doubted there was a soldier in that
massive square who was not feeling awed by the scene. Fear was

there too, but as a secondary emotion. Had these dark warriors been angels or demons he could not have been more amazed.

Having been in several battles, Seb was good at estimating the numbers of the enemy. Here today they were facing at least twenty thousand warriors. Most would be carrying spear and shield, of course, but a good number would be armed with Martini-Henrys captured in previous battles. Two thousand from Isandlwana, more from other Zulu victories in this strange war. The British army had lumbered, creaking and groaning, slowly, slowly across the landscape to be here today. The Zulus, usually swift in their move-ments, had chosen to wait for them to arrive. Now was the time for the final confrontation. If the British won, there would be an end to it. If the Zulus won, the British would come again and again, until they finally overwhelmed the warriors of the Zulu nation. King Cetshwayo could not win. The British were without number. Without end.

One of the Natal Native Contingent soldiers, a sergeant close to Seb, was quietly naming the regiments of Zulus he could see ahead of him.

'. . . umXapho, amaKwenkwe, inTsukamngeni, isaNgpu, uThu-lwana, uDloko, umCijo, uDududu – all here, all here.'

The man was probably a Zulu himself, one who had been disen-franchised by the Zulu nobility for some reason. Perhaps one robbed of his status or possessions. The Zulus were not a homogeneous group but a nation made up of various tribes, and no doubt this man was one of those whose clan had fallen out of favour. To Seb he sounded satisfied that he was now facing all these regiments of his former countrymen. He had a score to settle, it seemed, and he was ready to do that now. Revenge was a dish to be served hot today.

The red square moved ponderously forward as the massed regi-ments of the Zulus, with their waving headdresses and mapped shields, stepped out to meet it. Suddenly the Zulu movements became swifter and more concerted. They began to flow through the grasses to preordained positions. One or two regiments then sat down and quietly waited to be used, while the majority began to beat their shields with their spears and drum the earth with their feet. This sound created an even more uncanny atmosphere. Yet still undaunted the strange square formed of five thousand redcoats topped by white helmets continued to shuffle steadily up the long sloping plain.

The sunlight glinted on twenty thousand spearpoints. Commands were called, from chief to warrior in each regiment. This was their home and the enemy had come to destroy it. They could not let this happen. This was their king's village, the heart of their nation, and these white-and-red strangers from across the seas would burn it to the ground if they were given the chance. Without doubt every warrior who held a spear was intent on preventing that, willing to die to stop this atrocious invasion of their heartland. Who did they think they were, these impertinent pale weak men with skin like the bellies of fish? Were they to be allowed to make their own laws to govern the mighty empire of the Zulus? People, warriors of great prowess, individually strong and toughened by a lifetime of war and hunting. They could run twice as fast as any soldier. They could leap twice as high. They could kill wild beasts with a stick. They were magnificently athletic, with throwing and hand-to-hand fighting skills that were envied throughout Africa. Were they going to allow these puny white men to overcome them?

Not today. Not here. Never in a million years.

That same sun gleamed on five thousand levelled rifles that stuck out like blunt porcupine quills from the walls of the square. It was a human fort on the march. Discipline. Regimental pride. Training. These formed the mortar that held this structure together. Grim were the faces that glared out at the surrounding Zulus. Forbidding, determined, showing no fear. Faces made of stone. Was this monstrous living fort going to crumple under an attack from a primitive people who had no machines to assist them in their fight? A people whose technology was a thousand years behind? Good God, this was the British army, the pride of a nation that had conquered and carved out one of the greatest empires known to history. Were they going to let a bunch of savages overcome them?

Not today. Not here. Never in a million years.

Seb could see Buller's cavalry riding close to the Zulu lines, firing into the black masses with their carbines. Inside the square the guns were being unlimbered. Seb then heard the order 'Fix bayonets' and the sounds associated with the action. Sunlight soon sparkled on the blades at the ends of the rifles, flashing a bristling warning at the enemy who were preparing to charge. The square opened to let in the returning cavalry, now being chased by fast-running warriors. Once inside, the cavalry dismounted and clustered near the guns and transport. Those cartridge boxes that were not already open had their lids lifted and the ammunition made ready to pass on in handfuls to the soldiers. All was made ready for the impending charge of this bunch of 'savages' who had already outmanoeuvred and overwhelmed two thousand heavily armed soldiers of the Queen to destroy them utterly.

Inside the square there was great activity. Seb, who without a command was frustrated by how little he had to do, assisted with opening boxes of ammunition, though it was hardly the work of a commissioned officer. Bullets whined around their heads from the Zulu riflemen concealed in the grasses. One or two of the cavalry officers remained in their saddles, to get a better view of the battle. One casually smoked a cigarillo and peered out over the heads of the infantry with narrowed eyes. Another was standing in his stirrups, sketching the scene around him, charcoal skating over a pad, making a visual recording of the battle to present at dinner tables back home.

The doctors prepared their instruments, winding sheets and stood ready to receive the wounded and dying.

Corporal Evans was assisting the gunners, handing them shells, and he and Seb caught each other's eyes. Seb nodded and Evans winked. There was a warm comradeship between the ex-shepherd and the schoolmaster's son now. They had grown closer together than ever should an NCO and his commanding officer. Nothing was said, of course. Nothing could be said. But each knew that a friendship had developed, despite the rank and class differences, despite the fact that one was a belligerent Welshman not fond of the English and the other thought the English were God's own people. It was an unholy brotherhood, but one which was now undeniable.

The man who was sketching leaned down and showed Seb his drawing.

'What do you think, Ensign?'

Seb, whose pictures and sketches were of the highest quality, thought the drawing was well done, and said so.

'I think,' said the artist, 'they'll get a good idea from this when I show it to those back home, eh?'

It then suddenly struck Seb as horrifying to think that such a bloody encounter, where thousands of good honest men would die, had already died or lay in mortal agony, would become entertainment for ladies and gentlemen stuffed with lobster and beef, while they drank their coffee and brandy, their port, their sweet white wine. Away from the stink of war, the noise, the screams of pain, the gore splashing on white canvas, on shields and loincloths, on helmets and boots. Away from the bursting heads and flying fragments of skull. Away from the grating sound of a bayonet or speartip scraping along live bone, boring through hard gristle, sliding through soft spongy organs, driving through an eye socket into a brain. Away from the sight of legs and arms being catapulted from their torsos. Away, away from the aftermath of corpses piled into silent heaps. Away from all that, delicate ladies would find the retelling of the tale a fascinating experience, one they could pass on to their friends and children, and men whose experience of violence amounted to an argument with a cab driver over the fare would puff out their chests in pride and proclaim the British to be unbeatable.

The big guns opened up, startling Seb and making him jump. His ears rang with the sound. A soldier in the front line was shot and his body dragged in. The smoke of war drifted over Seb with its all-familiar pungent smell. He climbed up on the back of a cart and now saw that the Zulus were advancing slowly, surrounding the square of redcoats. Seb watched the shells bursting amongst the Zulu ranks and saw them stabbing at the smoke that ensued from the explosion. He had heard that some Zulus, unfamiliar with field guns, thought that soldiers hid in the big bullets that were hurled at them and sprang out to attack them from behind. It bemused the ensign. How could they think that a man would survive coming out of a hail of shrapnel that had killed and wounded men all around them? It did not make sense. Yet, not much about war did make a great deal of sense, and that was a fact.

Orders were going out, from officers to NCOs, from NCOs to their companies, calmly and firmly, as the enemy began to erupt into a full-throated, full-blooded surge towards the waiting soldiers.

Then the blizzard of bullets as thousands of Martini-Henrys spoke in concert, a sound that few men have heard. It quickened the blood in Seb's veins as he went into battle mode. He drew his sword and yelled encouragement now to the soldiers in the front line. Ranks of four in that monstrous square formation, with greasy smoke fogging everyone's vision now, as the kneeling ranks reloaded while the standing ranks fired over their heads. Gatling guns opened up on the corners. The big guns continued to blaze away. Rockets were fired into black masses.

Zulus began to go down in their hundreds. They were as brave as ever, charging into the iron wind, but falling, falling, falling. None even got as near as a spear's throw from the hated invaders. They tried desperately to cover the ground between them and the thick ranks of redcoats. It was an impossible dream. Zulu generals cried to their young men, 'Go, go, go.' And they went, and they died with a great leap into the air, or sank with a sigh to their homeland soil. Seb watched them drop with a lump in his throat. Yes, he wanted to be on the winning side, knew that his army was the greater and the stronger, but this was a slaughter equal to that of Isandlwana. As the front ranks fell, the following ranks surged forwards, and they too fell. It was relentless, as those the Gatling guns did not scythe down the rifles chopped away.

In the square the wounded were being attended to by bandsmen who were not handing out ammunition, and the dead were receiving their last rites from the chaplain. The edges of the square presented noisy order and within it was quiet chaos. Yet this was how it worked, containing the pain and death within the disciplined ranks. To the enemy they presented a formidable unworried face. This was a solid army, not to be moved by any wild charge. It was rock hard, unyielding.

Finally, the Zulu reserves were ordered forward by an impressive man on a white horse. These warriors too were shredded as a hailstorm of grapeshot and canister flew into their ranks, and several volleys from thousands of Martini-Henrys opened up to halt their last courageous charge.

There comes a point in every battle when all know it is over, when the defeated are aware they are defeated and the victors are certain they have won the day. There is a lull, and Seb knew they had reached that moment. The guns had finally gone quiet and the yells of defiance from the enemy had died away to a whisper of wind. After the moment had passed, Lord Chelmsford ordered the 17th Lancers to leave the square and pursue the beaten Zulus, some of whom were running for their lives while others stood dazed, bemused and broken. The cavalry were cheered out of the square by the infantry and others, sent on their glorious charge with shouts of encouragement and praise.

The horsemen did their work, chasing down the retreating warriors, cutting them, felling them like saplings. They saw this as necessary to prevent regrouping and counter-attack, but in truth the Zulus had lost all heart and had no more stomach for this unequal war. One or two small groups with rifles attempted to slow the horsemen, to allow their comrades to escape over the plain, but as usual their aim was high and they took few troopers out of their saddles. The cavalry entered the kraals, jumping the thorn fences and lancing any Zulus that ran from the huts or were hiding behind them.

In the square, still thick with smoke, the guns were limbered up and the carts loaded. Then just as ponderously as it had crossed the shallows, the great human fort shuffled over the river again. The wounded were carried on stretchers, or on the backs of carts, and the dead were lugged over likewise. Seb later heard that only ten redcoats had been killed in the battle, while on the slopes he could see at least a thousand Zulus lying in their open vault of air. There had to be more of them, in the marshes, in the kraals, out on the far plain. Indeed, almost eighty soldiers had been wounded, some of whom would undoubtedly die later, but the victory had been absolute, as naturally it should have been, mainly guns against spears, trained soldiers against warriors.

Twenty-One

It always took Seb a while to get over a battle. Even one where he had played little part in the killing. The conflicting emotions, of pride in being the victor and horror at the slaughter, were hard to reconcile. An engineer who builds a bridge can step back and admire his work, but a soldier having won a war cannot do the same. Relief and 'thanks be to God for life' are there, but he cannot look over a thousand broken dead men and admire his skill as a killing machine, not unless he has the kind of psychological bent that deadens all feeling of compassion.

The army plodded back to Natal, where the towns and cities, the villages and farms waited to greet them. It was all over. The perceived threat from the Zulu empire had been expunged. Perhaps they would not be greeted as heroes, but they had done the job they been asked to do, and in the end they had done it well. Some regiments would be staying in South Africa, others would be shipping back to Britain. Seb went to see Lord Chelmsford in Pietermaritzburg, bypassing Major Stringman. Surprisingly the general was willing to meet with him.

'Yes, Ensign, what can I do for you?'

'Sir,' replied Seb, 'I wonder now – now that the war is over – whether I am to continue as Provost-Marshal here?'

Lord Chelmsford lit a cigar and stared out of the window of his temporary quarters.

'There is an increasing need for a permanent post of policeman in this man's army, Ensign.' He waved his cigar. 'Of course, I'm no longer in charge here. General Wolseley is now the Commander-in-Chief, but I doubt he'll stay long now that there's no war to sort out.' There was a pause before, 'Still, I suggest you remain in post until you are officially relieved of it by someone with the right authority.'

Seb wondered whether he had found himself an oubliette, a pit where the occupant was simply forgotten, for he felt no one would come looking to relieve him of his post. For the moment this fitted in with his plans to bring Lunt to justice. He wondered if he should bother the general with his ideas and in the end decided it was necessary.

'Sir, I beg to inform you that I have discovered the murderer of Lieutenant Shepherd, the man killed in the duel.'

The general's eyebrows shot up.

'What duel?'

Generals are busy men and their plates are heaped high with problems, so it was not surprising that Lord Chelmsford had forgotten the details of the case.

'You will remember, sir, that before we left Landsman's Drift to begin the march to Ulundi, there was a duel in which a man deloped only to be shot down in cold blood.'

The frown which had appeared on the general's brow now disappeared.

'Ah yes, yes, I do recall it. You have evidence?'

'I know who the other duellist is, and will have the evidence shortly, sir.'

'And the man?'

'A Major Lunt, of the 5th Dragoons.'

'Any reason? The motive, I mean?'

'It involves some sort of secret society, sir – a ring. The dead man apparently would not take the oath which would have bound him to his brother members. A crime occurred in India, which necessitated all the officers binding themselves to each other with such an oath.'

Chelmsford's face clouded over again. 'I see.'

'Yes, sir, something like General Wolseley's Ring.'

'Well, we must not speak of things which are only hearsay, but I am now aware of the sort of abominable band to which you are alluding.' He became angry. 'Why do men, commissioned officers for God's sake, find it necessary to form these anathemas to the natural order of Her Majesty's army? Is not loyalty to the Queen enough? Loyalty to regiment? This is misplaced pride in some dark and slimy gathering which can only end in tragedy of some kind.'

'I have to agree with you, sir.'

'Well, then, get your evidence and then we can proceed with the court martial.'

'Yes, sir.'

Seb left the general, feeling a little confused. Yes, he had been given the authority to proceed with the arrest of Major Lunt, but then what? He was to remain as Provost-Marshal over an army that had been disbanded, half of which was to stay in South Africa and the other half to be scattered over the remainder of the planet? That was not how he had envisaged his army career progressing. He had been rather hoping for a hint of promotion from the general and a return to his regiment. Now he felt like a seed floating on the wind. Not destined for anywhere. It was not a pleasant experience. Perhaps he should have asked the general for a more definite direction, but he was an Englishman and awkward about putting himself forward without being requested to.

Of course, as bad luck would have it, the first person he ran into was Major Stringman.

'Ah, Ensign Early, I have it in mind to brief you on your future duties . . .' The major then glanced at the direction from which Seb had been coming. 'Where have you been?' came the demand.

The simple reply was, 'To see the general.'

Stringman went red in the face.

'That was very impertinent.'

'The general didn't seem to think so.'

'Well, *I* think so. I specifically ordered you *not* to approach Lord Chelmsford and told you that I was your immediate superior.'

'You weren't around, sir.'

'That does not give you the right . . .'

'Look, Major,' exploded Seb, 'every time we meet there's a confrontation between us. Now, that may be partly my fault, but it certainly isn't *all* my fault. Our chemistry doesn't mix. Aren't you tired of arguing with me, sir? It's very disturbing for both of us. Why don't you simply let me get on with my job, put in written reports for you, and act like any other officer with too much on your plate? There's no need to keep badgering me. You will reap the benefits of my investigations without continually interfering in the way I carry them out.'

Stringman stared at Seb for a few moments, before he asked, 'What did you see the general about?'

'Lord Chelmsford gave me permission to follow up my discoveries in the affair of the duel.'

A pained expression crossed the major's face.

'Did he now?'

'Yes, indeed he did.' Seb started to bend the truth now and added, 'He asked me to root out the canker of these officers who form secret societies, which I intend to do with the best of my ability.'

'Societies?'

'Rings, such as the Wolseley Ring.'

Stringman went a little pale and seemed agitated.

Seb said, 'Oh my God, you're not a member, are you?'

The major cleared his expression immediately.

'No, of course not, you idiot. I'm simply concerned that your target is rather high on the instep. If you think of going after General Wolseley . . .'

Seb laughed at this. 'No, no, not General Wolseley. That would be unthinkable. But there are other rings and my suspect is a member of one. The general regards them as abominations. I intend bringing three of them to justice for the murder of Lieutenant Shepherd. Lord Chelmsford is keen on me doing so.'

Stringman obviously knew when he had been checkmated and he nodded curtly saying, 'Keep me informed, Ensign.'

'I will certainly do so, Major,' replied Seb, saluting. 'Have a good day, sir.'

Seb left to collect Amasi at the army stables and set out for Landsman's Drift. It was nightfall when he reached it. He saw that his horse was catered for and then went to his tent. Sam was there, with Tom and Corporal Evans. He got them all together and then told them his plans.

'Tomorrow I am going to take Tom to the 5th Dragoons, where I hope he'll be able to identify the man I want.'

A shiver went through Tom and he looked scared.

Noticing this, Seb said, 'Don't worry, Tom. I shall be there, and Corporal Evans. We won't let anything happen to you. In fact I would like you to bring some of the other boys who were in the tree with you when that duel took place. Can you find them for me?'

'I can find Joe and Pincy,' replied Tom, eagerly. 'I can get 'em now, if you want.'

'No, tomorrow morning will do. Now, everyone get a good night's rest – and then we'll do the job.'

Seb himself went to his tent to settle down, but Sam Weary came to see him before he blew out the lamp.

'Boss,' said Sam, his face creasing with concern, 'you be careful there, when you go to arrest 'em. Them's bad people. They kill once, and they not afraid to kill again.'

Seb nodded. 'I know, Sam. They've had a go at me already. But we've got them where we want them, now.' He sighed. 'I don't know whether I'm going to manage to make the charge stick against the seconds, but I'm going to try. In my mind they're just as guilty as Lunt. Others don't see it that way, though. They think that only the man who squeezes the trigger is guilty. We'll see. Now, Sam, how's your family? You haven't spoken of them in a while.'

'Well, boss, they're fine . . .'

Once Sam had gone, Seb reflected on the fact that six months ago he would not even have considered enquiring after a black man's family, his servant or not. But the war against the Zulus had changed him. He had seen that the colour of a man's skin was no indication as to his character or his intellect. Sam Weary was just as honest, honourable and clever as Sebastian Early. All right, Seb was more worldly, had the wisdom of travel and the knowledge of books and an upbringing in an industrial society behind him, but his intellect was no greater than this man's, the amaXhosa who cooked and cared for him. And certainly courage was not a prerogative of the white man. The bravery shown by the Zulus was equal to, perhaps even surpassing, that of the best soldiers of the Queen Seb had ever seen. To charge into the barrels of guns with only spears! It had been done by the Light Brigade at Balaclava, but that had been the result of a mistake. The Zulus were magnificent warriors. Not soldiers. They had not needed to be soldiers until now. But certainly they had the hearts of lions. Sam was of their kind, a man as full of pride and honour as Seb was himself.

The following morning Seb and Evans took the three boys to the lines where the 5th Dragoons were temporarily camped. Seb sought out the colonel, an officer by the name of Witlow. Colonel Witlow listened to what Seb had to say, but his expression changed from bored uninterest to anger the more the ensign spoke. The moustache

on his tanned lean face bristled and his grey eyes hooded over. He
was an old soldier and protective of his regimental pride.

'Are you trying to tell me, Ensign, that you intend arresting
three of my officers?'

'They may not all be in your regiment, sir.'

The major ignored this and countered with, 'For *murder*?'

'I'm sorry to say that is the case, sir.'

'You overstep your mark, Ensign. I am the colonel of this highly
respected cavalry regiment. If you come applying to me, you will
find yourself leaving with empty pockets. I do not intend handing
over any of my men, especially my *officers*, to,' he looked Seb up
and down with an expression of disgust, 'an oik out of an infantry
regiment.'

Seb did not even flinch at the insult, being now used to senior
officers regarding him with contempt.

'I'm afraid, sir, you have no choice. My office gives me the right
to arrest anyone I suspect is guilty of a serious crime. If you insist
on protecting criminals then I shall have no option but to arrest
you too, pending an enquiry. You see before you an ensign, a junior
officer of an infantry battalion, but you forget the fact that I am
the Provost-Marshal, with powers that stretch way beyond my rank.
You will, if you please sir, lead me to Major Lunt, who I intend
arresting for murder.'

The colonel looked as if he were about to explode, but his adjutant laid a hand on his sleeve and gave it a slight tug. Witlow
glanced at his face and within a minute had taken control of his
temper. The adjutant knew they were dealing with someone with
a direct line to the highest command and his warning look was
understood.

The colonel's tone changed. 'Look here, Ensign – I understand
it was a duel . . .'

'You knew about this incident?' Seb cried. 'You knew it and
did not report it?'

'Hang it all, man. These were my officers!' cried the colonel,
indignantly.

'Did you also know that the dead officer deloped and was then
shot down in cold blood?'

The colonel clearly did not know this, for his face revealed the
shock he felt on hearing these words.

'No – but, look – Major Lunt's sister . . .'

'This has nothing to do with the major's sister. I should be surprised if he's even got a sister. Colonel, you are protecting a man who sent an assassin to kill me. Fortunately his aim was poor and I was hit in the shoulder. This officer could very well be responsible for two murders.'

'You have proof of this?'

'The would-be assassin has confessed.'

The colonel went very quiet and turned away, his face grey in the morning light. Tom and his two friends were agitated and shifted their bare feet in the dust. They looked as if they wanted to be a thousand miles away. Corporal Evans, standing at the back of the boys to make sure they did not bolt, laid a hand on Tom's shoulder.

'My regiment!' whispered the colonel to himself, still turned away. '*My* regiment.'

The adjutant, a major, now spoke for the first time.

'Ensign,' he said, softly, 'Major Lunt has resigned his commission in the army. He left two days ago. No one knows where he went. He did not leave a forwarding address, nor did he say which town was his destination.'

The news stunned Seb. His quarry had escaped? He cursed himself, thinking he should have anticipated such a move. Lunt had gone. This was a big blow. 'Damnation,' he groaned.

At that moment Pincy, a black boy of about eight years, pointed with a long thin finger at a lieutenant nearby.

'He's one of 'em, ain't he, Tom. One of them that was there.'

Tom peered at the lieutenant and got excited.

'He's right, sir,' cried Tom. 'That's one of them what was at the duelling.'

The third boy confirmed the fact.

Seb marched over to the young officer, who was about to mount his horse.

'Sir, you are under arrest for the murder of Lieutenant Shepherd.'

The man, one foot in the stirrup, one hand on the saddle ready to haul himself on to his horse, went very pale. He was a big fellow, almost twice the size of Seb, being bulky as well as tall. He looked down on this officer with a red sash around his shoulder before awkwardly taking his foot out of the stirrup, getting it caught in his scabbard on the way down, and then he stood square on to the Provost-Marshal.

'You can't do this,' he said in a deep, gravelly voice. 'I was at the duel, yes, but I wasn't the duellist.'

Seb took out his notebook. 'Your name, Lieutenant?'

The officer looked surprised.

'If you don't know my name, how do you know I was at the duel?'

Seb nodded over his shoulder. 'Those boys over there witnessed the killing. They were in one of the trees. You were recognized. Will you accompany me, please? You are most definitely under arrest.'

The officer looked towards his colonel, whose bleak, grey expression told him all he wanted to know.

'All right,' he replied, 'just let me find a man to take my mount – but I assure you, I was not the fellow with the pistol. That was . . .'

'Major Lunt. I know.'

A corporal came and took the officer's horse from him. Then the lieutenant fell in beside Seb, towering over him, but not over Evans who marched purposefully behind him bearing a rifle. The three boys trotted alongside, occasionally looking up in awe at the cavalryman with the huge stride.

Tom whispered audibly to his friends, 'He don't need no horse. He could jump Blood River with them legs.'

'Quiet, Tom,' ordered Seb. 'You three boys can go now. I'll find you later.' He turned to Pincy. 'You did well. You all did well. I wish I could reward you, but I can't because that would look bad at the trial. Thank you for your help, anyway.'

The boys went off, chattering amongst themselves.

It was a bright day, the blue of the big sky being particularly deep and even. It was hot too. Very hot. Seb led the officer to a grove of trees where they would be in the shade. He did not want to take him back to his tent because when he questioned the lieutenant they would be within the earshot of others. This had to be a private affair. Evans could be there, of course, to verify any facts later, but it would not do to make this interview general gossip amongst the troops. They found a spot under a large tree with broad leaves and Seb indicated that the sweating cavalryman should sit.

'I shall remain standing,' replied the officer, 'and to be frank I object to this corporal being present.'

'Corporal Evans is an assistant provost-marshal and it is imperative for him to be here, for your sake as well as mine. If at the trial there is any dispute about what has been said here, Corporal Evans will be able to put us straight.'

'But he's *your* man,' protested the lieutenant.

'He's not my man, he's the army's man. He's an honest NCO and would no more lie for me than shoot himself in the head. I don't know what kind of men you deal with, Lieutenant, but most of those I know are not blackguards and liars.'

The lieutenant went very red, but before he had time to speak again, Seb asked him for his name once more, which he had not yet given.

'Lieutenant Felix Darby.'

Evans moved round behind Seb, so that he was facing the accused man.

'Where's he going?' asked Lieutenant Darby.

'He wants to see your mouth,' replied Seb, writing the name in his notebook. 'He's deaf. Artillery.'

'And he's supposed to remember an accurate account of what we say here today?' sneered the officer.

Seb finished writing, then replied, 'I find that his disability enables him to pay *more* attention to the conversation. He's less interested in what I say. He knows the questions I'm going to ask. It's you he's watching. Now, I am Ensign Early, Provost-Marshal for Lord Chelmsford's army. I have good reason to believe you were Major Lunt's second on the morning of the murder of Lieutenant Shepherd.'

'It was a duel, man,' came the sharp, angry reply.

'It was murder. Lieutenant Shepherd deloped and was then shot down in cold blood. Do you deny that's what happened?'

Darby's face twisted into a wry smile and he folded his arms over his chest.

'I understand that it's my word against that of a bunch of snotty urchins, one of them a little nigger.'

Seb sighed. 'Oh dear, like so many cavalrymen with limited intelligence you are so very predictable, Lieutenant. Listen to me carefully. There were more than a dozen boys who witnessed that duel, most of them as white as you. A dozen would be enough to checkmate any false statements from you, I think. Furthermore I have absolute proof that Major Lunt sent a man to kill me. In point of fact the aim was poor and I was merely wounded. Major Lunt will certainly try to spread the blame of the killing on his fellows – he's that kind of a man, isn't he? – and as such you're in the firing line. You would be wise to tell the truth from the start in order to retain your own credibility. If the court is convinced of one lie, they'll not believe the truth when you tell it.'

Panic now replaced the smugness on the face of the lieutenant.

'Ensign,' said Darby, licking his lips and staring down into the face of the junior officer, 'I was present at that duel. What you said before is true. Lieutenant Shepherd fired into the air and then Major Lunt took deliberate aim and shot him through the heart. Lunt is a very good marksman. The younger man didn't stand a chance. Now, that's all I know about the affair. I do not and did not condone it. I was as appalled as you appear to be. It was indeed no way to act at a duel. There was no honour involved, only a desire for revenge.'

Seb was scribbling in his notebook, trying to keep up with the confession.

'Desire for revenge . . .' he repeated.

'Yes,' continued Darby, shifting from one foot to another, 'for the insult to his sister.'

Seb looked up, sharply.

'What?' asked Darby, spreading his hands. 'What did I say?'

Seb was thinking that he had heard about this insult to Lunt's sister from the colonel. The colonel then, had known about the duel, yet had not reported it. In fact, it was probable that most of the regiment's officers were aware that a duel had taken place and a death had resulted. None had reported it. As a policeman this offended his sense of duty, yet he knew that were he an officer in that regiment, he would not have told anyone in authority about the duel. How could he? Snitching on one's comrades in arms was very bad form. No one would have spoken to him again. He would have been ostracized by his fellow officers, friends and enemies alike. No, he would not have spoken out.

'Let me apprise you of something, Lieutenant Darby, I know about the ring, so let's drop this pretence about a sister.'

'Ring?' said Darby. 'What ring?'

'The secret society, headed by Major Lunt.'

Darby looked genuinely puzzled. 'I don't know what you're talking about.'

Seb studied the face of the man in front of him. It seemed that Darby really did not know about the ring, but he could be a very good actor. In the end he decided to believe he was dealing with an officer who had been duped along with everyone else.

'Lieutenant Darby, I'm sorry to have to inform you that you've been the victim of a very diabolical plot. Were you with the regiment in India?'

'No – didn't join until they came back to England.'

'Something happened in India, something ugly. Major Lunt committed a heinous crime and chose to hide it by forming a secret society, a ring of officers who were bound to silence by an oath. One man present on the night of the crime refused to become part of that ring, though he obviously didn't go to the authorities. That man was the officer shot dead in front of you by Major Lunt. I'm afraid that what began as a duel ended in murder. I intend bringing Major Lunt to book. You and your fellow second will also be charged with murder.'

'No – no, please,' said Darby, now pale with anxiety. 'I had no idea. I believed it to be an honourable duel, between two willing participants, one man seeking satisfaction, the other – the other defending himself against an accusation. I had no idea – no idea that there was some sort of history between the two men which did not involve Major Lunt's family. You must believe me. I'm new to the regiment. My father – well, you know . . .'

Seb did indeed understand. Fathers lived in a world where sons were perfect officers who brought nothing but honour and pride to one's household and family name. Fathers waited for news of their sons' exploits in the army, remembering their own imperfect service with an imperfect memory. Waited to hear that their sons had been awarded a medal for bravery, or had been promoted for their outstanding part in some famous battle and were coming home to England shrouded in glory. Fathers expected their sons to bring back that which they had never managed to achieve, in order to expunge from their minds that horrible thing that had lurked there since youth: *failure*.

Seb said to Darby, 'You didn't know about the ring?'

'I swear. I was with my friend, Willoughby, Captain Willoughby, when Major Lunt asked him to be his second. I volunteered as well, since they seemed keen for me to be there too. I thought it was a genuine duel. I know, I know. They're illegal now, but more senior and more important men than I are still involved in duels. Of course,' Darby licked his lips and his face creased in spiritual pain, 'when I saw what happened I was as appalled as anyone would be – a man fired into the air and then just stood there while his opponent shot him dead – but I thought Shepherd must have wanted to die, for his crime, you know, for violating Lunt's sister. That's a horrible thing to do to another officer's sister and I had nothing but contempt for the man.

'Yet now you say that wasn't true. Lunt lied to me. He told me he was so enraged by the thought of this man Shepherd raping his sister he had no control over himself, over his actions. His blood was heated to boiling point and he shot the officer in a red haze. I believed him. I did. You must believe me.'

'And you told no one about the incident.'

Lieutenant Darby laughed. 'No one? I told everyone. So did Willoughby. So did Lunt. Everyone thought Lunt had done the right thing, by avenging his sister. Of course we kept the fact of the delopement from certain persons, like the colonel, but certainly quite a few officers knew exactly what had happened. No one blamed him for his actions, thought them untoward. He was a hero. Everyone understood that his fury had taken over and he had no choice but to kill Shepherd.'

Seb had guessed that the whole regiment was aware of the crime, but they had concluded that Shepherd had got his just deserts. Certainly none would have thought of reporting the incident to the Provost-Marshal. Not Darby, not the colonel, not even Lunt's enemies – and every field officer has a few of those: none came forward. Any man who had done would have been despised by his fellows and cut dead.

'Lieutenant, do you believe that Captain Willoughby was a member of Lunt's Ring?'

'I have no idea.'

'If you were to guess.'

'I think – I think it probable. But if you're going to arrest

Captain Willoughby now, you won't find him here. A squadron has gone with a party to Isandlwana, to bury more of the dead there. Captain Willoughby is leading that squadron.'

'Lieutenant Darby, I feel sorry . . .'

Darby pursed his lips. 'Don't pity me! I don't need it.'

Seb nodded. 'So be it, but I shall need you as a witness when Major Lunt and Captain Willoughby are court-martialled. You have been unwittingly dragged into this mess, but unfortunately you are now part of it. I doubt you'll be charged with any crime yourself, but you'll have to look forward to at least a reprimand for seconding a duel.'

The lieutenant nodded, stiffly, and marched away. When he was about twenty paces from Seb, he turned and asked, 'Do you like your job, Ensign? I should hate it. I think it foul work for an officer.'

'Do I like it?' Seb was surprised to be asked such a question, for he had not thought about whether he enjoyed doing what he did. 'I'm sure I don't know. Do *you* like killing people? It's not a question of like, it's a question of duty. Oh, I know, no one is fond of a policeman. But people like criminals less, and someone's got to do the dirty work of bringing them to justice. To answer your question, I don't need to like it, I just need to do it to the best of my ability, as I would any job.'

Twenty-Two

Once again Seb turned to the Boer for assistance. Yes, he and Evans could have ridden out to Isandlwana together, but though the Zulus had been defeated many of them would not accept that state of affairs. Cetshwayo was their paramount chief – king was an epithet given him by the white men – but there were many lesser chiefs, some of them proud enough to have confronted Cetshwayo himself in their time. There would be clans out there quite happy to attack a lone British officer and his corporal. Zululand had not suddenly been transformed into a safe haven for white people, especially those wearing a red coat.

Pieter Zeldenthuis knew the country, knew the climate, knew the hidden dangers, and so it was to him that Seb turned. The Boer remonstrated at first, of course, said he was no longer employed by the British army and therefore had no obligations to anyone wearing a red coat, but Seb also knew that this frontiersman, this man of the African bush, could not resist an adventure. It took very little persuading to get him along on the trek. They left Evans behind and entered Zululand by the now well-trodden path which Chelmsford's army, subsequent suppliers and couriers had used.

The evening sun burned hot and orange in the wide sky. Game in that region was scarce, but they saw one or two interesting antelope as they walked their horses. The river had been low enough to wade across mounted and the two steeds had a ring of green scum end to end around their middles from the still-water reed beds on the Zulu side. Seb was wearing his oldest uniform, the one that had faded to a washed-out purple colour, and his dirtiest helmet. There was no sense in getting good clothes grimed and the seams stained by red dust. His attire was covered in small holes and tears, and his boots were so engrained with dirt they would never shine again. He looked a sad sight beside the Boer in his stiff cotton shirt and riding breeches, with his calf-length boots and wideawake hat tied around with a puggaree that flew like a banner from it.

Pieter was carrying his bolt-action .43 Mauser, a rifle which had accounted for several lives in this war. Seb had a Martini-Henry carbine, borrowed from a quartermaster who promised him hell if he did not return it in its perfect condition. Both men carried Webley revolvers and Seb wore a sword. Finally, Pieter had on his belt a hunting knife of which the late Jim Bowie of Alamo fame would have been proud.

Besides arms, the pair had water for five days, food for three days, and blankets for the night hours. They rode through the mellow light which burned the reddening plain ahead of them and gave the clouds a base of old gold. Lizards scuttled out of the way of the horses' hooves. Small mammals sought the sanctuary of rocks. Birds of prey swept the darkening blue with their feathered wings. A poet would have made much of that evening. It was quiet and still, an innocent evening with no blood on its hands, and it closed around the two riders enfolding them in a blanket of warm dust and air. But neither of these men was inclined towards poetry, not the sort of poetry of the written word, though both had expansive spirits able to feel the tranquil beauty. Their souls appreciated the loveliness of the scene, if not their minds.

'So,' said Seb, as they settled down to a supper of fried eggs and bacon before a campfire, 'how do you feel now that all the fighting's over?'

'Ag, it might be over for you, friend – but not for us. The Zulus will still be here when you've gone, and your countrymen keep pressing us, even though we've moved into the Transvaal. Seems your Queen is never satisfied with the size of her empire. She wants more and more.'

Seb gave the Boer a wry grin in the firelight.

'Not sure it's Victoria who wants it all. In fact I don't really know who does. Politicians, I suppose. It increases their power. But then they're a temporary lot, in and out like nobody's business. Merchants, certainly, want the advantages of privileged trade. India was ideal for that, until John Company started collecting taxes there, and began to treat it like a satrapy. Certainly I suppose it's nice for settlers to come to Africa and start a farm, but we're still heavily outnumbered here by you lot, and both the Boers and the Brits are outnumbered by the blacks, so the future is still unstable.'

'So, what's going to happen to you, bru? You still policing the place, now it's all over?'

'For a while,' replied Seb. 'Things haven't settled yet.'

'Wolseley going to stay here?'

'I don't know. I doubt it.'

'Somebody will probably shoot that Bartle Frere.'

'Well, if they do, I hope I don't have to investigate it. This case is bad enough. No one seems to want to bring a bad man to justice. He's up and flown, thinking he's out of my reach. I'm really not sure of my jurisdiction, but if Lunt thinks that by leaving the service I'll let him go, he's much mistaken. I'll bring him in and *then* decide whether I've a right to or not. If he's the kind of man I believe him to be, he'll think himself beyond military law. He'll think I'll be happy to have him out of my hair. Well, he's mistaken in Ensign Early. I'm a man who sees a job through and he won't wriggle off my hook.'

'Whoa, bru – you're singeing your own hair.'

Seb laughed at this, realizing he was taking himself too seriously, and picked a piece of bacon up between his forefinger and thumb, out of the sizzling fat. He held it over his mouth and dropped it. The fat burned his tongue but he kept the pain to himself. He had meant everything he had said. In fact, he had left Evans and Sam Weary the task of spreading the word that he was going to hunt down the ex-major. He wanted Lunt to know he was not getting away with murder. If it was the last thing Ensign Early did, he was going to drag Lieutenant Shepherd's murderer to trial.

The two men rolled themselves into blankets and slept the night through until dawn. They woke to find themselves ringed by armed black warriors creeping towards their camp. It was the horses that had stirred them awake, whinnying and shuffling in their hobbles. One of the warriors, on seeing that the men were now alert to the danger, tried to rush the camp and grab himself some glory, only to be shot dead by two revolvers that blasted almost simultaneously in the dawn. Seb had been right to think the war was not completely over. Here was a clan that was not ready to lie down and be trodden on by redcoats and Boers.

'How many?' cried Seb, lying behind the saddle he was using as a shield. 'Any idea?'

'Enough to keep us busy for a while,' replied his companion, who was sliding his Mauser out of its holster. 'My guess is around thirty.'

Several spears thudded into the ground around them, one striking a rock and sending sparks flying as it skidded away. The long grasses were at least eighty yards from the camp, so there was quite a bit of open ground between the now hidden Zulus and the defending pair. Behind them was rocky ground where there might be more warriors tucked away, but any boulders large enough to hide a man were at least two hundred yards from them. They felt they were in a good defensive position, in the donga Pieter had chosen for the night's camp. That feeling lasted at least until the first bullet zinged off a stone close to Seb's head and then ricocheted, clattering into more stones close to the horses.

'They've got a firearm,' muttered Seb.

'Maybe more than one,' replied Pieter.

Neither of them said, *Thanks to the British army*, but both thought it, as they fired in what they believed to be the direction of the man with the Martini-Henry rifle.

If these Zulus had been at Ulundi, they had learned little from the recent battle. They gathered for a charge and came roaring out of the tall grass, only to be met by rapid fire from the two rifles. After the first few had gone down, the remainder retreated back into the cover. There the two white men could hear them discussing in loud voices whether to attempt another charge.

'You know what they're saying?' asked Seb, prising a stubborn empty cartridge case out of the breech of his Martini-Henry.

'Yes, the loud one wants another go, his friend is telling the others that there's too many of us.'

'Too many? Two?'

'Well, the poor beggar needs an excuse, eh? He's saying there's more of us behind the rocks.'

'What rocks?'

'Like I said, he needs an excuse to run. Wait, wait, yep, there's one out there, running. They've lost the taste. Let's send a few more shots into the grasses and help the rest of them to make up their minds for good.'

This the pair did, blazing away happily into tall, swaying green grass that waved like the sea. The Zulus never emerged again and had presumably slipped away like eels through a weed island in the Sargasso. Nevertheless, the two men kept a vigilant eye on the landscape for more breakaway groups of warriors, keen to have a last whack at the whites. For some men the war is not over until *they* decide it is. Just as over in America there were Southerners who continued to battle on in small groups after Robert E. Lee had surrendered the main rebel army, so there were Zulu warriors whose pride would not allow them to stop fighting just because their king had told them the war had been lost. Pride is a fierce emotion. Especially the pride of a fighting man.

When the two white men arrived at Isandlwana they found British and South African soldiers digging graves and gathering pieces of kit to be carried back to Natal on ox-carts. There was a major in charge of the operation, to whom Seb reported, saying he had come to arrest Captain Willoughby of the 5th Dragoons. The major was naturally shocked and surprised to hear of the charge against the captain and told Seb that the squadron of 5th Dragoons led by the captain were out patrolling the surrounding countryside.

'They'll be back soon,' he said. 'I hope you're not wrong over this business, Ensign. To bring a man to his court martial and find he's cleared of the charge would leave you in an awkward position.'

'Oh, I don't think so, sir,' replied Seb, coolly. 'It's not my job to judge the man, only to gather as much evidence as I can and present the man and the evidence to the court. The court may decide there are mitigating circumstances allowing reasonable doubt as to his guilt. That's nothing to do with me. My duty as Provost-Marshal will have been carried out to the best of my ability, I hope.'

'But to accuse a fellow officer . . .'

'You must not think of me as that, but as a policeman. If it were my own father, I would take him in.'

The major stared at Seb, before saying, 'You must have ice-water in your veins, Ensign.'

Seb made no reply. He was not as cold-hearted as the major believed him to be. It took a great deal of resolve to arrest another officer, possibly one who had stood by his side in a recent battle, perhaps even saved his life without him knowing it. But he had to detach himself from those sorts of thoughts and feelings. If a man is believed to have committed a crime, he must be brought to judgement. Seb would be the first to shake his hand if he were found innocent of the charge, though the man himself would probably scorn that gesture, believing – as most men do – that there is personal motive in a policeman's actions. The Provost-Marshal sees himself as a disinterested body, carrying out his duty. The accused sees him as the enemy incarnate in friendly clothing, bent on ruining him.

Walking away from the major, Seb's gaze roamed over that haunted place known as Isandlwana, sensing the great sorrow amongst the soldiers who were cleaning up after the terrible defeat. He felt it too, deep down, the shame of being beaten, the dreadful loss of comrades. His regiment. His. He had once visited Culloden, in Scotland, where the Highlanders and the flower of Scottish pride had perished. There had been that same eerie atmosphere and sense of sadness. A feeling that this should never have happened to such brave men. This vast open-vaulted plain was now the graveyard of two thousand courageous souls. It was the very opposite in physical character to a cathedral crypt, but it had the same ambience. The same hallowed air and dark melancholy.

Here British pride had been trampled in the dust. Here were drummer boys amongst the dead. Boys disembowelled and hung by their drum straps, their light corpses left to swing in the wind. Here were soldiers who had fought to the last ounce of their energy, taking down warrior after warrior before joining them on the ground. Here too were the Kaffirs and other black Africans who had fought on the British side, their dismembered cadavers tangled with the arms and legs of their white officers. This hollow land of red dust and rock, with its moaning wind, would henceforth be a place of ghosts that would never know rest.

In England this battle would be fought over and over again, at a dinner table, or by classes of cadets, or by military academics and students of warfare. *This is what the commanders should have done,* they would argue in hindsight, *if they had done this, or that, they would have held them off, won the fight.* Battles are so easily won at the dinner table or in the classroom that were lost in the real world because of small blunders – or not even mistakes, just circumstances of the time. Another few minutes here, another several yards there, and all would have been different. The lines would have been tighter, the men better prepared, the tents struck, the ammunition more readily available. Then, instead of this great feeling of grief, there would be celebrations, a proud symbol on the Regimental Colour, another Trafalgar or Waterloo. Instead, the glory belonged to the Zulus, whose oral history had been enriched by a great victory.

Seb stared at a cloud of dust on the horizon and wondered if this was his prey, out there guarding him and the others. Then his thoughts were interrupted by a slap on his shoulder. He turned and was delighted to see the grinning face of Mad Henry before him.

'I thought the wind was blowing from the South-East,' cried Henry, surprisingly dressed smartly and soberly in his best uniform. 'How are you, young rooster?'

'Nervous,' replied Seb, smiling at the eccentric aristocrat. 'I'm here to arrest an officer.'

Henry presented his wrists and screwed up his face.

'Sorry, guvnor,' he said in a weak attempt at a cockney accent, 'I din't mean to do 'er in, 'onest.'

'Not you, you fool,' laughed Seb. 'No, sadly this is a real arrest. My man is out there, a Captain Willoughby, of the 5th Dragoons.'

'He done her in, did he?'

'Helped to do a lieutenant in – but, Henry, you know I'm not supposed to discuss cases with those not involved, so please forget I said that.'

'My dear boy, it hardly even goes in these days, let alone allowing it to go out.' Henry's face lost none of its cheerful expression, but he added seriously, 'Watch yourself, South-East. Willoughby is no frilled shirt.'

'I shall, Henry. Thank you.'

Later in the day the dragoons rode into camp looking tired and dusty. Seb saw a captain heading the squadron. He was a big man, tall and well-built, every inch a soldier. There was a scar down his right cheek and his nose was slightly crooked, a sure sign of experience in battle. The broad face, however, revealed an officer for whom constant displeasure was not very far below the surface and Seb knew instantly that his men would have suffered abuse under his discontented command. Willoughby barked at his troopers and they dismounted and led their horses away to drink. A servant took Willoughby's charger and the captain strode towards the major's tent at the same time as removing some heavily stained white gloves. Seb allowed the two men to converse for a while, the major nodding in Seb's direction, and the captain turning to stare at Seb. Then there appeared to be an altercation, after which Captain Willoughby marched towards Seb. The captain stopped and with a sneer on his face looked Seb up and down in a contemptuous fashion before saying, 'If you think I'm coming with you, you little guttersnipe, you're very much mistaken. I'll ride back to Ladysmith in my own good time.'

Some of the other dragoons heard the remark and came wandering across to see what the raised tone was about.

Seb tried to keep the tremor out of his voice, as he said, 'I'm sorry, Captain, but you do need to accompany me.'

'On whose orders?'

'I need no orders. I am the Provost-Marshal. I have the authority to ask any man to accompany me, whatever his rank or status.' Seb flicked his red sash. 'If you have any complaints, you can register them with the senior staff when we get to Landsman's Drift, or Ladysmith.'

'I said *no*. Are you deaf?'

At that moment there was the sound of a rifle bolt loading a round into a breech, then a tall shadow fell over both men.

A voice with a clipped accent said, 'Ag, you'll do as you're told, man. Stop causing a bloody fuss and get a fresh horse or I'll blow your fucking head off. I've not got all month to argue with a bloody snotnose Englishman's son. I've got a damn farm that needs my attention.'

Pieter Zeldenthuis now stood beside Seb. Seb glanced at the Boer and saw that his face was grim and unyielding. Would he shoot the captain? He just might. He was an unpredictable man, fond of shooting people. Seb was embarrassed by Pieter's intervention. It was hardly constitutional. Yet bullies like Captain Willoughby needed rougher treatment than an honourable officer deserved. There was clearly no dignity in the man. He was used to treating soldiers with lesser rank like scum and getting away with it.

Willoughby stared at the rifle in disbelief, then his face turned thunderous.

'Who the fuck are you?' he screeched, his hand going to the hilt of his sabre.

'Your arresting officer,' snapped Seb, stepping in front of the muzzle of Pieter's Mauser, just in case he *did* squeeze the trigger. 'Now remove your hand from your sword, if you please, Captain. You!' Seb pointed at one of the troopers now gawping at this amazing scene. 'Get the captain a mount. Now!'

The man looked at his commander, but just as Willoughby was about to shout something at him, the major called, 'Do as the Provost-Marshal says.'

The poor trooper seemed uncertain, but in the end turned and walked towards the corral where the horses were kept. Some of the other dragoons stepped in front of him, to prevent him going any further, but an order from the major had the ranks parting and letting him through. The line had melted very quickly. The captain was a 5th Dragoon, yes, but not a very popular one, as Seb had guessed earlier.

The trooper returned some minutes later with a horse saddled and ready to ride. During this time Captain Willoughby and Pieter Zeldenthuis had been staring at one another through narrowed eyes. Clearly Seb was not worth bothering about. The captain's enemy was this Boer with the rifle pointed at his gut, for Seb had stepped aside again, now that the immediate danger of a flare-up was over.

'Right, mount up, sir,' ordered Seb, in a husky voice, know-ing that the sooner they got this officer out of the camp, the better.

'It'll be dark soon,' growled Willoughby.

Seb replied, 'We'll ride until then.'

Willoughby mounted, then turned in the saddle, yelling, 'Well, some idiot get me some bloody water, will they? I haven't had a blasted drink yet.'

One of his men, his servant, ran up with a canteen and handed it to his officer.

'5th Dragoons,' snarled the captain, as the other pair mounted, 'I'll remember you did nothing when they took your commanding officer away.'

Someone, a man hidden by his fellows, made a derogatory remark in a low voice, and several others laughed at it.

'I'll remember that, too, Swanson.'

A trooper, presumably Swanson, cried out, 'That weren't me, sir . . . it was . . .' but nothing else came out, as the man no doubt recalled that if one snitched on one's comrades one was likely to get a beating from the rest of them.

Once out of the camp, with Seb alongside the captain and Pieter riding behind him, his Mauser unsheathed and the butt resting on his hip, Seb said, 'That was totally unnecessary. Have you no dignity, sir?'

'I'm not one of your biblical meek, Ensign.'

'I can see that.'

'Bloody angry bastard, if you ask me,' Pieter called from behind. 'Well, there's plenty of those in Africa, boyo, so don't think you're special.'

Seb turned in the saddle with a pained expression. 'Please, Pieter, you're not making things easier.'

'Good. I want this loskop to know where we stand.'

'Oh, I'm well aware where we stand, yarpy,' replied the captain without turning round. 'You may have cause to regret that later.'

Pieter let out a short harsh laugh, but no reply.

They managed to ride ten miles before the light faded. After they had made camp, Pieter came to Seb and suggested they tie up their prisoner. Seb refused. An officer of the Queen bound with ropes? It was unthinkable. He told Pieter that officers were always permitted their dignity and that open arrest was the normal way to deal with them. Pieter pointed out that just a few hours ago, Seb had said that the prisoner had 'no dignity' and that this was a case of murder. Seb replied brusquely that the prisoner was not being charged with the actual murder, but with assisting in the murder, which was a different thing altogether. They continued to argue, but in the end it was the Provost-Marshal's decision and Seb prevailed. Willoughby was permitted to roam around the camp free of any restrictions.

When it came time to bed down, Pieter said, 'I'll take the first watch.'

'Fine,' replied Seb, 'wake me in two hours.'

However, as the two men were talking, they heard the sound of a rifle being loaded, then the words, 'You can drop that Mauser, yarpy.'

The two men turned to look down the small black hole which was the muzzle of Seb's Martini-Henry carbine.

Pieter said angrily to Seb, 'You left your *weapon* in his reach?'

'Never mind the recriminations,' growled Willoughby, 'you can sort that out later. Just drop the Mauser.'

Pieter let his own rifle fall to the ground. Seb was staring in amazement and horror at the captain, his erstwhile prisoner.

'Do you know what you've done, man? Good God, you would most likely have never appeared before a court martial for the crime of assisting at Major Lunt's duel. You could have argued that you knew nothing about what he intended to do and that he was the senior officer there and you had to obey his orders. Most of the senior staff I've spoken to think the prosecution wouldn't have stood a cat's chance in Hell of success. It was only me, pursuing my duty. Now? Now you've changed the whole situation, and extremely gravely. To threaten a provost-marshal with a firearm? A dishonourable discharge at the very least.'

'I don't think it will come to that, Ensign,' replied Willoughby, 'you see, I intend killing you both.'

A trickle of fear went down Seb's back. The darkness was falling rapidly on the deep red plains of Zululand. Distant ridges of hills looked black and low on the horizon. The world was closing for the night. This was a lonely place, the only witnesses to murder the wildlife, and even that was few and far between. Everything had suddenly gone very still, as if in expectation of this heinous crime. Even the rocks and the tall waving grasses seemed to be watching and waiting for the event to take place. Seb stared at Willoughby's face, seeing only a harsh, uncompromising expression. This officer was clearly either insane or without conscience. He had dug himself a pit whose dirt would cover him with dishonour.

'You can't be serious,' Seb said.

The tall, battered-faced, well-built officer with the Martini-Henry obviously thought otherwise, because he smiled. 'I shall be extremely dirty and dishevelled when I ride back to Isandlwana to report that you were both killed by the Zulus, your bodies mutilated by the savages. Hacked to pieces, in fact, while I managed to escape on horseback, unable to help you at all because my weapons had been confiscated by the very men I could have saved. Oh, the irony of it will amuse those who despise policemen as much as I do, believe me. As you say, Ensign, once you're dead this whole case will be dropped, since the only one interested in bringing it to court seems to be you. My good friend Major Lunt will be able to re-join his regiment and we'll all be one big happy family again.'

'One big happy ring.'

Willoughby laughed. 'Oh, you know about that, then?' He raised the rifle and took aim at Pieter Zeldenthuis. 'You first, yarpy. I never could stand Boers. Uncouth, ill-mannered creatures. Worse than the niggers . . .'

'You'd better shoot good, loskop, because the moment you do I'm going to draw my pistol and blow your fucking head off.'

'HEY, YOU OVER THERE? ANYONE GOT A LIGHT?'

Captain Willoughby turned slightly in the direction of the voice, a frown on his brow. In the next instant there was the sound of a shot and his head jerked back, his helmet coming off and rolling away towards the tent. He fell like a pole, backwards to hit the dust with an audible thump. The rifle went spinning away from his fingers to land at the feet of a man who appeared out of the gloom. He was not especially tall, but he had the bearing of an aristocrat. His stride was confident, his gait languid and easy. He had an unlit pipe in his mouth.

'Henry!' cried Seb. 'Am I glad to see you!'

'I should hope so,' replied Mad Henry, striking a match which flared to reveal his unruffled features. 'You almost bought it there, young rooster.' He lit his pipe, puffed on it for a moment, then poked the body of the captain with his toe. 'Nasty beggar, eh? Never did take to him. Good shot, man,' he added, to Pieter. 'Quick on the draw, eh? I like the way you did that. You have to show me some time. Never know when it'll come in useful. Almost in the centre of the forehead. And in this poor light.'

In fact, Willoughby was still alive, and tried to say something, his mouth moving slowly and deliberately. Seb stared, fascinated, while the man worked the muscles of his mouth but made no sound, his protruding eyes fixed on Seb's own, as if they were exchanging secrets. Then the captain's body jerked several times, before going limp and still.

The idea that a man could still be alive with a bullet in his brain was unnerving and Seb stood there shaking a little, wide-eyed, staring down at the corpse. Then he shook himself and turned to join his companions. They were talking calmly.

Pieter had a smoking revolver in his hand, and was explaining to Henry what had followed the shout. 'My hand was halfway to the holster when you called. Without that distraction it would have been futile, but I couldn't just let him blow me away without trying.'

'Henry, how did you know? Why follow us?'

'Oh, I knew Willoughby very well. Know his family too. He's the second son of three. The other two are all right, but this one has been a little touched in the head since birth. I once saw him kill a girl's pet dog for fun, when we were both around twelve years of age. Couldn't shoot him myself, of course, that wouldn't have done at all. Family already displeased with me. This would have horrified them. So I had to rely on you, Sir Seldom-at-home. Good shot. Very good shot. Yes, I guessed he would try *something*, though I wasn't sure exactly what. Just a wee bit too fond of violence, you see. Watched him in battle. Actually enjoys chopping arms, heads and legs off, all that sort of thing. His face is suffused with passion when he does it. You'd think he gets some sort of sexual excitement from the act. Loony.'

That claim, coming from Mad Henry, was *very* ironic.

'Well,' sighed Seb, looking down at the dead officer, 'this won't be easy to explain, when we get back, but . . .'

Mad Henry stayed with the pair for the night, then set off back towards Isandlwana. Seb and Pieter strapped the corpse to the captain's horse and rode back with him to Landsman's Drift without stopping. There he reported to Major Stringman, who walked around the dead man on the horse with a glazed look in his eyes, as if hoping to find some sign of life.

'You *killed* him?'

'Yes, well no, not me. The Boer scout did that.'

'But he was threatening you with your own rifle? Captain Willoughby, I mean.'

'Yes, sir.'

'It was not a prank? I mean, the captain was not having a joke with you.'

Seb shook his head. 'He fully intended to kill us.'

'My God, what a mess,' murmured the major. 'What a dreadful mess. But,' he seemed to rally, 'you have a witness in Lieutenant Wycliffe. He's a reliable officer, isn't he? Well thought of by the general, I should think? Sober and dependable?'

'Um, yes,' came the reply, but Stringman seemed not to notice the doubt in Seb's tone. The major was too absorbed in the enormity of what had happened and in how it should be reported.

'There'll be an enquiry, of course.'

'Yes, sir, of course.'

'And thank God it was a Boer who killed him and not a brother officer.'

'I would have shot him, sir, had I the chance.'

Stringman wheeled on Seb. 'Yes, but you didn't. And don't say things like that at the enquiry. It won't do you – or me – any good. You know that. You're just trying to bait me. This is not the time for a war between us, Ensign. We have to stick together tighter than brothers on this one. You understand? This is the sort of thing that raises questions in the House back home. The man's family can raise all sorts of hell, however unjustified. If you value your reputation, you will follow my lead in this. Am I understood? The captain was . . . not himself.'

Seb realized the major was right. Whatever the justification for killing Captain Willoughby, a previously respectable officer from a good family had been shot down in cold blood. His family would be outraged, no matter that an ensign and a Boer claimed they were being held at gunpoint and threatened with execution. Friends, family, relations, even acquaintances and newspaper reporters would say, 'Couldn't you have disarmed him?' or 'Why didn't you just run away?' Stupid post-event ideas that had been utterly impossible at the time. Grief blots out reason. Even if the enquiry exonerated Seb, he knew there would be those who would say, 'No smoke without fire,' and think there could have been another, more honourable outcome.

'I understand perfectly, sir. Captain Willoughby fully intended to squeeze the trigger being temporarily unhinged at the time. Afterwards, he might have regretted his action, but war does strange things to a man's mind and causes him to act in a way abnormal to his nature. It was not his fault. He was ill. The massacre at Isandlwana had obviously been playing on his mind for some time and finally, when he went back, the full horror of what had happened there affected his mind.'

'Perfect, remember that speech for the court.'

Twenty-Three

There were three letters waiting for Seb at Ladysmith, which he took back to his quarters to savour. At least, two of them were to be opened and read slowly and carefully. The third was from his dead friend Peter's sister, Gwen. He ripped this one open and scoured the lines quickly, his heart beating fast. Yes, there it was, Gwen was pleased to tell Sebastian, her late brother's dearest friend and lifetime companion, that she had accepted an offer from her beloved 'Alfred'.

'*You will remember Alfred, Sebastian, he was the curate who assisted at your uncle William's funeral . . .*'

Seb did indeed remember good old Alf, who was to be congratulated on winning Gwen for his bride, a scenario Seb had prayed for if he had not initiated it with his last letter. However, as is so often the case with young men and their pride, now this event had come about, yes indeed, a fervently hoped-for result, he was a little piqued. There was no mention in the letter that Gwen was pining for him and had taken Alfred as a substitute after an interminable wait. Well, thought the ensign, that would have been a little too much, but perhaps *some* hint that she would have preferred Sebastian Early, the dashing officer of the 24th Foot, to a measly vicar-in-waiting with a penchant for grovelling at the hem of the bishop's robe? No hint of sadness, nor wistful complaint of what might have been. Just '*. . . I know you will be happy for me, Sebastian, now your childhood friend has found a perfect partner for life.*'

'Perfect?' Seb muttered pompously, wearing a frown, rustling the pages of the lavender-scented notepaper in irritation. 'As to that, I hope he makes her a reasonable husband and does not put upon her too much. These vicars expect their wives to run around the parish with pastoral gowns on, caring for the sick and poor night and day, without a worry for the health of their own family. If he does not treat her right, he will answer to me, this Alfred-of-the-cloth fellow.'

That said, he put the letter aside and completely forgot about both Gwen and her perfect Alfred within two minutes.

The next letter, the first of the savoured, was from Seb's father, who was still devastated by the news of Isandlwana, but proud of his son's promotion to Provost-Marshal.

'Not so much a promotion, Father, as a punishment,' murmured Seb.

Finally there was a long, long letter from his older sister, Megan, who missed him greatly and wished he would come home soon. Megan was married to the owner of an ironworks and had moved to Derbyshire to raise her own family. She now had two children, Seb's nieces, delightful little girls with shrill voices. Megan, he was sure, was making a wonderful mother and a dutiful wife. Her husband Roger was a boring fellow with a voice that droned, full of good advice to young soldiers, but fortunately he was not fond of writing letters. Megan, though, seemed happy, and was left to raise the girls in her own way, her husband being far too immersed in business matters to interfere. Had there been a boy, or if a boy should come along next, well that would probably be entirely different.

That evening, while Seb was warming a glass of squareface with his hands, Corporal Evans arrived in Ladysmith in the company of Sam Weary and young Tom. Seb was pleased to see his crew, having slipped into a maudlin state with the gin. He greeted them with soft words and even shook Sam's hand, saying he was glad the war was over. Then he sparred with Tom for a few minutes, leaving the delighted youngster gasping for breath, and went for a walk with Evans to talk over the possibility of tracking down their arch-enemy, Major Lunt.

'No need for that, sir,' shouted Evans. 'He's sent you a note.'

'Sent me a note?' The hair on Seb's neck rose. 'I don't understand.'

Evans came to a halt under the light of a lamp and signed his next few sentences.

This Lunt beggar is at the farmhouse of that woman who came to see you, the Scotch lass. He says for you to come and get him. He says to go alone. If you don't, he'll kill the girl certain sure. I say we take a troop down there and get him, sir, before he harms the lass.

'Mary?' whispered Seb, shocked to the core. 'He'd hurt a woman to get to *me*?'

I reckon he hates you for making him leave the army, sir, that's what it is.

Seb signed, *No troopers. I don't want anything to happen to Mary. I'll have to do as he says and go alone.*

He'll shoot you dead, sir – the advantage is with him, like, since he's there and you've got to approach him.

The ensign looked his corporal in the eyes. 'That's true, Evans, but what choice do I have? That farm is on a flat plain. You can see someone approaching from twenty miles away. If I go with soldiers, he'll have time to kill her and escape. I can't put her life at risk. I must go alone.'

'I'll come too,' bawled Evans. 'You got to have me to watch out for you, sir.'

I know your courage, Evans, and I'm mindful of your dedication to duty, but this situation is too delicate. I may be at a disadvantage, but at least I know I'm at a disadvantage. I must just hope to get the better of this desperate man, who seems to have no conscience.

Seb took the note from his corporal and studied it under the lamplight. It did indeed say all that Evans had conveyed to him. But how on earth did Lunt know of Mary Donaldson, and Seb's attraction to her? Oh, wait, he thought. Of course. That was where the Indian, Gupta, had trailed him to. Private Gupta must have told Lunt about the farmhouse and the man and woman who lived there. And what about Mary's father? There was no mention of the old man in the note. Had Lunt already killed Mr Donaldson? It was all rather bad.

'I'll set out in the morning, Evans. I'm relying on you not to tell anyone about this, especially not Major Stringman.'

I'll be in big trouble if you don't come back.

'No, you won't. No one will know you're involved. All you have to say is your officer rode out to the home of his lady friend. If I'm not back in a week, I expect you'll be asked where I am. You have my permission at that point to send a troop after me.'

'Yes, sir. Good luck.'

'Thank you, Corporal.'

The next morning, Seb saddled Amasi and set out towards the farm owned by Mary Donaldson's father. He rode through the streets of Ladysmith, observing the peacetime activities of the soldiery. Bands of redcoats were enjoying rowdy strolls through the markets, calling after pretty women and making a thorough nuisance of themselves. A soldier is never at his best when idle amongst the civilian population. If he is not already by nature a restless beast, he has been turned into one by participation in bloody conflict and army adventures. He has marched over waterless deserts, tramped up mountain ranges, forded savage rivers, lost himself in thick forests, all purely for the purpose of killing strangers, or getting himself killed by one. His philosophy is that once let off the leash he is entitled to a certain lawlessness of behaviour and if the damn civilians don't like it, they can go hang themselves.

Seb avoided a cart by going up on the boardwalk for a moment, Amasi's hooves thumping on the planks. The town was busy once again and commerce and business was thriving. Now that the 'threat' of a Zulu invasion was past, those who had fled the town were returning. Mostly they were British colonials, but there were some Boers amongst them, and of course indigenous people. Out of this throng of carts, wagons, horses and people a rider came towards Seb. It was Pieter Zeldenthuis and Seb knew instinctively that Corporal Evans had disobeyed his orders and had informed the Boer of Seb's mission.

Pieter fell in beside Seb. 'Ag, how are you, bru?'

'I'm fine. You can't come with me.'

'Man, you need some help here. This rooinek major, he's a dangerous fellow.'

'I know,' replied Seb, 'and don't think I don't appreciate your offer, Pieter, but I've got to do this myself. If Lunt sees you, he'll kill Mary. And anyway, this is my fight, not yours.' He reined in his mount and stared Pieter in the eyes. 'We haven't always agreed, you and me – but I do look on you as a friend now, Pieter. You've come through for me many times. Not this one, though. I really do need to take care of Lunt myself.'

'I can't see you killing one of your own kind, Seb.'

'What must be done, must be done. I will if I have to. Especially to protect a lady of whom I've grown rather fond.'

'St George, eh?' said Pieter, grinning.

'Our patron saint? If you like.'

'Ag, good luck, man – I'll see you sometime.'

'You too. Look after yourself.' Seb paused before saying, 'There's stirrings in the Transvaal, amongst Paul Kruger's people. We might end up on different sides in the near future.'

'I would think that's almost a given.'

'Well, I'd like to tell you now, if you're ever in my rifle sights, I won't shoot you, not on purpose.'

'You might have to, bru.'

'Well, I won't and that's that.'

Pieter laughed. 'Let's hope it never comes to that.'

Pieter then turned his mount and walked it through the crowds of citizens hemming the marketplace. Seb weaved on, towards the edge of the town. Once in open country he spurred Amasi on, in the direction of the Donaldson farm. The sky was big and open, with puffs of cloud like burst shells amongst the deep blue. Seb's senses were fully alive on that ride, taking in every detail of the veldt as he went. A small mammal crossed his path, one he did not recognize. There were reptiles everywhere, which scattered at his advance. Once, he saw a huge vulture wheeling slowly above him and wondered if it knew something he did not. Could it smell death on this young man riding out over its land?

That night he camped against some ruin or other: he could not tell what it had been, a chapel possibly? The west wall still half-stood and offered some comfort. He woke in the early morning cold, but grateful that he was alive to watch a big orange sun rise above the horizon. Out here in the wilds of Natal the farms were well apart, with plenty of space between them. Once back on Amasi he could see for miles. On occasion he saw people in the distance: one or two men, some women in Indian saris of pastel shades, seeming to float along the skyline. He loved the mix of cultures and races here, feeling he was privileged to witness the wider world.

At noon he came to the Donaldson farm. He rode straight up to a doorway framed by blue wisteria. There was no sight or sound of any occupants. He half-expected to be shot as he came into the yard, but also guessed that Lunt wanted to savour his victory. Seb had been the cause of his having to leave the profession he loved. The Provost-Marshal knew how he would feel if he had been forced out of the army into the life of a drifting civilian in a foreign land. The army kept you closeted, within their family. One could enjoy Africa from a relatively safe standpoint. Outside there were no friends to watch your back or to offer assistance when you were in need.

Seb dismounted and knocked on the door.

'Anyone there?' called Seb. 'Mary? Mr Donaldson?'

A voice behind him made him jump.

'So, the provo? You came.'

Seb turned and straightened, before saying in the tone of an official on business, 'Major Lunt, you are under arrest.'

The big handsome ex-cavalry officer, dressed now in buckskins and broadcloth, gave him a sardonic smile. He held a revolver in his right hand, which was pointed at Seb's chest. He was also wearing a sabre, the hilt glistening in the noonday sun.

'You forget, I'm no longer a commissioned officer in Her Majesty Queen Victoria's army, though still a loyal subject and a patriot.'

'A patriot?'

Lunt gave Seb a dark look. 'Of course a patriot. I am an Englishman, sir, proud of my country, proud of my heritage. Eton- and Oxford-educated. From a very old family. My father is Sir Ebenezer Lunt, the Member for Derby. I am a monarchist and support every branch of the nobility. You must understand who you are dealing with here, Ensign. I am not John Dobbs of Sloe Farm, nor the half-baked son of some rural schoolmaster. I am Bradford Lunt, a highly respected man in my county. One whose status is far above yours. Do you really wish to draw the enmity of a powerful family down upon your head?'

'Where is Mary Donaldson?' snapped Seb. 'Where's her father?'

Lunt folded his arms and slouched. 'I have not the faintest idea.'

Seb was puzzled. 'But you said in your note . . .'

'Merely the bait, which you took. You came to arrest me, but you are an army policeman. I'm no longer in the army. If I have committed a crime, it should be a civilian who arrests me. I'm going to defend myself against an illegal action by an overzealous provo.'

'You were in the army when you murdered a man, who was also a brother officer in the same army.'

Lunt's face stiffened to a mask of loathing.

'Enough. You and I are going to duel,' he said.

Seb stared back with the same abhorrence that Lunt obviously felt for him.

'Are you going to shoot *me* in cold blood too?'

'You will have your chance, as did that stupid lieutenant. I told him before the duel what I was going to do. He threw away his opportunity to shoot me and deserved all he got. I didn't ask him to delope. It was the act of an idiot or a coward, hoping that because he had done so, I would not continue. He was wrong. I promised to kill him and I did. Just as I promise to kill you, today.'

Seb felt a shiver of apprehension trickle down his spine.

'So, here and now?' he said. 'In this yard?'

Lunt gave the ensign another look of distaste.

'Not on foot. I am a dragoon, sir. You will meet me at full charge on your horse. There must be no quarter. Either you will die, or it will be me – but looking at you . . .' the contemptuous gaze went up and down Seb's much shorter stature '. . . I'm quite sure who it will be.'

The ex-major then strode off, towards the Dutch barn that Seb and his company had once slept in. There he mounted a heavy horse and drew his sabre. He walked his mount to an open pasture nearby and waited patiently in the far corner of the meadow for his adversary to join him on the killing ground. When Seb did not follow him immediately, he took out a long thin cigar and lit it. While he drew and puffed on it he slashed with his sword at the blue smoke which trailed from its end. Lunt had been in many battles, killed many men, and this was all in a day's work for a rogue dragoon.

Seb was an infantry officer. He could ride well, yes, but was not a trained cavalryman. There was a choice, of course. The ensign did not have to play the major's game. He was entitled to draw the carbine from its holster on Amasi and shoot a resisting criminal down in cold blood. But then he would be no better than Lunt, and he despised the man, fervently. No, he could not do that. It was against all his principles and the moral foundations given him by his father.

Seb knew he was going to have to go along with the murderer's plan, or ride away empty-handed. He gently spurred Amasi forward, the milk-coloured steed obeying the command immediately. They trotted to the far corner of the lea where Lunt was waiting. Once in position Seb drew his revolver, leaving his sword in its scabbard. He stared around him. Birds were singing in the orchard's fruit trees. A goat was wandering around the edge of the house, eating anything it could find on the ground. The sky was cobalt-blue without a cloud. Somewhere in the near distance an ass was braying. A fine warm day.

Lunt spat out the cigar and drew a handgun.

He started to trot forward, sword in his right fist, pistol in his left.

When he was halfway across the meadow he yelled, 'CHARGE!' and spurred his mount into a canter.

They came hurtling on, horse and rider, and Seb could see the face of his opponent, suffused with blood, eyes burning with battle-fever.

A shot sang past Seb's ear. Then another snicked his thigh. Lunt's normally good aim was of course poor when taken from the back of a charging warhorse.

Seb murmured to Amasi, 'Steady boy,' and levelled his firing arm. His own mount remained unmoving beneath him. One more round zipped somewhere around Seb's head. He felt calm and detached as he took careful aim at the big man thundering towards him. An incandescent moment. He squeezed the trigger once, then again, feeling the revolver buck in his hand with each deliberate shot.

Lunt jolted in his saddle, his arms flew up releasing the sabre and the pistol almost simultaneously. They spun through the air on either side of him in two arcs. Then with wide eyes full of surprise, he fell backwards, out of his stirrups, and landed with a thud on the grassy lea. His horse continued on, galloping towards a fence, and crashed through horizontal timbers and into the next field, where he came to a halt, wheezing and snorting. Still, Amasi had not moved an inch from his position in the corner of the meadow.

His heart beating fast now, Seb dismounted. He went to the supine ex-major, who was staring up at the sky. Lunt's chest was soaked with his own blood. The eyes moved as Seb's shadow fell on him.

Then he spoke.

'Damn you!' croaked the ex-major. 'I'll fix you . . .'

'Not a chance, old chap,' replied Seb. 'You're dying.'

And indeed, within a few moments the life had gone from the dragoon.

While Seb stood over the corpse a shout came from nearby, and Seb looked up to see a man riding an ass. He recognized him as Mary Donaldson's father. Glaring, Mr Donaldson shook his fist at Seb.

'I saw that!' he cried, furiously. 'I saw you kill that man.'

Seb replied, calmly, 'Yes, you did, sir. He is Major Bradford Lunt, of the 5th Dragoons, and I'd kill him again if I could, for once is not enough for a brute like that.'

The puzzled colonial farmer's mouth fell open as he took in the scene, of a young unrepentant officer wearing a scarlet sash standing over the body of a large man with a hole in his chest.

Afterword

There was no such regiment as the 5th Dragoons taking part in the Anglo-Zulu Wars. The 5th Dragoons (not to be confused with the 5th Dragoon Guards or the 5th Royal Inniskilling Dragoon Guards) was disbanded for mutiny in 1799 and stripped of its seniority. Its honours passed to a regiment raised in 1858, the 5th (Royal Irish) Lancers. I have thus used the 5th Dragoons as a fictitious vehicle for the villains of this novel. Similarly, there was to my knowledge no Border Rangers taking part in the battles, a regiment I have invented for the purposes of this novel.